THE SPY IN THE SILVER PALACE

EMPIRE OF TALENTS BOOK ONE

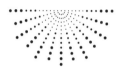

JORDAN RIVET

For Chelsea.
I'm happy we're sisters,
but I'm even happier we're friends.

CONTENTS

MAP

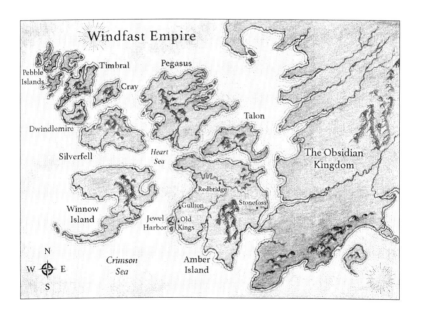

CHAPTER ONE

Mica wore her own face as she ran across the cobblestones. The assembly hall rose ahead of her, the burnished bronze dome glowing like a second sunrise. She squeezed through the visitors making their way to the ceremony, noting interesting features along the way: a set of high cheekbones, a pair of protruding ears, a scarred lip.

She dodged a small family, catching a snippet of their conversation.

"Are we going to see real Mimics today?" one of the children asked.

"Hush, darling," said the mother, clearly distracted by the crowds.

Mica filed away the details of the woman's appearance out of habit: thick black hair, a wide mouth turned down at the corners, a lean brown hand clutching her younger child.

"You see Mimics every day," said an older boy (similar mouth below a flat, sunburned nose). "You just don't know it."

Mica didn't hear the child's reply as she pushed onward through the throng. She should have arrived long before the guests, but she had only just escaped the ramshackle inn where her family was staying. They had traveled on horseback for three days to reach the town of Redbridge from Stonefoss Infantry Base, and she had skipped the celebrations in the Academy dormitory to spend the night with them. Her parents and four brothers had smothered her with hugs and good wishes before letting her leave that morning.

"It's not every day your baby sister graduates from Mimic Academy," her brother Aden had said, nearly crushing her with his unnatural strength.

"You're not supposed to call it that," Emir had said. "You'll get Mica in trouble."

"Everyone calls them Mimics," Aden said. "Even Mica."

"Not where my instructors can hear it," Mica said.

Aden shrugged. "You *Impersonators* have no sense of humor."

"That's enough of that," their father cut in. "This is Mica's day. You should be proud to have an Imperial Impersonator in the family."

Mica had rolled her eyes for her brothers' benefit, but she was secretly pleased. As the youngest of five—and the only girl—she wasn't used to being the center of attention. She was surprised that her parents and all four brothers had managed to secure leave from the base to travel the length of Amber Island for her Assignment Ceremony. She hoped she'd make them proud.

She reached the assembly hall at the center of the town square and darted up the granite steps, escaping the early-summer heat for the cool, echoing interior of the ancient building. Voices issued from the main hall, where she glimpsed the families of the graduates gathering beneath the bronze dome. She ducked down a side corridor, nerves wriggling in her stomach.

She shouldn't be too concerned. She had worked hard at the Redbridge Academy for Professional Impersonators, the best institution of its kind in the empire, and she was near the top of her class. She was sure to get a good assignment. The question was whether it would be the one she had coveted since her very first day at the Academy.

Mica turned a corner and found her classmates lined up by a side door, waiting to be called into the assembly hall. The torchlit corridor echoed with the voices of a hundred anxious young Impersonators preparing to receive their first missions. Their nervous babble nearly drowned out the scraping benches and tapping feet inside the hall itself. The air was thick with the smell of sweat, torch smoke, and just a hint of last night's liquor.

Mica squeezed into line in front of a familiar woman with raven hair, an aquiline nose, and perfect curves.

"You made it," the woman said in a throaty purr.

"Am I the last one?" Mica asked.

"Not even close." The raven-haired beauty rubbed her eyes, which were a luminous shade of lavender. "Half the cohort didn't even go to bed last night. A few more will stumble in."

"Where's Danil?"

"Still sleeping it off, I expect. Tiber stole a crate of brandy from his mother's cellar. Oh, strike it." Suddenly the woman's figure flattened and stretched into a taller, more athletic shape. The raven hair faded to an ashy blond, and the aquiline nose shortened and widened. In seconds, a tall, fresh-faced girl, who was cute rather than stunning, had replaced the alluring beauty. This was the true face of Mica's friend Sapphire.

Mica grinned. "Changed your mind, eh?"

"You were right," Sapphire said. "We should look like ourselves today. Also, it's too much effort to hold that figure with a headache." She rubbed her eyes, which remained lavender rather than their natural blue—possibly to hide how bloodshot her real eyes were. The throaty voice was all hers, though it sounded scratchier than usual after the night's revels.

"You look gorgeous," Mica said. She surveyed their hundred-odd classmates, many of whom were wearing their favorite faces today. They had been developing those faces for the past five years, training their features to morph into ever more difficult variations. Some Mimics preferred their impersonations to their normal appearances, and the crowd in the corridor contained an unusually high percentage of staggering beauties. "People really went all out."

"That elfin look over there is new." Sapphire nodded at a girl who'd sharpened her features to look like a fairy from a story, complete with shimmering blue hair. "I wonder who that is."

"Probably won't be the most useful face," Mica said, "unless she gets assigned to one of those fancy performance troupes."

Mica's Talent enabled her to change individual features at will, and she'd been taught to create a collection of practical looks she could slip into without thought. There was the plain-faced cowherd's daughter. The big-eyed and buxom barmaid. The lad with foppish hair and a twinkle in his green eyes. The lean old soldier. The humpbacked crone. Most important of all was an array of faces from the Obsidian Kingdom, a land of pale eyes and paler skin, where the people stood out against the dark, rocky landscape like doves in a tar pit.

Mica had studied more Obsidian faces than anyone else at the Academy. Impersonation was useful in a wide range of professions, but she had trained with a single goal in mind: to serve the Windfast Empire as a spy in Obsidian territory. Windfast, also known as the Empire of Islands, encompassed a dozen small island nations that had banded together against their larger, more powerful neighbor to the east. The Obsidian Kingdom had been a looming threat over Mica's homeland for generations. Windfast spies served as the first line of defense against the dark kingdom, the secret agents whose work in the shadows could save thousands of lives. If everything went according to plan, Mica was about to become one of them.

"I hope my hand-to-hand results don't set me back," she whispered to Sapphire. Combat had been Mica's weakest subject at the Academy. Her build was slight, and though she was nimble and quick with a knife, she had little hope of overpowering enemy combatants.

"Master Kiev knows what you can do," Sapphire said. "Besides, the ability to disappear is more important than being strong enough to knock someone out."

"I hope you're right." Mica worried the spymasters on the front lines in Obsidian would be expecting the Academy to send them only skilled fighters. She'd hate to be stuck working as a body double in a field unrelated to espionage. They couldn't all be spies.

"Shh!" Sapphire held up a hand. "They're quieting down."

Mica held her breath, listening to the sounds inside the assembly hall. Applause broke out on the other side of the wall.

"It's starting!"

"Master Kiev must be walking up to the stage now." Mica pictured the Head of the Academy climbing the platform with his uneven gait and raising his hands to silence the applause.

She and Sapphire exchanged excited glances as Master Kiev's deep voice rumbled through the wall, the cadence familiar even though they couldn't make out the words. He must be welcoming the guests, many of whom had traveled much farther than Mica's family to reach the northern heartland of Amber Island for the Assignment Ceremony.

"Get back in line!" The message was whispered down the torchlit corridor from the Academy instructor who'd been posted by the door. "Master Kiev will call you in two minutes."

The students straightened their clothes and made last-minute adjustments to their faces, a little extra color here, a few more lashes there. Mica bounced on the balls of her feet, fidgeting with the pockets in her sturdy gray skirt, the best one she owned. She hadn't altered her appearance at all today, despite her skill. She wore her own snub nose, hazel eyes, and nut-brown hair, which just brushed her shoulders. She had prepared for a life of secrecy, one where she could go months without ever showing her true face to anyone. But on this day, she wanted to look like herself.

"Danil's going to miss the whole thing." Sapphire stood on her toes to search for their friend amongst the students, though she towered over most of them anyway. "What is he *doing*?"

"He'll be here." Mica scanned the corridor, absently making her bottom lip grow and shrink. She half expected one of the other students to sprout curly dark hair, revealing that Danil had been there all along. It wasn't like him to be late. Barrel-chested and merry, their friend was one of the most reliable people Mica knew.

"Will they give him his scroll later if he doesn't make it?" Sapphire asked.

"I hope so." Their instructors weren't known for being lenient, but surely they wouldn't withhold Danil's assignment for celebrating too hard last night.

Mica, Sapphire, and Danil had been inseparable since their first day at the Academy. They had helped each other through some arduous tasks on their five-year journey to become Imperial Impersonators. It was strange to think that this morning's ceremony marked the end of their time together. As an Obsidian spy, Mica would spend most of her career overseas, while Sapphire and Danil both had their sights on assignments in the empire. She pushed aside a hint of melancholy at the prospect of not seeing them often. This was a day for celebration.

"It's time," called the instructor at the front of the line. "Quit yammering, everybody."

Mica squeezed Sapphire's hand as the door at the end of the corridor opened at last, allowing them to hear Master Kiev's voice just as it reached a crescendo.

". . . to present the graduates of the Redbridge Academy for Professional Impersonators!"

Applause erupted around the assembly hall as Mica and her classmates entered to the sound of blaring trumpets. Light filled the vast space beneath the bronze dome, spilling from windows set high in the granite walls. A platform had been set up directly beneath the dome, the sides draped with banners bearing the Redbridge Academy crest and the Windfast flag. Heavy wooden benches surrounded the stage, every seat filled except for the front rows, which were reserved for the hundred graduates. Mica felt a thrill of pride as she marched down the aisle with her cohort, hardly able to believe this was finally happening.

Benches scraped against the granite floor as the guests stood to get a better look at the Impersonators. This was the only time some of them would ever see real Mimics—at least as far as they knew. More than a few jaws dropped at the sight of so many beautiful young people parading toward the front of the hall. For a moment, Mica regretted not assuming her most beautiful face for the occasion. Beauty was a tool like any other, but the best Impersonators knew that going unnoticed was often more important—and took more skill—than being the prettiest person in the room. Besides, she wanted her family to know it was her.

The trumpets faded as the students took their seats at the front of the hall. Mica and Sapphire left a space between them for Danil in case he made it at the last minute. They looked up at Master Kiev, who leaned on a wooden podium on the center platform. He was a huge man, with black skin and wild white hair. The Academy instructors sat on his right—many of them also wearing their best faces for the occasion. On his left sat a handful of dignitaries who had traveled from the capital city of Jewel Harbor to represent the emperor. One of the seats on stage remained empty.

"Welcome, Impersonators," Master Kiev began. "Today we are gathered to ..."

Mica couldn't concentrate on the words of his speech. Her focus was drawn to a stack of scrolls on the podium, rolls of parchment bound with simple black ribbon. There they were. The assignments. In a matter of minutes, Mica would know whether the life she had worked toward for the past five years would be hers. She would embark on a great adventure across the sea, facing countless perils in service of her homeland. She would use all the faces she had practiced at the Academy and more, wearing and discarding features like so many cheap hats.

She studied the pyramid of scrolls intently, counting them, trying to read the names scrawled on the sides. Her entire future rested in one of those scrolls. It was impossible to think of anything else. She tuned in to Master Kiev's oration only when he was clearly drawing to the end.

"Most people in the empire will never know your names." He paused to meet the eyes of several of his students in turn. "They will never see your best works or speak of your greatest deeds. That is your purpose, your mission. This may be one of the few moments when you will receive public recognition for the skills you have trained so hard to acquire. This is your day, Impersonators. May you thrive."

"May you thrive," the students intoned. Then someone whooped, and applause echoed through the assembly hall once more.

Mica tore her eyes from the scrolls long enough to seek out her family in the crowd. Her mother caught her eye and waved. The details of their assignments would be kept private, and the Impersonators would be unrecognizable for most of their careers. This was truly their only chance for acknowledgement.

When Mica turned back to face the platform again, Master Kiev was introducing one of the visiting dignitaries, a man in his late fifties with thick gray hair, a prominent nose, and a finely sculpted beard. Mica took special note of the shape of the nose.

"Lord Ober has been a stalwart supporter of all Talents in Emperor Styl's court, including our fellow Impersonators," Master Kiev said. "We are honored he could be here today to help us present the assignments."

"Thank you, Master Kiev," Lord Ober said. "May I also introduce my lady wife, Euphia, and esteemed guests Lord Riven, Lady Lorna, and my nephew, Lord Caleb of the Pebble—hmm, it looks as though Lord Caleb hasn't made it this morning." Lord Ober gestured at the empty chair and chuckled. "I believe he made the most of your celebrations last night. In any case, we are all proud of our young Impersonators. Talents form the backbone of this empire, and I'm pleased to witness this momentous occasion as you complete your training. May we work together toward the good of the Windfast Empire and of His Imperial Majesty Emperor Styl."

Lord Ober relinquished his spot at the podium, positioning himself so he could shake hands with the Impersonators after they received their scrolls from Master Kiev. The other three nobles watched the proceedings with indifference, occasionally fanning themselves or looking down at their fingernails. Nobles were usually too busy with the courtly frivolities of Jewel Harbor to concern themselves with working Talents. If Lord Ober's admiration was genuine, he was a rare breed.

Master Kiev reminded everyone one last time to be discreet about their assignments, picked up the first scroll from the top of the pyramid, and read out the name.

"Tiber Warson."

Cheers erupted as Tiber sauntered up to the podium. The son of a prosperous innkeeper, he was the only student in their cohort who was actually from Redbridge, making him a local hero. He shook hands enthusiastically with Master Kiev and Lord Ober and took his time returning to his seat, clearly enjoying the adulation of the townsfolk in the audience.

Tiber was one Mimic Mica hoped never to see again, whether in his own face or in one of his impersonations. Broad-shouldered and blond, he was what Sapphire called "objectively handsome." He had excelled in every class, and Mica had seen him working on his pale Obsidian faces a little too often for comfort. Even though she knew several members of their cohort were likely to receive assignments in Obsidian, she couldn't help feeling that she was competing against Tiber for a spot.

He ripped the ribbon off his scroll on his way off the stage, and he was beaming at whatever it said by the time he reached his bench. He had clearly gotten what he wanted.

"Stop scowling," Sapphire said. "Your face will stick like that."

Mica jerked her head at Tiber's broad back. "It just occurred to me that we'll have to work together if we both get Obsidian assignments."

"I know you have a few faces even *I* haven't seen," Sapphire said. "You can avoid him if you really want to."

"Good thing Obsidian is a big kingdom."

"Mmm." Sapphire craned her neck, searching the hall for any sign of Danil, whether in his natural form or in one of the dozen others they'd seen him wear.

"I'm sure Master Kiev won't take away Danil's assignment, Sapph," Mica said as more names were called and the graduates received their scrolls one by one. "This is just a formality."

"It's not that," Sapphire said. "I'm worried he's avoiding me."

"Why?"

Sapphire glanced around at their classmates, her face going pink. "I'll tell you after."

It dawned on Mica that something must have finally happened between Sapphire and Danil last night. The two had been dancing around their growing attraction to each other for a while now. Mica had skipped her evening impersonation exercises many times to listen to one or the other talk through their feelings on late-night walks through Redbridge. But as the day of their graduation neared, she had begun to doubt whether either one would ever make a move.

She was busy sorting through what it would mean for her two best friends to form their own bond when Sapphire nudged her.

"You're up."

"Huh?"

"Master Kiev just called your name."

Mica's stomach plummeted. A hundred faces turned to look at her. Tiber wore a condescending smirk. Master Kiev cleared his throat expectantly.

"Micathea Graydier."

Mica got to her feet. She felt her features shifting, and she struggled to master them as she edged past her classmates and walked to the stage. Her nose used to grow and her jawline change shape when she was nervous. She thought she had kicked that habit. She took a deep breath and ascended the steps to the platform.

"Congratulations, Micathea." Master Kiev's deep voice rumbled through her. "You have done well."

Then the scroll was in her hands, the thick parchment smooth against her skin. It was lighter than she expected. Did that mean something?

She felt cold and clammy as she moved on to shake hands with Lord Ober. His eyes twinkled, and his firm handshake pumped a little life into her.

"I hope you got a good one," he said.

She blinked at him, at that fine specimen of a nose, and turned back to the assembly. Faces blurred together as she stomped off the platform. She had pictured herself waving to her family, perhaps giving a jaunty bow to her friends, but she barely felt in control of her body as she stumbled back to her seat. The whole point of being a Mimic was to be able to control every inch of her body. She clutched the scroll tight, willing her hands to stop shaking.

Sapphire returned to her seat while Mica was still staring at her scroll, at the simple black ribbon and the scrawl of her name.

"You didn't have to wait for me," Sapphire said. She also clutched a scroll now.

Mica shook herself out of a daze. Her friend had been called up right after her, and she'd missed seeing her walk up to the podium.

"Are you ready?" Mica asked.

Sapphire looked around, perhaps hoping Danil had made it. It felt strange to do this without him. "On three?"

"One." Mica's hands stopped vibrating at last.

Sapphire grinned, her eyes suddenly turning back to their natural blue. "Two."

"Three."

The scrolls unfurled together.

CHAPTER TWO

Mica stared at the words on the parchment. She was still staring when the last name was called, still staring when Master Kiev invited everyone to adjourn to the town green for a picnic. She didn't understand. In swirling letters scrawled with the finest ink, she read:

Princess Jessamyn
The Silver Palace
Jewel Harbor

Sapphire tugged on her arm. Mica was vaguely aware of her friend saying something, but she couldn't concentrate on what it was. She was still trying to process the words written on her assignment scroll in black and white.

"There's my mother," Sapphire said after failing to get a coherent response. "We'll talk later."

"Wait, did you—?" But Sapphire disappeared into the crowd before Mica could ask if she got the assignment she wanted.

The rest of their classmates were dispersing to greet their families. Mica blinked at the commotion as if she'd just awoken from a deep sleep. The Assignment Ceremony was over. She was now a fully-fledged Imperial Impersonator. But she was not an Obsidian spy.

Mica looked down at her assignment scroll. The parchment was supposed to have a single name on it, Master Black, which was how the Academy notified Impersonators assigned to the Obsidian Kingdom. They would then be called in for individual meetings to discuss the sensitive details of their missions. The other scrolls would name the noble or business that had requested the services of an Academy-trained Impersonator— for which they paid handsomely. Some wanted informants, while others used the Impersonators as body doubles or pawns in their schemes. A few prestigious theaters even used them as actors.

As Mica ran through all the jobs she could have been assigned, a hollow feeling opened in the pit of her stomach. She read her paper again.

> *Princess Jessamyn*
> *The Silver Palace*
> *Jewel Harbor*

Despite all the time she had spent worrying over her assignment, she had never truly believed she'd fail to get an Obsidian mission. She was near the top of her class. She had practiced that pale Obsidian look more than anyone else. And while she wasn't the best or biggest fighter, spies rarely needed to fight anyway.

The parchment crinkled in her hands. She wasn't even sure what this assignment involved. It made sense that Emperor Styl's daughter, Princess Jessamyn, needed an Impersonator. Many important nobles employed them as doubles for safety or to fulfill their less enjoyable tasks. The nobles with Lord Ober could easily be Impersonators, if the real lords and ladies hadn't wanted to leave the comforts of Jewel Harbor. But the Academy Masters wouldn't waste Mica's abilities on an assignment like that, would they? There had to be some mistake.

A mistake. Of course. Mica stuffed the parchment into her pocket and straightened. She must have been given the wrong scroll. She'd talk to Master Kiev. He would clear this up.

No sooner had she put away the scroll than two identical men barreled into her, nearly knocking her off her feet.

"Did you get it?" her brother Wills asked.

"You got it, didn't you?" crowed his twin, Rees.

"Let me see it!"

Mica swatted their hands away, though of course it didn't hurt them. Like all of her family members, the twins were Talents, people born with one of four supernatural traits. Theirs was impervious skin.

Emir, the second oldest brother, appeared before them, seemingly out of thin air. "You heard Master Kiev. She has to be discreet."

"I'll get it from her." Suddenly, Mica was grabbed from behind. Aden, the oldest of the Graysons, lifted her into the air as if she weighed nothing at all. To him, it was just about true. He tried to snatch the scroll from her pocket.

"Put me down," Mica snapped, more sharply than she intended.

"No need to be snippy just because you're a fancy spy now." Aden set her back on her feet.

Mica hadn't meant to let on that she was upset. She squeezed her eyes shut for a second, and when she opened them she wore Aden's features on her face (heavy jaw, hazel eyes, knobby forehead). She stuck her tongue out at him.

Aden roared with laughter.

"Do us! Do us!" the twins called.

Mica engaged the muscles in her face, and soon she was flashing their own grins at them. She knew the subtle differences in their twin features well. Rees tensed his jaw more often and had a more prominent muscle in his cheek, and Wills had a unique twinkle in his eyes. The face she wore now was half of each. Wills and Rees applauded enthusiastically, and it made Mica feel a bit better.

"I've never seen you look uglier," said Aden. The twins tackled him, and he held them off easily with his unnatural strength.

"Take that roughhousing out to the square." Their father, Gray, had arrived. Like Emir, he moved so quickly he seemed to appear out of nowhere. "You don't want to embarrass our little Impersonator."

"They have food outside, you know," Mica said.

"Say no more," Wills called. "Race you." He extracted himself from the tangle of his brothers and charged off, heedless of injury. Rees and Aden followed, narrowly avoiding knocking over an elderly man with a patchwork of scars on his face.

"You'd never know they're grown men," their father said, shaking his head ruefully.

"The allure of free food has no age limit," Emir said. He hadn't bothered running after his brothers. He was so much faster than the others that he never joined in when they raced each other.

"Can't argue with you on that." Their father surveyed Mica for a moment and put his hands on her shoulders. "Micathea, I am so proud of you." His voice went hoarse. "I remember when you were small enough to sit on my shoulders." He stepped back and flicked a handkerchief out of his pocket, hands moving so fast they blurred.

Emir rolled his eyes as their father blew his nose loudly enough to make strangers look over. "All right, now *you're* embarrassing me." He clapped their father on the back. They had the same slim build and dark hair, as well as the same abnormally quick movements. "Let's go see about that free food."

"Good idea." He sniffed. "My daughter, an imperial spy."

Mica watched her father and Emir stroll out of the assembly

hall, weaving through the little knots of people gathered around each graduate. She didn't have the heart to correct her father. He hadn't doubted for a second that she had received the assignment she wanted.

Her mother, Cora, had been standing back until then, watching Mica closely. She could always figure out what her daughter was thinking, regardless of the face she wore.

"You don't have to talk about it now, if you don't want to," she said softly. Then she wrapped her arms around Mica in a bone-crushing hug. She had a calming presence, steady as a mountain and just as strong. Mica sighed into her mother's shoulder, allowing her features to return to normal as she breathed in the familiar smells of home: earth, fresh-cut grass, and clean leather.

"Thanks," Mica mumbled. "I'm still figuring it out."

In truth, she felt a bit queasy. Her family had used up their precious yearly leave and come all this way to celebrate with her. She didn't want to let on how disheartened she was with how the day had gone.

The two of them caught up with her father and brother and joined the families and curious locals spilling out of the assembly hall and into the sunlit square.

The town of Redbridge was packed with Talents this week. Many of the graduates' families showed signs of the hereditary abilities. Some darted across the square unnaturally quickly or moved in the careful manner of those born with tremendous strength. Only one out of every ten people in the empire had a Talent—never more than one—and it was rare to see so many Talented people in one place. The notable exception was on military bases like the one where Mica had grown up.

Her brothers and parents were all Talents enlisted in the Imperial Army. Her mother and oldest brother, Aden, were Muscles, known for being abnormally strong. Her father and second-oldest brother, Emir, were Blurs, capable of extreme speed. The twins, Wills and Rees, were Shields, their skin utterly impervious to injury. Her parents had received their own little house on the base when they got together as an incentive to have exceptional children. They had done their duty, producing four Talented soldiers for the Imperial Army—and Mica. She was the only Mimic in the family as well as the only daughter, indicated by her patronymic: Graydier.

Mica had grown up among soldiers, learning a keen sense of loyalty to the empire. As the daughter of two career soldiers, it had never occurred to her that she would have an assignment that *wasn't* in direct opposition to their greatest enemy. She had thought she was destined to infiltrate the evil kingdom that had threatened her homeland for her entire life, serving Windfast in her own way. She didn't see how the words on the parchment in her pocket fit that birthright.

"So when do you ship out?" her father asked as they crossed the cobblestone square toward the town green.

"Huh?"

"I'm not asking you to reveal any imperial secrets." He winked at her. "Just wondering if you might have time to stop at the base before you report for duty."

"It's not on the way."

"Eh?"

"Jewel Harbor," Mica said dully. "Stonefoss isn't on the way."

Her father stared at her—not noticing his wife giving him a death glare for bringing it up. Yes, Cora had already figured out that Mica hadn't received the coveted assignment.

"You've been assigned to the capital?" her father said when he found his voice at last.

Mica nodded.

"But you always said you wanted—"

"It's not up to me," Mica said. "The Academy decides the assignments."

She studied the cobblestones beneath her feet so she wouldn't have to see the disappointment on their faces.

"But the capital," Emir said. "That's really prestigious, isn't it? You'll be working for real lords and ladies there."

"Is that right, Micathea?" her mother said. "Will you be working for the nobility?"

"Yes." Mica glanced up in time to catch a rather impressed look on Emir's face.

"I always knew you'd make us proud," her father said.

Mica was speechless. It hadn't occurred to her that this assignment could be an honor. She touched the crumpled scroll in her pocket. Maybe Master Kiev thought this was an honor too! Maybe she could explain to him that she'd prefer a dangerous foreign mission over an accolade any day. She was sure the princess could make do with a different Impersonator.

"*I'm* proud no matter what assignment you get," her mother said.

Emir winked at Mica. "Always knew you were the favorite."

She grinned and tried to elbow him, but he easily danced out of her reach.

She wondered what her family would say if she told them she had been assigned to Princess Jessamyn herself. They hadn't asked who the Jewel Harbor noble was. Military folk didn't mix with the lords and ladies at court, and Mica probably couldn't name ten nobles herself, even if she counted the four who had been introduced during the ceremony. Well, five including Lord Caleb, the one who hadn't even bothered to show up.

They reached the green in the center of town, where the Academy Masters had provided a luncheon for the graduates and their guests. A river burbled alongside the grassy expanse, and venerable old willow trees swayed gracefully in the summer breeze. The elegant form of the red stone bridge was visible to the west, the bronze dome of the assembly hall overlooked the square in the east, and fine townhouses and inns bordered the remaining sides. Though not too large, the town of Redbridge was prosperous thanks to the Academy, and far prettier than the grim, functional Stonefoss Base where the Gray family lived.

They found the others lining up at the long buffet table on the green.

"There she is!" called Aden. "Hurry up and get some food before I eat it all." He was at the front of the line, busy filling his bowl with chicken legs and crusty bread. Crumbs trailing down his tunic suggested he had already helped himself to a few bites.

"Will you do the twin face again, Mica?" Wills called from farther back in line. "I want to show my new friend here how good my little sister is."

He was chatting with a delicate red-haired girl, whom Mica recognized as one of the common guises of an Impersonator called Jack. He winked at Mica, and she grinned. Nearby, Rees had secured a spot in the shade of a large willow tree and glared at anyone who tried to encroach on it. Aden thudded down beside him and began digging into his meal. In an instant, Emir was between them, already halfway finished with his first drumstick.

Mica and her parents joined her brothers beneath the willow tree, and the afternoon passed in a blaze of sunshine. Mica hoped her setback was temporary, but she was still too nervous to finish her meal, the roasted chicken and bread sticking in her mouth. Even so, she pretended everything was fine, smiling and laughing along with her brothers. She'd always felt the need to put on a tough face around the boys.

After they ate their fill, her brothers began circulating among the other guests, making friends in the manner that had always come easily to them. Her father stretched out in the shade of the willow tree to snooze. Her mother settled back against the tree trunk beside him, her hands folded comfortably over her belly. Mica sat beside them, fidgeting with the pockets of her skirt.

"Go on then, Mica," her mother said. "I'm sure you want to see your friends."

"Are you sure?"

"We'll be fine here."

Mica thanked her and leapt up, intending to look for Master Kiev first. She hurried across the green, where her classmates were relaxing with their own families or swearing to each other they'd keep in touch after they left the Academy. She answered vaguely when anyone asked about her assignment.

She spotted Sapphire with Danil's younger sister over near the bridge. The little girl had similar curly hair and round features. Mica didn't see Danil, but he had to be here by now. There'd be plenty of time to catch up with her friends later—hopefully when she had better news to share.

Master Kiev was nowhere to be found. She didn't think he'd assume a different face on such an important occasion, but she began looking more closely at the people spread around the green and the cobblestone square, trying to judge by size rather than features. The primary limitation of impersonation was that a person's mass always remained the same. A slight girl like Mica could become a perfect copy of a broad fellow like Tiber Warson, but at half his size. Mass was one of the factors the Academy took into account when they doled out assignments. Tall, strapping Sapphire wouldn't be much use as a body double for a child, for example.

There were ways around the limitation. They had all practiced making themselves appear bigger or smaller than they were. Mica could make herself look like a tall man, providing no one noticed she had squeezed her waist as thin as a wrist beneath her shirt, and taller Impersonators could thicken their legs in order to make themselves appear smaller. Mica wondered if her relatively small size had something to do with her assignment. It shouldn't matter. If anything, it ought to be better for a spy to be slight, able to pass as a serving boy or little old lady. They needn't all be hulking brutes.

Speaking of which . . .

"Ho there, my Mica!" A rotund matron by the assembly hall steps suddenly morphed into Tiber Warson. "You get the scroll you wanted?"

Mica grimaced. She should have recognized him. She'd seen Tiber impersonate a similar woman before, but this time he'd used a prominent nose that looked suspiciously like Lord Ober's.

Tiber stepped into her path. "Well? We going to be working together, or what?"

"None of your business." Mica wished she hadn't let word get around that she was after an Obsidian assignment.

"I reckon we'll make a good team," Tiber said. "You think we'll be sent to the same city? I hear they usually send new assignees to the—"

"Have you seen Master Kiev?" Mica interrupted.

"He was avoiding that Lady Euphia," Tiber said. "Look for a bald fellow with a long scar down his cheek."

"Thanks."

"Wait, you didn't answer my question!"

Mica pretended she didn't hear him. She should have adopted a different look before searching through the crowd. She could turn herself into a shambling madman when she wanted to make sure people would turn the other way. She wasn't sure what to make of Tiber's overtures of friendship. It was possible he didn't realize how irritating Mica had found him since their first week of school, when he had taken to shouting, "My my Mica!" whenever she arrived at a lesson.

She doubled back across the square, keeping an eye out for the bald, scarred man Tiber had described. She spotted Lord Ober and Lady Euphia and decided to work from there. A ring of Impersonators and their families surrounded the nobles, some apparently acquainted with the guests of honor already. Lady Euphia's fine silk gown and her husband's elegant coat looked out of place on the Redbridge green. A handful of students from noble families studied at the Academy, but the

Talent strain occurred more frequently among the common people.

Mica had never paid much attention to nobles, but she was curious about what they were discussing. She made a few quick changes, lightening her hair and multiplying the freckles on her skin, an impersonation of a morose cowherd's daughter she had seen once on the road from Stonefoss. It was the kind of face a group of nobles and hangers-on would never look at twice. More important than the physical change was the way she altered her stance, drooping her shoulders and making her nimble footsteps heavy. Impersonating someone was about a lot more than looking like them. The bearing had to match the appearance. Beautiful people carried themselves differently than plain ones. The same was true of soldiers compared to shepherds compared to nobles. She had the least experience with nobles. Until she opened her assignment scroll, she hadn't thought it would matter.

Her transformation complete, she shuffled into the crowd surrounding the noble pair.

"So good to be back at the Academy," Lord Ober was saying. "I used to visit often, but I've been busier than ever these past few years."

"Emperor Styl relies on us," Lady Euphia said. She had a high, simpering voice that sounded a bit affected. She appeared old enough to have gray hair like her husband's, but it was dyed a brassy bronze. Her face powder stuck in her wrinkles, and her lip stain was a shade too pink.

"He'll have to do without us for a few more days, darling."

"We're honored you could be here," said a man in the crowd with receding hair and soft pouches under his eyes. "Our son will be along in a moment. We'd love to introduce you."

"It would be a pleasure," Lord Ober said. "I wonder where my nephew has gotten to. I want him to meet the empire's *best* Impersonators."

The man preened as if Ober had named his son the best of the Impersonators.

"I daresay Lord Caleb has found companionship," Lady Euphia said with a titter. "Some of these lovelies wouldn't look out of place at a palace gala. They are simply marvelous."

The drawn-out way Lady Euphia said marvelous made Mica grind her teeth. The noblewoman talked about Mica's friends and classmates as if they were dolls in a toyshop. The other two nobles, Lord Riven (black hair, fine-boned nose) and Lady Lorna (buxom, with pouty lips), stood off to the side, gazing haughtily at the country folk around them. Mica had no desire to live among people like that, prestigious assignment or not.

A shimmer of sunlight on a bald pate drew her eye. A thickset man with a gruesome scar on his cheek hovered a few paces away from the crowd around the nobles. Mica hurried over to him, and he acknowledged her with a nod. Master Kiev had helped her work on the stance for this impersonation, and he knew it well.

"Miss Graydier. I hope you are enjoying your first few hours of post-Academy life." He hadn't altered his usual voice, the deep tone matching this face as well as his own.

"Master Kiev, I need to talk to you about my assignment," Mica said.

"Go on."

"I was wondering if, well, if there's been some mistake?"

"Oh?"

"You know I've been working on my Obsidian impressions, and I thought . . . I thought maybe I got the wrong scroll."

Master Kiev studied her gravely. She had always thought she was among his favorite students, but she wondered if she'd gotten the wrong idea. He was a guarded sort, with a long history of hiding his true thoughts.

"There was no mistake," he said at last. "I chose you for this assignment myself."

A little piece of her deflated. "So . . . so it wasn't supposed to be a Master Black scroll?"

"I'm afraid not," Master Kiev said. "I assumed you'd be honored to work for a member of the emperor's family."

Mica blushed, struggling to keep the red flush from overcoming her fake freckles.

"I appreciate the honor. But . . . will this just be body double work?"

"Just?"

"I didn't mean that," Mica said quickly. Serving as a body double was supposed to be as valuable as being a spy, but she couldn't help feeling it was a job that could be accomplished by a less skilled Mimic. She wasn't the best of them, but she liked to think she knew her own worth. "I mean . . . did you only choose me because I'm the same size as the princess?"

Master Kiev's sigh rumbled in his chest. "I remember the day you arrived at the Academy, Miss Graydier," he said. "You were sitting in your very first class when I outlined the possible careers a well-trained Impersonator might pursue in the empire."

"You were my favorite teacher." Mica wasn't sure where this was going.

Master Kiev smiled, stretching the false scar on his face. "I recall how starry-eyed you became when I described the work of a covert operative in Obsidian territory."

Mica remembered it well. The drafty classroom with shared desks. The window with a view of the bronze dome. The gangly girl sitting beside her whose hair changed color when she got excited. Sapphire had long since grown out of that habit. They'd been thirteen at the time, and they could hardly wait to start learning to use the ability that set them apart from almost everyone they knew. She remembered the burst of exhilaration she'd felt at the thought of herself as an imperial spy. She'd get to see the world. She'd have adventures full of daring and intrigue.

Most of all, she'd show her annoying older brothers that she could be just as important as them.

"I also remember, though you may not," Master Kiev continued, "how you were so caught up in the idea of being a spy that you did not listen to what I said about the other ways to serve the empire, many of them just as vital as foreign espionage."

"But—"

"Miss Graydier, do you wish to defend the empire against threats posed by the King of Obsidian?"

"Of course."

"Think about it carefully. Is that truly your aim?"

Mica hesitated. Truth be told, the prospect of adventure, of doing something grand and important occupied more of her daydreams. Master Kiev must realize it. But she wanted to help the empire too. The Obsidian King enslaved Talents like Mica and her family. He forced them to labor in his mines and build his cities under terrible conditions. He was constantly seeking to expand the reach of his dark dominion, to swallow up the islands of Windfast one by one. Mica's family would lay down their lives to prevent that from happening. She wanted to show that she could do the same.

"Yes," she said. "I want to use my Talent for the good of Windfast."

"Then I am going to tell you something, and I trust you will understand my meaning." Master Kiev looked around, well aware the people nearby could be wearing faces that were not their own. He lowered his voice. "The last Impersonator employed by Princess Jessamyn was not especially skilled. Her mastery of her Talent was adequate for the task."

Mica's stomach lurched, and her features slid out of shape on her face. Was he saying she was nothing special too? What if she *wasn't* among the best Impersonators in her year at all, and she'd been too proud and naïve to see it?

But Master Kiev fixed her with a piercing gaze. "I believe your mastery of your Talent is also adequate for the *task* at hand."

Mica frowned. Had the task of serving the princess changed since she last employed an Impersonator? Could there be more to this assignment than just being the princess's body double when she didn't feel like going to royal balls—or whatever imperial princesses did?

Master Kiev watched her steadily for a moment longer. Then his scar disappeared and white hair burst from his skull as he resumed his usual appearance.

"I believe you will do well in Jewel Harbor," he said. "I will send more information when I have it. In the meantime, keep your eyes open for anything unusual."

"Yes, Master Kiev," she said, hope stirring within her once more.

"Good. I will arrange for you to travel to the Silver Palace with Lord Ober. You will need to study the mannerisms of the nobility carefully. And Miss Graydier?"

"Yes?"

"Do not underestimate anyone you meet in the capital."

CHAPTER THREE

Mica had planned to show her family around Redbridge in the days after the Assignment Ceremony, eager to introduce them to her second home, but they ended up spending most of their time helping to look for Danil. Her curly-haired, merry-faced friend had never surfaced to collect his scroll. His father and sister, who had traveled all the way from Dwindlemire for the event, were positively frantic. Mica, Sapphire, and their families helped them comb through the town, searching all their old haunts and trying to reassure themselves that his absence wasn't sinister.

"Maybe he was sent on an early assignment," Mica said as she, Sapphire, and the twins walked through a pasture outside town where they used to practice hand-to-hand combat. "One Master Kiev can't talk about."

"Maybe," Sapphire said. "But don't you think, well, that Danil would tell me anyway?"

"Did he have a chance?"

"We were together most of that night, until—never mind." Sapphire kicked at a tuft of grass.

"What?" Mica checked to make sure her brothers were too far

away to hear. They were busy throwing old cow pies at each other by the pasture gate. "You can tell me, Sapph."

"Fine." Sapphire kept her attention on the ground, her hair shifting gradually through different shades as the story came out. "We kissed. It was late, after the festivities were winding down. We were standing on the bridge, and I just got the feeling that it was my last chance to tell him how I feel. I turned toward him to say something, and before I could get a word out, we were kissing. I'm not even sure who started it."

"Was it nice?"

Sapphire blushed. "Yes. Or it was for me. Now I'm worried that maybe he—"

"Don't even say it. He's been wanting to kiss you for ages too."

"Then why did he vanish into the night afterwards? He was supposed to go back to his dormitory, but no one has seen him since. I thought maybe he didn't like it."

"That's ridiculous," Mica said. "I'm sure there's a reasonable explanation. We'll figure it out."

"The other possibilities aren't much better," Sapphire said. "What if raiders from Obsidian . . ."

She trailed off, but Mica knew what she was getting at. Windfast Talents had been known to disappear along the eastern border of the empire. The Obsidians enslaved any of their own people born with the supernatural abilities, and they paid handsomely for captives from the empire.

"We're nowhere near the coast," Mica said firmly, trying not to let Sapphire see her own apprehension. "They couldn't get him in the middle of Amber Island."

They went over every theory a dozen times as they continued to search, but Sapphire still acted as if it were somehow her fault, as if one kiss had sent Danil straight into the clutches of darkness.

By the third day, it became clear that Danil was not in Redbridge, and none of the townsfolk or students had seen him depart. They could only hope that he would return from wherever he had wandered to that night of his own volition.

"He probably just got nervous," Mica's brother Aden reassured her on their final evening before everyone had to go their separate ways. "Maybe he was afraid he'd get sent to Jewel Harbor."

"Thanks a lot."

Mica still hadn't told her family she would be working for Princess Jessamyn herself, not wanting to reveal too much until she knew more about her mission. Her brothers were already having too much fun teasing her about becoming a proper lady. As a child, she had tried to prove she was as rough-and-tumble as the boys. She thought she'd grown out of that at the Academy, thanks in large part to Sapphire's influence, but she fell back into old habits around her brothers.

The night before their departure from Redbridge, Mica and her brothers stayed up in the ramshackle inn's common room after their parents went up to their room, drinking ale and chatting as the fire burned low.

"Don't get all snooty on us in the capital," Aden said. "Wearing silks and gems can do that to a person, I hear."

Mica rolled her eyes. "I'll still be a working Talent, not some indolent lady."

"You have to introduce us to all your fancy lady friends, though," Wills said.

"He has a point." Rees gave a wolfish grin. "You can demonstrate in advance how handsome we are."

"I don't know if I'll be *friends* with the ladies," Mica said.

"They wouldn't be interested in the likes of you, anyway." Emir stole a leftover roll off of Wills's plate. "You spend too much time getting covered in sweat and mud on maneuvers."

Aden nodded. "Yes, they all want sweet-smelling lordlings with big ... estates."

"Ah, strike off," Wills said. "I bet even fine noblewomen appreciate a good-looking man in uniform."

"Hear! Hear!" Rees said. The twins clinked glasses.

"That's the whole point of being a soldier," Wills said.

"How'd that work out with the redhead from the picnic?" Mica said sweetly.

Wills quickly drained his ale, muttering something about Mimics and their tricks, while the others roared with laughter.

They stayed up talking late into the night, even though they all had to be up before dawn. The boys swapped stories about the young men and women in their companies. Muscles and Shields, like Aden and the twins, were the most common Talents found in the infantry. They trained together, never as effective alone as they were in a unit. Blurs had their place too, mostly as couriers and scouts, but also as elite fighters. Mica had watched Emir and their father train with sword and spear, twirling so fast it was impossible to connect the thwack of the weapons with the individual movements. Speed trumped strength in a one-on-one contest—unless one was fighting a Shield, of course.

Mica used to wish she were a different kind of Talent, until she realized that being a Mimic set her apart from her brothers, giving her a chance to thrive on her own. But as she watched her family ride away the next day, back to where they'd once again train with their comrades to defend the empire, ever ready to march to the front lines, some of her old jealousy surfaced. Instead of becoming a warrior, she was about to enter a world she knew precious little about.

After her family disappeared in a cloud of road dust, Mica walked down to the expensive inn on the main square where the nobles from the ceremony had been staying. True to his word, Master Kiev had arranged for her to ride to the Silver Palace with them, a three-day journey for anyone who wasn't a Blur. The inn was the fanciest one in Redbridge, owned by Tiber Warson's mother. Tiber had departed yesterday, presumably for Obsidian. Though Master Kiev had reassured her about the importance of her mission, Mica couldn't shake the feeling that Tiber was off winning glory without her.

It's not about that, she reminded herself firmly. *It was never supposed to be about that.*

A trio of enclosed carriages waited in front of the inn, the horses stamping impatiently. They were scheduled to depart at dawn, but the nobles had not yet emerged. Mica waited beside the carriages as the sun rose over the dome. She had a small pack of belongings on her back, and she wore her own face. It was customary for Impersonators, even those who habitually enhanced their looks, to greet their employers in their natural state. She had on a sturdy brown skirt that was specially designed to turn into a cloak with a few quick adjustments. She wore trousers underneath and a loose white shirt suitable for a man or a woman. The nondescript clothes were typical for an Impersonator. They needed to wear outfits that could be adjusted as easily as their faces.

Activity began to pick up around town. Redbridge was busier than usual as the members of the Academy's latest graduating cohort headed off to their new lives, but there was still no sign of Mica's traveling companions. She paced back and forth in front of the inn, wondering if she should go inside and try banging on Lord Ober's door.

"Mica! You're still here!"

Mica turned to find Sapphire jogging toward her across the green. She looked bleary-eyed, as if she had slept poorly. She threw her arms around Mica's neck, the too-tight hug betraying her worries.

"Danil still hasn't turned up?"

Sapphire shook her head, and Mica winced at the fragility in her friend's expression.

"I'm sure he'll contact you as soon as he can."

Sapphire pulled at a tangle in her hair. "I wish you were going to Obsidian in case he got taken there. You could keep an eye out for him."

"Danil will be okay," Mica said. "Don't fall apart, or at least make it look like you're not."

Sapphire smiled through a film of tears. They used to say that to each other before tests. *Don't fall apart, or at least make it look like you're not.* The reminder brought home the fact that they were parting ways here. Saying goodbye didn't feel right without the third member of their trio. None of this was turning out quite how Mica had imagined.

She knew Sapphire had even greater cause to fear for Danil's safety. She was missing not just a friend, but someone with whom she'd hoped to share a future. That future had now been cast into uncertainty. The least Mica could do was put on a brave face for her friend.

"Send word when you hear from him," she said cheerily. "*When*, not if. And write me to let me know how you're doing. You'll be rich enough to pay for a Blur messenger!"

Sapphire had been assigned to a wealthy trading outfit on Winnow Island. She would be paid handsomely to travel around the empire in various guises to make sure its investments were in good condition.

"Have fun in the palace," Sapphire said. "Don't let that princess push you around."

Mica laughed. "I have four older brothers. I can stand up to one little princess."

Sapphire cracked a real smile at last. "Oh, Mica, you have no idea what you're getting yourself into."

Just then, the five nobles emerged from the inn in a jumble of sleepy expressions and bright clothes, already snapping orders. Mica hugged her friend one last time and hurried to the carriages. The first was reserved for the nobles, while the other two were for their baggage and servants. Mica would ride in the third one, with the baggage.

No sooner had she settled amongst the trunks and parcels than Lord Riven and Lady Lorna climbed in after her.

"Oh! I'm sorry," Mica said. "I thought this was the servants' car—"

"You're fine," grumbled Lord Riven. Suddenly his thick black hair receded into his scalp, and his fine-boned patrician face seemed to melt as he transformed into a paunchy middle-aged man with a bulbous red nose.

"You're Mimics!" Mica said.

The former Lord Riven mumbled something incoherent, slumped against a large hatbox, and went straight to sleep.

Lady Lorna's Impersonator dropped her pouty lips and doe eyes, becoming a squat little woman who wouldn't be out of place running a village bakery.

"Don't mind my husband, dear," she said. "Lord Ober kept him up all night. That man has more energy than someone his age has a right to. I'm Edwina, and this is Rufus."

"Mica Graydier."

"Oh yes, we spoke to Master Kiev about you. I must say I don't envy you. I hear that princess is a whirlwind."

The carriage lurched into motion. Mica steadied the trunk swaying beside her and leaned toward Edwina. "Do you spend a lot of time in the palace?"

"Goodness, no." Edwina chuckled. "We're freelancers based less than a day's journey from here. Lord Ober hired us for the ceremony. I don't know that he even asked the lord and lady if they wanted to make the trip. Most noble folk don't bother with the likes of us."

Mica didn't like the sound of that. Didn't the nobles know their safety and prosperity relied on people like them?

"But that's really Lord Ober and his wife?"

"Oh yes. And Lord Caleb is himself too, though he seems an elusive chap."

Mica hadn't actually seen Lord Ober's nephew, come to think

of it. He was probably one of those lords who didn't respect her profession.

The carriage trundled across the square, over the red stone bridge, and into the rolling countryside. Farmland surrounded the town for miles, and the smell of hay and cattle filtered in through the carriage windows.

"I must say it was good to be back at the Academy," Edwina said as she settled in for the ride. "We trained there ourselves nigh on twenty years ago. Kiev joined the Masters Council the same year we got our first assignments. What a legend he is!"

As Redbridge receded behind them, Mica and Edwina chatted about the Academy, where she and Rufus had met, and about Jewel Harbor. Mica was disappointed to find that the cheery Impersonator didn't know much about life in the Silver Palace itself. Princess Jessamyn, who was a few years older than Mica, had been a toddler when Edwina and Rufus moved out of the capital to raise their children in the country.

"That was before the emperor's wife died. Oh, I hear that girl needed a mother's firm hand to rein her in. I expect it's too late now."

"Rein her in?" A memory popped into Mica's head of her mother lifting Wills and Rees straight into the air seconds before they released a jar of poisonous spiders in the kitchen. They'd collected them with their bare hands, not understanding that the rest of the family didn't have impervious skin like theirs. Somehow, she doubted that was the kind of thing Edwina was talking about. "Is she that bad?"

"You know how ladies are, dear."

"Uh . . ."

"Reminds me of my first assignment as a double for Lady Maren of Winnow Island. What a temper that woman had! Little wonder she needed protection."

Edwina babbled on about Lady Maren—who sounded fearsome—as they rumbled down the road toward the western coast of Amber Island. Mica felt troubled at Edwina's description of the noblewoman, especially after what Sapphire had said about how Mica didn't know what she was getting herself into. How did *she* know, for that matter? Sapphire had grown up in a wealthier family than Mica's, but she was not a noble. Maybe the habits of elegant ladies were discussed more regularly in households that didn't include four brash boys with far too much energy and supernatural ability.

Still, it was nice to talk with someone who had worked in various impersonation fields over the years, and when Edwina and Rufus were let off in their town that afternoon, Mica was sorry to see them go.

"Good luck with your assignment, dear," Edwina said, patting her hand. "And stay safe in the big city, you hear? Talents can't be too careful these days."

"What do you mean?"

"You hear things, you know? Disappearances and the like."

Mica sat forward. "Disappearances?"

"Aye. More than usual. These are strange times."

"I reckon you'll be safe in the palace," Rufus said. He had roused himself at last, and he heaved a trunk out of the way and helped his wife climb down from the carriage.

"Can you tell me more about—?"

"Hurry up back there!" the carriage driver shouted. "You're keeping His Lordship waiting."

Rufus grumbled an imprecation then looked back at Mica. "Just keep your eyes open."

The carriage door slammed, leaving Mica alone with the baggage.

The journey became less enjoyable after Edwina and Rufus departed. The nobles paid little attention to Mica. Lady Euphia complained relentlessly about the food and accommodations whenever they stopped, and Lord Ober spent much of his time appeasing her. He had called Talents the backbone of the empire during his Assignment Ceremony speech, but now he barely seemed to notice Mica. Lord Caleb slept through their early stops and stumbled straight to his room in the inn the first night. Mica caught a glimpse of tousled brown hair and a shuffling walk, but she never saw his face.

She tried making friends with Lady Euphia's handmaids, who were her best chance to learn about the life she was about to embark on amongst the nobility. The three handmaids were all older than Mica, and they looked oddly alike. Their hair, though different colors on each—black, red-gold, and chestnut—had the same sleek sheen, as if treated with a potion, and all their eyes had a sharp glint, somewhere between haughty and distrustful. They rode in the middle carriage and moved in a giggling group whenever the carriages stopped.

Mica approached them in the crowded common room at the roadside inn where they stayed the first night. The nobles had been given a private booth removed from the ordinary travelers. After making sure all of Lady Euphia's needs were met, the maids gathered at a table by the window with thick bowls of stew.

"Mind if I join you?" Mica said, coming over to the table with her own stew. "It's been lonely in the baggage carriage."

The women turned as one and looked her up and down, their eyes lingering on her skirt. Mica fidgeted with the coarse brown material. The maids wore surprisingly expensive-looking dresses with complicated lace-up fronts emphasizing their womanly features.

"Can I sit, or . . ."

Mica trailed off as identical sneers twisted across rosy lips.

"*Who* are you?" one of the maids said at last. She had red-gold hair, deep-set eyes, and a mole on her cheek.

"I'm Micathea, from the Academy. Well, originally from

Stonefoss, but I've been at Redbridge for five years. I've been riding with—"

"Stonefoss?" A red-gold eyebrow arched. "How quaint."

And the women turned right back to their conversation.

Mica gaped at the backs of their heads. She had been trained to pay attention to appearances, and while it was easy to see she didn't belong in this group, she hadn't expected outright rudeness. What was their problem?

She was tempted to plop down at the maids' table no matter what they said. Instead, she left the noisy common room and sat on the steps of the carriage to eat her stew alone, pushing away the growing fear that this assignment was going to be a disaster.

She couldn't refuse her posting without being liable for the full cost of her education. Employers paid a percentage back to the Academy during the first years of a professional Impersonator's service, and Mica's family didn't have the money to settle a debt like that. She could only hope most of the people she'd encounter in Jewel Harbor wouldn't be like her traveling companions.

Mica missed Sapphire and Danil more than ever as she ate her stew in the gloomy stable yard, listening to the laughter rising from the common room. Danil had to be back by now. She couldn't bear the thought of anything happening to her friend.

Talents can't be too careful these days. Edwina's words repeated in her mind. *Disappearances... More than usual.*

Were the Obsidian raiders getting bolder? The possibility that their enemy was becoming more aggressive only strengthened Mica's feeling that she was traveling in the wrong direction.

CHAPTER FOUR

Over the next two days, Mica rode alone in the swaying carriage among the trunks and hatboxes. The scenery changed from rolling farmland to windswept coastline, occasionally interrupted by settlements, and the salty tang of the sea replaced the smell of hay and manure.

The night before they arrived in the capital, they stayed in a bustling seaside town called Gullton. Their inn, located on a steep sea cliff, was packed with people traveling to and from the big city. Mica was given a cot in the servants' quarters above the common room, where the maids slept six to a room. She turned in early, hoping for a good night's sleep before she reported to the palace. But the women in her room chatted late into the night, gossiping relentlessly about their employers and ignoring her requests to keep their voices down. After the fourth time the sound of shrill laughter jolted her awake, she gave up and left the room.

The common area was just as noisy as the servants' quarters. Mica found herself missing the ramshackle tavern where she'd stayed up late with her brothers on her final night in Redbridge. She hadn't expected to feel isolated among so many people.

You'd be alone in Obsidian too, she reminded herself as she searched for an open seat. *This is the life you signed up for.*

She spotted Lord Ober drinking port with a handful of other men, all wearing fine clothes suggesting they were nobles or perhaps wealthy merchants. Ober carried himself with a sense of assurance that reminded Mica of the commanding officers back in Stonefoss. They had confidence bordering on arrogance, as if they had never doubted their place in the world. Mica squared her shoulders and adopted a similar stance, hoping the dominant bearing would help her feel bold inside too.

Then someone bumped into her roughly, knocking her hip against a table.

"Watch out," said a low, gravelly voice.

Mica stepped back as a man with white hair pushed past her, carrying a brimming tankard of ale. She did a double take at the sight of patchy scars covering his face and hands, as if he'd been splashed with burning oil.

"Excuse me, sir," she said quickly. "I didn't mean—"

"This is no place for a young woman at this hour," he grumbled, continuing on to a table at the back of the common room.

Mica sighed, shoulders slumping. So much for her dominant stance. It seemed no place was quite right for her on this journey. Admitting defeat, she slipped out of the inn doors to go for a walk.

Other raucous establishments surrounded their inn on the main Gullton thoroughfare. Mica strolled past them, peeking in windows to catch glimpses of the faces within. Light spilled out onto the sandy street, and the clatter of voices almost drowned out the sound of waves crashing below the town. She wondered if this was what Jewel Harbor would be like. She had never actually been to a city as large as the capital.

Mica walked until she escaped the commotion, keeping the sea to her right. A stiff wind carried fog through the outer edges of Gullton, glowing white as the moon rose high above it. The cacophony of the inns faded as she left the town boundaries and strode along a pathway beside the cliff. Soon all she could hear was the wind and the waves.

She found a large, flat rock overlooking the water and sat cross-legged on it to exercise her faces. She was supposed to practice her impersonations every day, cycling through features the way a singer practiced scales. As the moonlit fog swirled around her, she engaged the muscles in her face one by one, calling on her Talent to change her eyes from hazel to green to blue, first dark and murky and then as pale as a late-summer sky. Pale blue turned to yellow, darkening to brown to black, then gray, lavender, and on through increasingly unnatural shades. Next she morphed her eyebrows, thinned, thickened, arched in different places depending on the mood she wanted to convey. Her mouth was next, followed by her skin tone and then the bone structure of her face. It was soothing to stretch her features from shape to shape as the wind blew sharp across her cheeks.

After completing her "scales," Mica stood up on the rock at the cliff's edge and practiced her regular rotation of impersonations. The cowherd's daughter, the buxom barmaid, the mischievous lad, the lean old soldier, the humpbacked crone. She became a fat little boy, a devastating beauty, a miniature version of Master Kiev. She couldn't bring herself to practice any of her Obsidian impersonations. Taking on those shapes reminded her too much of the excitement and anticipation as she'd prepared for her espionage career. She tried to hold on to the hope that Master Kiev had something big in mind for her in Jewel Harbor, something only she could do.

The roar of the waves breaking against the cliff below filled her ears as the night deepened. The fog was like a living thing, morphing and curling around her in an elegant dance. The chill raised bumps on her arms.

Mica began to grow tired. Impersonation took effort, just like lifting heavy objects or walking long distances. But she needed to stay sharp, especially because she would need to learn a whole new cast of impersonations in the palace. She tried out a few of the people she had seen on the journey, mimicking Rufus's paunch, Lord Ober's nose, the haughty maid's mole and red-gold hair. At last, she shifted back to her own form: slight build, snub nose, nut-brown hair.

"That one's my favorite."

Mica jumped as a strange man stepped out of the fog. She was still standing on the rock, and as she whirled to face him, her foot slipped off the edge. Her arms flailed wide, her balance tipping too far, too fast. The waves crashed against the cliff far below.

The stranger reached her so fast he might have been a Blur, grabbing her hand before she toppled into the sea. He pulled her to him as if on reflex.

"I'm so sorry! I—"

"You startled me." Mica wrenched away from the stranger and retreated from the dizzying drop, heart thudding wildly. "You shouldn't sneak up on people like that."

"I didn't mean to scare you. I was just admiring your work."

"Oh." Mica straightened her clothes, hoping he hadn't seen her nose grow an inch when she slipped. At least the young man sounded genuinely apologetic. She cleared her throat. "How long have you been standing there?"

"Long enough to see that wrinkly old lady impression."

Mica winced. She was supposed to keep her impersonations private outside of the Academy. They wouldn't be any use if people knew them all. She looked the stranger up and down, cataloguing his features as well as she could in the darkness: windblown hair, slightly pointed ears, broad shoulders. He wasn't very tall, but energy seemed to fill every line of his stocky body.

He accepted her scrutiny unselfconsciously. "I've never seen a Mimic go through so many faces so fast."

"I thought I was alone."

The man didn't take the hint, regarding her with frank curiosity.

"I'd love to ask you about your Talent." He sat on the large rock, sticking his boots over the cliff edge, and beckoned to her with a square hand. "Would you care to join me?"

Mica didn't move, remembering Edwina's words about how Talents can't be too careful these days. She was all too aware of how remote this location was.

The stranger looked up at her, as if surprised she didn't immediately sit beside him. "I promise not to push you off the cliff."

Mica hesitated, thinking of Danil disappearing without a trace and the scarred man's comment about young women being out at this hour. Would Lord Ober and his entourage even notice if she didn't take her place in the carriage the next morning?

"I have to get back to town," she said. "I have an early start in the morning."

"Oh. Okay." The man sounded disappointed though not in a particularly sinister way. "May I escort you?"

"It's not far." Mica started to go, but something held her back. The stranger had sort of saved her life by pulling her away from the cliff, even though he'd put her in danger in the first place. His eager curiosity and open expression didn't seem nefarious— though she knew not to be fooled by people's faces.

The wind picked up, sweeping away the fog that had helped to light her way. It was getting darker by the minute, turning the cliff edge into an ominous maw. Mica figured the young man was probably a local, who would know if there were any hidden drops on the way back to town.

"All right then," she said. "Are you coming?"

The stranger flashed a smile and scrambled to his feet. He fell in beside her, and they headed back toward the lights of Gullton.

"So what do you want to know about Talents?" she asked.

"It's *your* Talent in particular," he said. "Impersonation. I've known plenty of Blurs, Shields, and Muscles, but Mimics are much more secretive."

"That's kind of the point."

"What does it feel like to change your face?"

"Like squeezing a muscle, though my bones and skin change as often as my facial muscles."

"What about your eyes?"

"That feels like squinting. Then I just visualize the color I want."

"How can you tell you got it right?"

"It's difficult to explain. That's like asking how you know when you've scratched an itch enough. You just do."

"Hmm." The young man lapsed into a thoughtful silence. Mica matched her steps to his, an exercise she'd learned in her first year at the Academy. It always took a few paces to get a stranger's stride just right. His walk was like a soldier's, purposeful and straight though not too fast. He clearly wasn't worried about the rocky landscape, even in the dark.

They reached the town and strode onward through patches of light from the windows. The young man remained at Mica's side, still discussing what it was like to be a Mimic. She found herself slowing her steps to prolong the conversation as they drew near to her inn. It was surprisingly nice to have company after the lonely ride with indifferent traveling companions. The stranger was an agreeable sort, and his questions were keen—and numerous. She sometimes forgot that most people didn't spend much time around trained Impersonators, at least as far as they knew.

"And can you always control it?" he asked as they paused in front of the door to the inn's common room.

"Now, yes," Mica said. "Control is something you can improve through practice. Blurs and Muscles practice too. Those who don't never reach their full potential."

"Huh. Did you learn that at Redbridge?"

"How did you know I went to Redbridge?"

The man gave her a puzzled look. Before he could answer, the inn door burst open, releasing a torrent of laughter. A trio of drunken sailors tumbled out, singing sea shanties at the top of their lungs. One of the sailors spotted Mica and lurched toward her with a lascivious grin.

Mica's companion stepped forward at once, clapping a firm hand on the sailor's shoulder and steering him back toward his friends. But Mica had already turned into a lean old soldier at the first sign of a threat and slipped through the door.

She paused in the common room and peered back outside. The young man was looking around for her, brushing a hand through his wind-tousled hair. She could see him better now—and he was quite good looking. She hesitated, wondering if she should resume her own face and invite him for a drink in the common room. But the hour was late, and Edwina's warning lingered in her mind. She retreated to the servants' quarters, leaving the handsome young local behind.

CHAPTER FIVE

The road became clogged with traffic as Lord Ober's convoy trundled toward Jewel Harbor. Mica had woken early that morning and spent nearly half an hour rearranging the trunks in her carriage so she would have a better view out the window. They were heavy, and she was grunting and swearing by the time she finished, but it was worth it.

She leaned all the way out of the window now, coughing in the dust of passing horses. They were still on the coast road, but she could only smell the barest hint of sea salt, hidden beneath the musk of the horses and the thick aroma of sweat. She tried to memorize the features of passersby but was quickly overwhelmed by the endless parade of strangers. They were all so different from each other! She wondered how she was going to come up with some proper city-folk looks when they hardly seemed to have a single thing in common.

Mica forgot about the people entirely when the carriage rumbled around a bend and she got her first view of the capital city. Jewel Harbor was located on a crescent-shaped island so built up it was almost impossible to see the ground beneath the buildings. The city was a glittering, chaotic place, rising from the water like a jagged knot of crystal and stone.

When the Windfast Empire formed, it was agreed that the capital shouldn't belong to any of the individual kingdoms that made up the original coalition. It was built on a formerly uninhabited hunk of rock and quickly blossomed as the political seat, cultural hub, and center of commerce for the empire. Space on the island was limited, so the city grew up rather than out over the generations, with towers built on top of each other in teetering piles. Teams of Muscle builders were constantly being called upon to reinforce structures so they could stretch farther into the sky. The streets were warren-like, half of them covered by the outcroppings of yet more additions to the buildings.

The harbor itself was sheltered between the crescent landmass and the western coast of Amber Island. Another city, Old Kings, spread along the Amber coast, directly across from Jewel Harbor. It had more space for sprawling estates and wide avenues, but most people preferred to live in the imperial capital itself, where the action was.

Mica's caravan rumbled down the broad streets of Old Kings to a noisy dock, where ferries waited to carry them across. After a few shouted negotiations, the carriages lurched onto one of the larger ferries. They swayed precipitously as they crossed the churning harbor toward the city. Boats of all sizes and shapes careened around them. Sailors cursed elaborately at one another whenever they came close to a collision, which happened frequently.

Mica marveled at the cacophony. Jewel Harbor was busier than she could ever have imagined. How could anyone even *think* in a place like this?

It only got noisier when the ferry bumped against the opposite dock and they rumbled off into the city itself. The streets were narrow and packed, and voices echoed off the buildings looming overhead. Mica could have sworn the walls themselves trembled under the onslaught of sound.

Faces whizzed past her so fast she felt dizzy. Fire-red hair, protruding ears, black mustache, harelip, red lip, black braid, protruding nose. On and on, features morphing, mixing. She had to clamp down on the instinct to catalogue everyone she saw, or she might be sick.

Instead, she tried to spot the Talents in the crowds. Here and there, Blur messengers darted through the throng, moving side to side as often as forward. A pair of Muscles carried huge stones across the road, forcing traffic to come to a halt until they passed. Mica wondered what they were building. There hardly seemed to be room for so much as a hut in this chaos.

Shields were more difficult to identify. Just because they couldn't be injured didn't mean they were any stronger or fitter than anyone else. But they carried themselves with a certain self-assurance mixed with brash abandon, a trait that had made Mica's brothers especially popular with the girls back in Stonefoss.

Once, she caught a glimpse of a fellow Mimic down an alley-way. He was performing a complex rotation of impersonations, standing atop a crate with a hat for coins at his feet. Mica felt faintly embarrassed for him. He must have failed out of his Impersonator training if he had to resort to being a street performer. There were beggars in the alley too, some missing limbs or eyes. Barefoot children watched the fine carriages pass with hungry gleams in their eyes. Safe in the bubbles of Stonefoss and the Academy, Mica had never seen such poverty before.

The carriage turned another corner, and she lost sight of the Mimic and the beggars. They jolted along a broad street lined with apothecaries and potioners shops. A myriad of scents filled the air, and colorful steam issued from the windows. She detected rosemary and sage, cedar and cinnamon, poppy, eucalyptus, and the heady aroma of incense. Potions were costly, and

Mica had only seen them used on rare occasions. She could hardly imagine a city wealthy enough to fill an entire street with them.

They left the potioners street, the mixed aromas lingering in the carriage, and entered a lane of prosperous townhouses and fine stone buildings. Crystal shone in the windows, and elegant trimmings adorned the walls. It was just as busy here as in the poorer streets, and the endless parade of faces continued. Sleek hair, jeweled earrings, powdered cheeks, sharp eyes. Mica could hardly believe there were this many people in the whole empire.

They turned at last toward the Silver Palace. Located at the apex of the crescent, the palace was a grand, sprawling place, bigger than the assembly hall back at the Academy. There was a wing for every point of the compass, radiating from a central tower. A dome topped this tower, plated in pure silver so dazzling Mica had to shade her eyes as they approached.

Guards, likely Shields, waved them through the palace gates into a broad courtyard. Once inside, the first carriage turned right, delivering Lord Ober and the nobles to a shaded portico where they could disembark. The servant and baggage carriages turned left and continued on through a stone archway. At last they came to an abrupt stop, and Mica tumbled out into a crowded stable yard.

She hoisted her satchel of belongings onto her shoulder, wondering where she was supposed to go next. Everyone seemed to be in a rush. Lady Euphia's maids darted one way, and the carriage drivers went the other, already shouting at the stable boys to hurry up and attend to their horses. Mica had thought she could ask Lord Ober for further instructions, but he must have already disappeared into the depths of the palace. She wasn't even sure which archway around the stable yard led back to the front gates.

"Move yer feet!" shouted a scrawny man, elbowing past her

with a massive bale of hay balanced on his shoulder as if it weighed no more than a teapot.

She jumped out of the Muscle's way and was nearly trampled by a fine stallion. The nobleman on its back didn't notice her at all. She realized with a start that it was the real Lord Riven. Rufus had captured his features well, but he hadn't included the imperious air Lord Riven adopted as he looked right through the stable boy rushing up to take his horse. He dismounted and sauntered toward another archway, walking as if he expected everyone in the crowded yard to move out of his way. They did exactly that.

Mica tried to follow the arrogant lord, figuring Princess Jessamyn would be wherever the other nobles were, but the gap was already closing behind him. She couldn't force her way through the throng, and she got turned around, no longer sure which way Lord Riven had gone. Most everyone else seemed to be palace employees, and they were all far too busy to talk. One guard leered at her when she asked where to find the princess.

"In my bed, naturally!"

Mica retreated, taking refuge in an archway to try to get her bearings. She wished she'd asked Master Kiev for more details about how to actually report for duty. She had no idea the Silver Palace would be this big and bustling. She might as well be invisible.

Then she had an idea. She closed her eyes, shutting out the riot of faces in the courtyard. She concentrated, squeezing her features into new shapes, eyes widening, lips plumping, chest expanding as her waist dwindled to waspish proportions. By the time she opened her eyes, she was a passable copy of Lady Lorna. She lifted her nose into the air and sauntered straight across the courtyard.

It was like magic. The crowds parted before her, servants leaping aside to make room, some dipping into curtsies and bows. Mica tried not to look at them. That seemed to be the most common trait of the nobles she had seen so far. They didn't look at anyone but each other.

As the way cleared before her, she spied another archway that appeared to lead into the palace proper. She marched straight toward it, wishing she'd had a chance to observe Lady Lorna's walk. Did noble ladies sway their hips, or were they supposed to process in a statelier fashion? She'd find out soon enough.

Once she made it inside the palace, the crowds thinned. She walked down a plain stone corridor lined with doors and stairwells at regular intervals. The clatter of pots and pans echoing down the corridor indicated she was near the kitchens. A passing scullery maid gave her a strange look, which Mica took to mean that Lady Lorna didn't frequent this part of the palace. She slipped into a doorway and changed back to her own face before continuing on.

Mica hadn't made it another ten paces before a young woman with frizzy black hair and wide, frightened eyes bounced out of a nearby stairwell and seized her hand.

"Are you the Mimic? I've been looking everywhere for you! Hurry along! She's expecting you."

"How did—?"

"Don't stand there gaping like a goldfish. Come with me."

The girl tugged her into the stairwell and led the way up the steps. She had a panicked way of moving that Mica had noticed in many of the servants in the stable yard too, as if she were trying to outrun an angry wildcat. She kept up an anxious patter as she hurried up staircases, turning into corridors seemingly at random.

"She's in such a state this morning. Lord Riven went riding when he was supposed to be visiting with Lady Ingrid, which means Lady Ingrid was in the conservatory instead of her parlor. Nearly ruined everything! Fortunately, she sent in Lady Elana, and Lady Ingrid can't stand to be in the same room with her after everything that happened in Winnow Bay last summer. Oh dear, can't you walk a little faster?"

Mica picked up the pace, trying to process the flood of information burbling from the girl's mouth. She had completely lost track of where they were, though she noticed the corridors becoming wider and airier in this part of the palace. She caught glimpses of the city out of the windows, but she wasn't sure which wing of the palace they were in now. She'd never be able to find her way out.

"What's your name?" Mica said when the girl paused to take a breath.

"I'm Brin, Her Ladyship's handmaid. I do errands and carry messages when the Blur isn't needed. Oh, I wish I were a Blur. Quickly, it's this way!"

Mica jogged after her into the widest corridor yet. Decorative lanterns in sconces lined the walls, and additional light flooded into the corridor from panes of thick glass set directly into the stone ceiling. Before Mica could ask about the skylights, Brin grabbed her arm again and stopped her in front of an especially large set of doors. She slipped a key out of her pocket, fumbling it in nervous hands.

"Don't tell her it took me so long to find you. And do try not to breathe so hard so she doesn't realize we ran all the way. She hates it when servants run." Brin was trying to fix her frazzled hair and fit her key into the lock at the same time.

"I'm not really a servant," Mica said, finding her voice at last. "I trained at the best academy for professional—"

The lock clicked. "Got it! Shh, don't speak unless she speaks to you." Brin turned the knob, and a small door set into one of the larger doors swung open. Then she ushered Mica through it and into Princess Jessamyn's chambers.

CHAPTER SIX

Mica's first impression was of a meadow of wildflowers. They entered a huge sunlit room in which every surface was covered with vases overflowing with blooming lilies, crocuses, and lupines. Deep plush carpets spread across much of the tile floor in muted shades of rose, tan, and pale green. Assorted couches and tables were arranged in clusters, enough to seat at least two dozen people at once.

Elegant tapestries adorned most of the walls, except for one made entirely of glass. The massive windows looked out on the crescent harbor, with a view of Amber Island beyond. It wasn't long past noon, and the sun shone bright above Old Kings and the glittering harbor.

"Psst. Over here." Brin tugged Mica toward a round table dominated by a massive vase of yellow roses.

As they approached, the vase rose from the table, hiding the face of the woman carrying it. Her long indigo skirts swished as she tottered under the weight of the flowers. A voice came from deep within the roses.

"Who does he think he is? He expects me to believe he picked these flowers for me himself? Does he think I am as dumb as this cheap Dwindlemire crockery?"

Abruptly, the vase soared through the air and shattered on the tile floor with a terrific crash. Roses and shards of porcelain scattered all the way to the window. Mica's eyes snapped back to the woman who'd thrown the vase.

Princess Jessamyn was exactly Mica's height. She had a similarly slight build, though it looked less boyish and more delicate on her. Her hair was a pretty shade of dark red that reminded Mica of summer cherries. Her cheeks were flushed, her brown eyes bright, and she had some of the thickest and most expressive eyebrows Mica had ever seen.

"Can you believe he had the gall to claim he went riding to pick me some roses—roses!—and that's why he failed to call upon poor Lady Ingrid?"

Brin dipped her head nervously. "No, Princess Jessamyn." She elbowed Mica, who dipped her head as well. The princess didn't seem to be speaking to either of them.

"And to think I was forced to skip my dancing lesson this morning to make sure Lady Elana would go to the conservatory." The princess stalked over to the puddle by the window and began kicking the roses, porcelain crunching under her slippers. "My life is *such* a trial."

"I'm so sorry, Princess Jessamyn." Brin swallowed audibly and approached the irate lady as if she were a rabid animal. "Princess Jessamyn? This is the—"

"And I'm supposed to have a new Impersonator by now!" Another rose flew across the floor. "Why is it taking Ober and Caleb so long to get me one? I thought they were the only reliable men left in the empire. Apparently, I was wrong!"

"Princess Jessamyn!" Brin said, her voice taking on a desperate edge. "This is the Mimic His Lordship brought from the Academy. Her name is . . . is . . ."

"Micathea Graydier," Mica said before Brin could fly into a full-blown panic. "I'm a recent graduate of the Redbridge Academy for—"

"At last something goes my way!" Jessamyn spun to face them, her skirt swirling over the battered roses. "But Brin, you mustn't call them Mimics. They get so tetchy about using the proper terms."

Brin looked as though she might burst into tears. Jessamyn waved off her apologies and swooped closer to Mica, scrutinizing her from head to toe.

"She's the right size." She pursed her lips. "I don't like that skirt. Dreadful color."

Mica felt a muscle pulsing in her jaw as the princess walked in a circle around her, examining her as thoroughly as if she were a horse at market.

"Well?" Jessamyn said when she completed her circuit. "Impersonate something. I don't have all day."

"Who would you like me to—?"

"Just show me what you can do," she said impatiently.

Mica's mind went completely blank. She couldn't remember a single one of her impersonations. She was still reeling from the city, the palace, the endless procession of strange faces.

Think, Mica. Don't just stand there.

Jessamyn tapped her silk slipper on the floor. Brin looked as though she was about to vomit.

"If you can't even—"

Mica shook herself then quickly squeezed her features to look like the first person who popped into her head, the young local she'd met on the cliff's edge near Gullton. She was smaller than he was, so she made the shoulders less broad and squeezed in her waist beneath her clothes to get the extra height she needed.

Princess Jessamyn blinked in surprise. "Well, he'd find *that* amusing."

Mica wasn't sure what "he" Jessamyn meant. Maybe the man who'd sent her the flowers? She quickly switched to a different impersonation: the humpbacked crone. Jessamyn grimaced and started to turn away. Mica scrambled, trying to think of what would impress the princess. It took a lot of skill to change the curve of her spine and make all her skin sag. Maybe Jessamyn didn't realize what a complicated impersonation that was.

The princess was already losing interest. Poor Brin hovered anxiously beside her, as if she expected her lady's displeasure to break over her like a sudden rainstorm.

Feeling slightly panicked, Mica looked around at the chamber full of flowers, the elegant wall hangings, the view overlooking the city. And then it hit her. Jessamyn obviously loved beautiful things. She didn't care about the intricacy of the impression. She cared about the beauty.

Mica summoned the most gorgeous face she knew, a woman so perfect that she couldn't be real. In fact, she wasn't. This was a face Mica had created herself, trying enhancement after enhancement until she found the perfect balance of features. Her hair became the pale gold of a moonbeam, growing thicker and falling all the way to her waist in soft curls. Her eyes grew, losing their plain hazel to become a shade of soft green that was a little unrealistic but not enough to be unnerving. Her features became more delicate, and her skin took on a dewy, translucent hue. It was an Obsidian look, exotic and ethereal.

Jessamyn raised one of those magnificent eyebrows. "Interesting choice."

Belatedly, Mica realized she probably shouldn't have selected an idealized version of their greatest enemy to show the princess of the empire. Beauty could come in many different forms, but she'd been taught to make judgment calls about what her audience found attractive. *Great. I'm going to lose my assignment for sure.*

Then Jessamyn said, "This one is exquisite. You have better taste than the last girl, Micathea Graydier."

Mica opened her perfect rosebud mouth, surprised Jessamyn had recalled her name. "Does that mean—?"

"Yes, you'll be useful, if you can stop gawking like a country lass."

"I—"

"You'd best take that look off before any of the lords see you, or you'll never have a night's peace." Jessamyn swept off toward an ornately carved door at the back of her chamber. "I must prepare for my afternoon tea. Brin, see that our new Impersonator finds her room. I'll send for her later. Now, I must go put on that new green gown. It will make Lady Amanta curl up and *die.*"

And she was gone in a whirl of skirts and pealing laughter.

Mica stared after her, not quite sure what to think of her new lady. At least she had passed the test.

Brin tugged on her sleeve. "Come on, then. Your room is just through here." She pulled back a large tapestry directly across from the windows, revealing a hidden door.

"I'm staying in the princess's quarters?"

"It's so she can call when she needs us." Brin led her into a narrow corridor behind the walls. It was lit with plain lanterns and lined with several doors. "These are the other two hand-maids' rooms, and that one is for her Shield. His name is Banner." Brin blushed deeply as they passed that door. "The servant staircase is at the end, next to my room. And this is you."

She opened the door to a small, furnished bedroom, no bigger than the one Mica had shared with the twins when she was young. It was clearly a maid's room. A bell hung next to the narrow bed, with a silk cord leading into the wall.

"You must come the moment she rings," Brin said.

"Do I have on-duty hours or—?"

"Don't make her wait," Brin said. "It's easier for everyone that way. I must go help her dress. We'll talk later."

And the maid scampered off, leaving Mica to catch her breath for the first time since arriving in the palace.

Mica was lost in a deep sleep when the bell sounded by her bed. She had only intended to take a quick nap before venturing out to explore the palace. The hard cot reminded her of the simple beds in the cottages back at Stonefoss, and she had drifted off thinking of home.

The abrupt clang of the bell made her jump so high she nearly rearranged her organs. She scrambled out of bed and tripped over the low stool where she had set her satchel. She rubbed sleep out of her eyes, trying to figure out whether it was still daytime or if she had slept right into the night. Then she remembered where she was.

She dashed out through the servants' corridor and back to the flower-filled antechamber. Red-gold light drifted in through the wall of windows, hinting that the sun was setting on the opposite side of the palace. Old Kings looked hazy on the eastern horizon, already cloaked in purples and blues. Mica must have slept for hours.

Princess Jessamyn was storming around her room, wearing the pale-green gown she had chosen for her tea. The shattered vase and roses had vanished.

"Impersonate a Blur messenger and deliver this note to Lady Ingrid." Jessamyn held up the letter without looking at Mica, forcing her to dart across the chamber to take it. "Make sure she knows it's from Lord Riven, and find out who she's dining with tonight."

Mica took the fine parchment, still feeling disoriented from her abrupt awakening. Blurs looked just like regular people. Was there a specific one she was supposed to impersonate?

"Excuse me, uh, Princess Jessamyn," she began. "How do you want—?"

The princess gave her an exasperated look, as if she had interrupted a very important train of thought. "I'm not going to tell you how to do your job, Micathea."

"But I don't know—"

"The Head of the Academy assured me he'd send me a better Impersonator than my last one." The princess made a shooing motion. "Don't waste my time with inane questions."

Mica swallowed a retort about how she wasn't here to be a messenger. She put the note in her pocket and hurried out into the corridor before the princess could dismiss her on the spot. As much as she'd prefer a different assignment, she didn't want to be fired on her first day.

She halted outside the door, staring down the broad corridor. The palace was vast, and she had no idea where anything was located yet. Unfortunately, Brin was nowhere in sight. Surely it wasn't reasonable of the princess to expect her to know her way around a few hours after she arrived?

A throat cleared gruffly behind her. She turned to find a tall, middle-aged man with a drooping mustache and deep-set eyes looking down at her.

"May I be of assistance?"

"Oh, uh, I'm supposed to deliver this to a Lady Ingrid."

"I believe her quarters are in the south wing on the fourth floor. Someone there can direct you to her room."

He had a melodious voice and an unflappable bearing. Mica already felt steadier in his presence.

"Thank you," she said. "Which way is it from here?"

"Go to the end of the corridor. Take your first left and walk around until you reach a large stone archway and turn left again. That's the south wing. Take the stairs down to the fourth floor. We're on seven now."

"Thank you, Mister . . . ?"

"Banner. I am the princess's Shield."

Mica was surprised. From the way Brin had blushed when

she pointed out Banner's room, she had imagined him being much younger.

"I'm Mica, the new Impersonator."

"A pleasure." Banner inclined his head politely.

"Oh, one more thing," Mica said. "She asked me to impersonate a Blur messenger. Is there a specific one?"

"Hmm. There's a lad about your age. Perhaps three inches taller, with bright-red hair. I very much doubt Lady Ingrid will be able to tell the difference beyond that."

Mica thanked him again and set off, morphing her features into the mischievous lad in her regular rotation but with red hair a few shades brighter than the princess's. She also unfastened her skirt and looped it over her shoulder as if it were a cloak, revealing the trousers beneath.

Even with Banner's instructions, it took her a while to find the correct corridor on the correct floor. She marveled at the opulence of the palace as she wandered down marble halls and caught glimpses of grand rooms trimmed in silver and gold. Sculptures decorated the corridors, some made of stone, others of crystal. The palace even smelled rich, as if costly perfumes and incense were in use at all times. Her brother's joke about sweet-smelling lordlings might not be far off.

The scurrying servants she had noticed before were evident here too, numbering at least three for every noble. With the exception of the ladies' maids, most wore uniforms with the imperial crest embroidered on the arm in silver thread. Clothing was going to be an issue here during acts of impromptu espionage. Her Mimic's garb of versatile materials in simple colors wouldn't be as useful where the commoners wore livery and the nobles bedecked themselves in jewels and silk. She expected she'd do more than just deliver notes when Master Kiev got in touch. She was eager to find out why she was really here.

When she reached the fourth-floor corridor in the south wing, she asked a puffy-cheeked servant to point her toward Lady

Ingrid's room. He gestured to the appropriate door with the candle he had been using to light the lanterns along the corridor.

Mica made sure her impersonation was in place and knocked. The door opened a mere crack, and a woman with brown skin and large eyes framed with thick lashes peeked through.

"Yes?"

"I have a note for Lady Ingrid."

A slim brown hand emerged. "Give it here."

"I'm supposed to deliver it to her personally."

"She is dining with a companion, and she does not wish to be disturbed."

Mica didn't move. She couldn't leave without finding out who was dining with Lady Ingrid.

"I can wait," she said, not entirely sure whether that was true. How long had it been since she left the princess's quarters? She probably expected Mica back by now.

"That won't be necessary," Lady Ingrid's maid said. She had a soft voice, and those large, framed eyes made her look frightened. But she didn't budge, and Mica couldn't see past her into the room.

"It's from Lord Riven," Mica said desperately. "He told me to give it—"

"Who is that out there?" came a haughty voice.

Lady Ingrid's maid stepped back, cringing slightly, and a woman with a familiar mole on her cheek appeared at the crack in the door. Mica recognized the sleek, red-gold hair of Lady Euphia's maid. She felt a moment of alarm before she remembered the maid would have no way of connecting her current face to the princess.

"I have a personal message from Lord Riven for Lady Ingrid."

"We will take it." The maid snatched the letter from Mica's hands before she could move. "Now run along, boy. The ladies are busy."

Mica didn't argue. This had already taken too long. She raced back through the palace, making at least two wrong turns before she found the east wing. She was out of breath by the time she reached the top-floor corridor. The lanterns were all lit now, and stars were visible through the panes of glass in the ceiling. Mica stole glances at them as she ran back to the princess's quarters and resumed her own face. Banner admitted her through the small door set in the main one with a polite nod.

Jessamyn had changed her clothes again, now wearing a luxurious black dressing gown. She sat on a plush couch near the vast windows, giggling over a glass of wine with another noblewoman. Mica got a glimpse of bouncing blond curls and round cheeks before she remembered to dip into a curtsy. Only then did it occur to her that perhaps she should have returned through the servants' staircase. She had no idea how to reach it from the other end.

"*Finally,*" Jessamyn said. She snapped her fingers. "Well, who was our mysterious dinner companion?"

Mica grinned. "Lady Euphia was the one dining with Lady—"

"That will be all, Micathea," Jessamyn interrupted sharply. "I don't need you for the rest of the night. Lady Bellina and I have *so* much to discuss."

"Yes, Princess Jessamyn." Mica crossed the room, silently kicking herself. Of course she shouldn't say Lady Ingrid's name around the other lady. She'd been lucky that she recognized Lady Euphia's maid, but she should know better than to divulge any more details than the princess explicitly requested in front of a stranger.

She felt as though she'd been infected with some of Brin's nervousness. She wasn't exactly making a good impression. To top it off, she couldn't remember which tapestry hid the door to the servants' chambers. She pushed aside two others before finding the correct one.

"Wherever do you get your maids?" Lady Bellina said, not bothering to lower her voice. "You always end up with dimwits."

Cheeks blazing, Mica escaped through the hidden door and closed off the sound of the ladies' laughter. She trudged back to her room, feeling embarrassed and overwhelmed, and collapsed onto her bed. She stared at the stone ceiling as her breathing slowed, desperately hoping Master Kiev would get in touch with further instructions soon.

CHAPTER SEVEN

Master Kiev had warned Mica to keep an eye out for anything unusual. The trouble was everything about the Silver Palace was exceedingly strange. Her first week was a blur of frantic errands and wrong turns. People moved as if they were constantly on the verge of disaster, yet nothing seemed to actually happen but tea parties, diverting walks through the conservatory, and balls. Apparently, whenever people weren't attending a ball, they were gossiping about what had happened at the last one. And they all spoke so fast! Mica decided to add a few vocal exercises to her nightly impersonation drills in an effort to accurately capture the way people talked here. She had taken classes on accents at the Academy, but speed and syntax were proving to be just as important.

Mica relied on Brin's help to find her way around the palace, though the girl seemed to be in danger of a breakdown at all times. It was difficult to get anyone else to stand still long enough to give her directions, and she occasionally had to turn herself into a lord or lady to get answers. But the nobles themselves were following an intricate set of rules determining where—and with whom—they should and shouldn't be seen. Mica realized pretty quickly that pretending to be the wrong noble in the wrong corridor could create ripples that would reverberate through the palace for weeks afterwards. The only person who seemed capable of following all the nuances was the princess herself.

Mica had thought she'd have a little more independence as a professional Impersonator. Even soldiers had designated free time. But she was beginning to understand that she was little more than a servant in the eyes of the nobility. Jessamyn was a demanding mistress, the sort who told her handmaids they should never have to rush about the palace, then sent them off on ambitious errands that would take all day if they didn't run. At first Mica couldn't tell if she acted on pure impulse or if there was a method to it all.

The princess expected Mica to repeat every conversation she listened in on verbatim and become a perfect copy of people she had only seen in passing. Mica tried to explain that she needed to see people move and hear them speak in order to form a truly accurate impersonation. Jessamyn waved her off as if *she* were the one being unreasonable. She nearly had a fit when Mica told her she couldn't impersonate Lady Bellina, whom she'd only glimpsed that first night.

"Why must everything be so difficult for me?" Jessamyn exclaimed. "All I want is for people to do the jobs I hired them to do. Is that so much to ask?"

"I'm sorry, Princess Jessamyn," Mica said. "If there's a way I could study the—"

"Do you expect all the ladies to line up for your perusal? Honestly, Talents are so entitled these days."

Mica briefly fantasized about pushing the princess out one of her vast windows. "I just need to see them for more than a few seconds and hear—"

"Wait!" Jessamyn flung up a hand. "Lining up! Of course. You ought to have thought of it sooner. You must attend a dancing lesson. You *can* dance?"

"Some," Mica said. "Not court dances."

Jessamyn looked at her blankly.

"I mean, I can do a jig," Mica said, "but I don't know any—"

"A jig?" Jessamyn closed her eyes and took deep, longsuffering breaths.

"I learn quickly," Mica said. "I'm sure during the lessons, I can pick up—"

"No one goes to dancing lessons to actually *learn* dancing. Really, I must speak to my father about increasing funding to the Academy. If they're not even teaching you how to dance . . ." Jessamyn shook her head. "Very well. Watch from the promenade until you can impersonate all the important lords and ladies. Brin will give you a list of names."

"That . . . would be helpful, actually. Thank you."

The princess was already rushing off for yet another outfit change in her inner rooms. She wore a minimum of three different dresses every day in addition to the costumes required for her other activities: riding, harbor cruises, the occasional racquetball match in the palace gardens. Mica hadn't seen Jessamyn's dressing room yet, but she imagined it was bigger than the antechamber and the entire servants' corridor combined.

The next time Jessamyn attended a dancing lesson in the ballroom at the center of the palace, Mica took up a spot on the promenade overlooking the dance floor. The ballroom itself was circular, and it filled one entire level of the Silver Palace's central tower. The palace consisted of the central tower, which had three expansive levels, and four wings, each with seven floors. At the top of the central tower, beneath the vast silver dome, was Emperor Styl's throne room. A banquet hall filled the bottom level, and the ballroom was in the middle.

Mica leaned on the promenade's stone balustrade, Brin's list clutched in her hand, and studied the people strutting across the polished hardwood dance floor below. She wore her own face, not bothering with an impersonation when no one knew who she was anyway. As the nobles assembled, the ladies greeted each other with kisses on the cheek, and the lords exchanged jubilant handshakes. They milled around for a long time before they actually started dancing, forming groups and dispersing in a different kind of ballet. Most of them kept quarters in the palace itself, rarely spending time in the islands they represented, and they maintained an intricate web of alliances and rivalries Mica was only beginning to unravel.

She started her study with the four people she knew on sight: Princess Jessamyn, Lord Riven, and Ladies Lorna and Bellina. She examined their features and mannerisms, parsing out their voices from the chatter echoing around the ballroom.

Lord Riven was tall and broad enough that she didn't think she could do a convincing impression of him unless she sat down and hid most of her body beneath a table. She'd have a better chance with the ladies, so she paid special attention to the shape of Lorna's pout and the shade of Bellina's curly hair. Identifying a person's most notable feature made it easier to pull off an impersonation. From the way Bellina tossed her hair, it was clear she was proud of her golden curls, and that was likely how others would identify her as well. And if Mica could get the shape of Lorna's features exactly right, she doubted a casual observer would notice she couldn't quite fill out the lady's generous curves.

After Mica felt confident with those impersonations, she began working her way through Brin's list, which included a few notes to help her recognize the various nobles. Unfortunately, Brin wasn't quite as keen an observer as the average Mimic, so the list included entries of dubious use, such as "Lady Ingrid: black hair" followed by an entry for "Lady Amanta: long black hair."

Mica made her lower lip grow and shrink as she tried to figure out which of the *four* ladies with black hair could be Ingrid and Amanta. She wished Brin had been free to watch the dancing lesson with her, but the maid was off on an errand, and Mica knew it would push her luck with Princess Jessamyn to request a helper.

She missed her friends from the Academy as she lurked on the promenade alone. It would be so much more fun to watch the ladies dance with Sapphire and explore the endless corridors with Danil. She'd barely had time to think about her missing friend since her arrival. The longer she went without news, the more she feared something terrible had happened to him.

She pushed away the worry, attempting to focus on the task at hand. She hated feeling two steps behind, as she had since the day her carriage pulled through the palace gates.

"She looks like an Ingrid," Mica muttered, spotting a woman with black hair piled on top of her head, a hawkish nose, and severe cheekbones. "Now which one is Amanta?"

"Lady Amanta isn't here today."

Mica turned to find a young man in a well-cut silk waistcoat standing beside her. He had tousled brown hair and a familiar smile. It was the young local from that evening in Gullton!

"You guessed right about Ingrid, though," he said. "I never thought about how much she looks like her name."

Mica gaped at him, momentarily at a loss for words.

"I didn't startle you again, did I?" he said when she didn't speak.

"Some people say hello before they jump right into conversations, you know."

"Do they? No wonder I'm always surprising people off cliffs."

Mica couldn't help grinning. "A common problem, is it?"

"You have no idea."

The young man brushed a hand through his hair, and Mica found herself cataloguing the planes of his broad face, the way his hair fell around his slightly pointed ears. The light was much better than it had been atop the cliff, giving her a better look at his handsome features. Her impersonation hadn't done him justice.

"That one is your real face, isn't it?" he said, studying her features in return. "That's how you looked when we walked back to town."

"Yep, this one's mine." On a sudden impulse, she turned her right eye bright blue and then back to its usual hazel, a Mimic's version of a wink. "Like it?"

He tipped his head to the side and scrutinized her closely, as if he'd never seen anyone quite like her. "I do, actually. Very much."

Mica blushed, suddenly feeling a little shy. She probably shouldn't be so forward. She didn't often flirt with handsome young men in her own form. Seduction was a time-honored skill among Impersonators, but it was usually done in disguise, with a specific mission in mind. But she'd felt lonely in the midst of the hectic palace life, and it was nice to talk to someone familiar.

Then the music drifting from below changed, and she remembered where she was. "What are you doing in the Silver Palace, anyway?"

"I live here most of the year," the young man said. "My quarters are over in the west wing."

"Your quarters . . ."

The puzzle pieces clicked together in Mica's mind as she took in his fine waistcoat and remembered how he'd walked her straight to the inn where Lord Ober's party had stayed in Gullton.

"You're Lord Caleb! I'm so sorry, my lord, I didn't realize who you were before."

He chuckled. "I did figure that out. I'm not in the habit of approaching young women alone in the darkness. I wouldn't have bothered you back in Gullton if I knew I was a complete stranger to you. Please accept my apology."

"It's . . . it's all right." Mica felt slightly mortified. She had spoken too familiarly with him, both in Gullton and a few moments ago. She had been in the palace long enough to know she wasn't supposed to make casual conversation with the lords.

But Lord Caleb didn't seem bothered. He rested his hip against the balustrade beside her and took the list of names from her hand.

"May I?"

Mica watched him read through it, thinking back through their conversation on the cliff. Had she said anything bad about the nobles in front of the young lord? She was pretty sure she hadn't. She should be safe.

Then he read aloud from the parchment. "Lord Caleb: messy hair, square face."

"I didn't write it," Mica said quickly. "One of the maids is helping me study."

She tried to take the parchment back from him, but he held it out of her reach with a grin. "Is this normally how you do it?"

"I don't usually learn so many impersonations at once. It's . . . challenging."

"Is there a limit to how many you can learn?"

"Not really." Mica gave up on trying to snatch the paper. "Faces come in infinite varieties, but it's easy to get them confused."

"How many could you do right now?"

"I have about thirty standard impressions." She nodded at the list in his hand. "I'm working on another thirty now."

Caleb read through a few more entries with that same frank curiosity Mica had noticed back in Gullton, and then turned it over to examine the other side. He looked up.

"Princess Jessamyn only wants you to learn lords and ladies?"

"We're starting here. Then there will be servants and guards and probably other people I haven't thought of yet." Mica broke off, worried that she was starting to sound frazzled.

"Sounds like a lot of work."

"I'll figure it out."

"Why are you working in the palace? Did you apply for this job?"

"You ask a lot of questions."

Caleb chuckled. "You sound like my uncle."

"I'm sorry, my lord," Mica said quickly. "I didn't mean to—"

"It's all right." He met her gaze steadily. His eyes were deep blue, like the sea at twilight. "And you needn't call me my lord, if that isn't too forward of me to say."

Mica wasn't sure what was forward or not. She was walking on unfamiliar ground with this noble who looked directly at her and spoke to her as if she were an equal.

"Go on then." Caleb moved a little closer, and Mica felt a flutter of nerves in her stomach. "Why don't you ask *me* some questions?"

"Okay." Mica cleared her throat, searching for a neutral topic. "Why did you miss the Assignment Ceremony?"

"I was ill during the beginning of our journey."

"How did you know who I was?"

"My uncle pointed you out at the inn. It was crowded. You may not have noticed me."

She was certainly noticing him now. "Did you follow me in Gullton?"

He seemed taken aback, and she instantly regretted asking. If there *was* a line of propriety here, she may have just crossed it.

"I didn't," he said before she could backtrack. "I was going for a walk when I came upon you doing your exercises."

"And running into me today?"

"A mere happy accident."

Mica blushed, glancing down at the paper he held. Caleb's hands were square and strong, distinctive enough to please any Impersonator. She met his eyes.

"Here's another question for you. Princess Jessamyn told me no one goes to the dancing lessons to actually learn dancing," Mica said. "What does that *mean*?"

Caleb burst out laughing, and a few of the nobles glanced around as the sound rang through the ballroom. They were taking a break, and they had scattered into clusters around the dance floor below.

Caleb leaned out over the balustrade, inviting Mica to join him.

"Take a look at that group of ladies there." He gestured to where Lady Ingrid and another one of the ladies with black hair were listening to the animated whispers of a sharp-nosed redhead in a bold red dress. "What do you think they're talking about?"

Mica shrugged. "Dresses?"

"Well, Lady Elana, in the red, probably *is* talking about dresses. But Lady Wendel, the very tall one, comes from Pegasus Island, where the primary exports are mutton and wool. A disease severely reduced the sheep population a few years back, and Pegasus wool production suffered. The fashion in Jewel Harbor has been shifting to silk in the meantime, which comes from outside the empire. Even though the farmers on Pegasus are building up their sheep population again, the market for their products has shrunk. But if Lady Wendel can convince Lady Elana to wear fine-spun wool dresses this winter, she will in turn influence the fashion in the capital. That fashion will slowly spread to the other cities in the empire, helped along by Lord Dolan over there. He's influential in the merchants' guild, and you may have noticed that Lady Wendel was dancing with him earlier. Before you know it, Lady Wendel's people will enjoy the prosperity they once had as demand for fine-spun wool dresses explodes throughout the empire. And all because Lady Wendel *always* wants to hear about Lady Elana's dresses at dance class."

Mica's eyebrows had been steadily rising throughout this speech. She admitted she hadn't thought these nobles were doing anything important. She knew they came from the many different islands making up the empire. They kept quarters in the Silver Palace and spent half the year or more in the capital. She assumed they were there to enjoy the decadent lifestyle and

Emperor Styl's famous hospitality. Apparently, they had other goals as well.

"What about you?" Mica said. "What are you hoping to accomplish at these dancing lessons?"

Caleb shot her a grin. "I'm here for the company."

Mica smiled back, and a thrill of warmth went straight to her toes.

Then a voice doused the feeling like a pitcher of cold water.

"Caleb, darling! You've been avoiding me!"

They turned to find Princess Jessamyn herself standing on the promenade. Mica ducked into a curtsy, but Jessamyn barely glanced at her. She launched herself at Caleb, flinging her arms around his neck in what looked like a genuinely warm hug.

Mica blinked in surprise as Caleb lifted the princess right off her feet before setting her down. "Jessa, you get lovelier every day."

"Oh, stop. How long has it been since you dropped by for tea?"

"Too long, my princess."

Jessamyn put her hands on her slim hips. "What could you possibly be doing that's more important than visiting your very dearest friend?"

"You know I was traveling with Uncle Ober and—"

"And you've been back for *a week*."

Caleb offered a deep bow. "Forgive me for depriving you of the pleasure of my company."

"Don't let it happen again," Jessamyn said, slapping him on the arm. "Oh, I see you've met my new Impersonator. Isn't she adorable?"

Mica tried not to let her features shift out of place as they both looked at her.

Lord Caleb's voice was perfectly polite as he said, "Miss Micathea was very kindly answering my questions about her Talent."

"You ought to hire your own Impersonator, darling," Jessamyn said. "I know how Talents fascinate you. Anyway, you've already missed half the lesson. Lady Bellina has been asking about you again."

"We'd best not keep her waiting." Lord Caleb dipped his head at Mica before following Jessamyn back down to the dance floor.

Mica watched him go, feeling slightly bereft in his absence. It was the first time since she'd arrived in Jewel Harbor that someone had taken the time to pause and speak with her. Lord Caleb may only be interested in her Talent, but at least he had looked at her like a fellow human. He was a member of the nobility, though. She'd likely never speak to him with her own voice again.

When they returned to the princess's rooms after the lesson, Jessamyn made Mica demonstrate every face she had studied while no fewer than three handmaids fussed over the princess's outfit and wove her hair into an intricate pile to support a silver tiara. Then Jessamyn was off for yet another social engagement, trailing yellow ribbons in her wake.

Mica retired to her room in the servants' corridor at last. Every muscle in her body was sore from cycling through so many new impersonations, and she was looking forward to going to sleep early.

But when she opened her door, Master Kiev was sitting on her bed.

CHAPTER EIGHT

"**G**ood evening, Miss Graydier."

"Master Kiev! What are you doing here?"

"I assured you I'd give you more information about your mission as soon as I had it," Master Kiev said.

"I was expecting a letter." It was utterly surreal to see the Head of the Academy sitting in her tiny bedroom. A rush of excitement washed away Mica's fatigue. At last she would find out why she'd been positioned here, why she'd been denied the future she had worked so hard to achieve.

But Master Kiev wasn't smiling.

"I'm afraid this matter is too sensitive to put into writing. You'd best check for eavesdroppers before we begin."

"Yes, sir." Mica quickly made sure the corridor was empty before pulling the stool out from under her bed and sitting at Master Kiev's feet. For the first time, she noticed that his face was thin and drawn, and his neutral brown trousers and white shirt hung loosely on him, as if he'd lost weight.

"Talents have been going missing," Master Kiev began. "You know raiding parties from Obsidian have kidnapped and enslaved our people on occasion. In recent months, the number of missing Talents has increased dramatically."

The last of Mica's excitement drained out of her, replaced by a queasy sense of dread. "My friend Danil . . ."

Master Kiev bowed his head. "No one has seen Danil Fairson since the night before the Assignment Ceremony. It is likely he is with the others."

"In Obsidian?"

"That is what we are trying to determine. The disappearances are not limited to coastal towns. I believe Obsidian agents are operating within the empire, possibly in Jewel Harbor itself."

Mica pressed her hands together between her knees. She had been so certain Danil would turn up, hopefully appearing on Sapphire's doorstep with hat in hand. The middle of Amber Island was supposed to be safe from such dangers.

"They'd risk reaching this far into the empire?"

Master Kiev looked at the wall, as if he could see through it to the city beyond. "Talents along the coast are well aware of the danger, and they take precautions to avoid capture. The Obsidians may want to snatch less vigilant targets from deeper in the empire, including the capital."

"And then?" Mica lowered her voice, the thought almost too horrible to speak aloud. "Are they taking them to the slave camps?"

"Our spies there are trying to ascertain that now," Master Kiev said. "So far, they have not reported any noticeable increase in the number of Windfast citizens being held against their will in the Obsidian camps. We fear there is some new scheme afoot."

Mica noted the reminder of how important the Obsidian assignments were. She wondered if Tiber Warson was even now infiltrating one of the infamous work camps.

"So why am I in Jewel Harbor?"

"The majority of the recent disappearances have occurred in this region, including several in the city itself. An Obsidian

Impersonator could easily go unnoticed here while preying on vulnerable Talents far from home."

"They're using Impersonators?"

"It seems likely," Master Kiev said. "None of the abductions have involved signs of struggle. I don't believe Talents are being hit over the head and dragged out of their homes. Foreign agents could be playing any number of roles to lure their targets away quietly."

Master Kiev rubbed his temple, and his hair shifted through different shades of gray. He must be very stressed to let his control slip like that. Unease roiled in Mica's stomach at the worry on her old teacher's face. The man was a legend. Nothing should faze him.

"What are they doing with them?" Mica asked.

"I wish I knew, Miss Graydier. The important thing is we must find their supply route and block it. They are smuggling the captive Talents away under our noses. We must figure out how. The fate of the empire depends on it."

She straightened her back. "What can I do to help?"

"You must do as you were trained," Master Kiev said. "Become invisible. Fulfill your duties as the princess's Impersonator, and keep your eyes and ears open for information about the Talent disappearances. You will report directly to me."

Mica glanced around her little servant's room, which didn't have so much as a window. Her eyes fell on the bell that kept her jumping at Jessamyn's every whim. "Wouldn't it be better for me to be posted out in the city, where I'd have more freedom to move around?"

"Why do *you* think I assigned you here?" Master Kiev asked, adopting his old teacher voice.

"It doesn't seem like the best place to watch out for Obsidian infiltrators, unless . . . you think someone in the palace is involved?"

"The Silver Palace is a hub for the powerful. There has been suspiciously little outcry over the disappearances, and reports about the abductions are being suppressed. Someone of great influence must be helping to smuggle the Talents out of Jewel Harbor."

"An imposter?"

"Or a traitor. We mustn't discount the possibility that the Obsidian King has found a way to buy the loyalty of one of our own."

"I understand." Mica thought of Danil, who had left his humble home in remote Dwindlemire and traveled all the way across the empire to study at Redbridge. He'd often come home to stay with her family on high days because his own was too far away. He deserved better than to be betrayed by some greedy and powerful noble. She clenched her hands into fists. "I'll find them."

"Focus on gathering information for now," Master Kiev said. "Do not take action without my approval."

Mica schooled her features to stillness, even though she wanted to object. She couldn't stand back and let more Talents be taken. But she had trained to be a spy, not a soldier, and information was a powerful weapon.

Master Kiev raised an eyebrow, as if he sensed her resistance. "Micathea?"

She sighed. "Yes, Master Kiev. I will listen and report, as you taught me."

"Good. I have great confidence in you. When the position opened by the princess's side, I couldn't think of a better student to send here."

Mica looked up at her old teacher. He seemed so out of place in her tiny palace bedroom, with his bulk and his carefully nondescript garb. "Master Kiev, you don't just work for the Academy, do you?"

He met her eyes, his expression betraying nothing. "Let us say that the Masters of the Academy do far more than train professional body doubles and dole out job assignments."

"And imperial spies are needed at home as well as abroad?"

"Something along those lines. We prefer to be discreet about the details." Master Kiev patted his pockets, as if searching for something. "Remember, we have no idea what form these kidnappers may take, whether they are Obsidian Impersonators or traitors to the empire. Pay special attention to *anyone* asking questions about Talents."

Lord Caleb's face flashed before her at once. He had done nothing *but* ask her about her Talent. He had shown interest in her, unlike every other member of the nobility. And he had been at the Academy when Danil went missing.

She sighed, heart sinking. "I may have a lead."

She pushed away the disappointment at perhaps losing one of the first people to treat her as a friend here. It was more important to find her *real* friend and rescue him from whoever had stolen him away in the middle of the night.

Master Kiev stood, groaning as his knees popped, and withdrew a slip of paper from his pocket. "I must go. I have other . . . former students to visit this evening." He handed her the paper and folded her fingers around it with his callused hands. "Here is the address of a Blur messenger. Peet will take your findings directly to me without charge."

Mica studied the paper, which was written in one of the codes taught at the Academy. When she looked up again, Master Kiev had transformed into a red-faced woman with meaty hands and flaxen hair. He produced a cook's apron from a pocket and tied it around his waist.

"You must be careful, Micathea," he said in his own deep voice. "It is easy for a young person to get lost in a city such as this. Our enemies are taking advantage of that fact. And remember that anyone you meet could well be an Impersonator."

"Yes, sir. We'll find them."

Mica closed the door behind Master Kiev, feeling the weight of the responsibility he'd given her. She may find the palace overwhelming, but Master Kiev had chosen her for this assignment, and she intended to live up to his confidence in her. If she proved she could handle this task, maybe she would get sent somewhere else next, even if it was another domestic role.

She had always thought of spies as people who went into enemy territory, but with her assignment, the Academy Masters had secured a pair of eyes in the chambers of Emperor Styl's own daughter. Mica wondered how much the emperor and the princess even knew about their activities. She was glad the Masters were looking out for the missing Talents, even though their rulers were consumed only with the affairs of the powerful.

Interesting though Master Kiev's spy network was, as Mica fell into bed, she thought mostly of Danil and her family back in Stonefoss. They were potential targets of these kidnappers too. She had to get to the bottom of the Talent disappearances before she lost anyone else.

She already knew where to start.

CHAPTER NINE

Investigating Lord Caleb's interest in Talents turned out to be more difficult than Mica anticipated. Now that she had learned a few noble impersonations, Jessamyn sent her on ever more elaborate missions. She attended a tea party as Lady Amanta (of the long black hair) and let slip a few carefully constructed rumors about who was invited to the princess's next private dinner party. She walked in the conservatory with dough-faced Lord Dolan in the guise of Lady Lorna to make young Lord Fritz jealous. She put on Lord Fritz's boyish good looks and blond hair to listen in on the gossip between Ladies Elana and Wendel —it was indeed about the latest in wool-based fashion—and reported back to the princess about every detail.

"Are you certain Elana said her dress for the next ball was indigo?"

"An indigo skirt, with a pearl bodice."

"Pearl-colored fabric, or pearls on the bodice?"

"Uh..."

"And if there are pearls on the bodice, who is the supplier?"

"She didn't say, Princess."

"Must I think of everything myself? Run along to Elana's

quarters. If you look like *anyone* except Lady Ingrid, she's sure to invite you in for tea. Now where is Brin? We must rethink my gown for tomorrow night."

Mica raced off to find something to wear to tea, kicking herself for not pressing for more information. It was tricky to know which details would be most important to the princess in the midst of trying to keep all the nobles and their connections to each other straight. There was hardly any time left for her own enquiries.

While Mica sipped tea with the ladies and strolled arm in arm with the nobles, she studied the handmaids, menservants, Shield guards, and advisors who accompanied them. In the long run, posing as trusted servants would likely yield more useful information than impersonating the nobles themselves. It seemed less essential to get those impressions right, though, as the nobles tended to look right through their attendants. They didn't guard their words as much as they should around their perceived inferiors, especially in a place where anyone could have been replaced with an Impersonator. Still, Mica had to treat everything she heard with skepticism because many nobles used their own Impersonators to get out of unsavory tasks.

"Wasn't Lord Nobu acting strange at Lady Velvet's luncheon," she heard the hawkish Lady Ingrid say as she strolled around the ballroom promenade with Lady Bellina and Mica—who was impersonating Ingrid's big-eyed maid—before a dance lesson. "I thought I must be talking to his Mimic. It's difficult to tell with that fellow."

"I'm sure he's just worried about the news from Dwindlemire," said Lady Bellina. "I hear there's unrest near his family's estate."

Lady Ingrid snorted. "They are overly dramatic in Dwindlemire. He should try owning property in Talon."

"He has a right to worry about his home."

"A lord of Nobu's stature ought to keep his composure better than that. It *had* to have been the Mimic."

Lady Bellina twirled a finger through a golden curl and didn't argue. Ingrid was among the most influential and assertive ladies at court, and people rarely stood up to her for long. She was from Talon, a rocky island located almost within shouting distance of the Obsidian coast, whose citizens were known for being tough. Of course, Bellina herself could have been an Impersonator too. Mica knew there must be tricks to work out which nobles were acting as themselves—yet another layer of information she had to keep straight.

She wrote down the exchange about Nobu's recent worries in Academy code and sent it to Master Kiev anyway, unsure which little tidbit would help. She doubted a whisper about unrest on faraway Dwindlemire would help him identify whoever was abducting Talents right from the capital, but she couldn't keep back any details. If the Obsidian King had sent agents into the Silver Palace itself, she could leave no possibility unexplored.

She reported everything she overheard to Jessamyn too, though she wasn't sure why the princess needed all this information. She clearly enjoyed playing matchmaker with the younger nobles, but some schemes didn't have anything to do with romantic pairings. For example, she had Mica impersonate Lord Dolan's hired Shield and "accidentally" knock over one of Lady Euphia's sleek-haired handmaidens without stopping to apologize. The encounter was rather satisfying for Mica, but what was it supposed to accomplish? She didn't yet know enough about the inner workings of the imperial court to figure it out. With representatives of noble families from every one of the far-flung imperial islands gathered beneath the palace's shining silver dome, all the relationships were rife with opportunities for offense.

Mica sometimes felt as if she'd been tossed into the sea and she was barely keeping her head above water. It reminded her of her final years at school, when her lessons had become increasingly complex. She, Sapphire, and Danil had spent long hours studying together before exams. They used to meet on the assembly hall steps to practice their impersonations, performing for each other as if they were actors on a stage. Danil would play a game where he'd morph through increasingly ridiculous impersonations while Mica and Sapphire tried not to laugh. Mica always cracked first, and she'd be doubled over and wheezing by the time Sapphire gave in. Sometimes it was the sudden appearance of bright-pink hair that did it. Other times, he'd turn himself into one of their instructors and deliver a brilliant parody of an Academy lecture. In the end, he'd always turn back into their curly-haired, merry friend and grin bashfully while they laughed so hard their features slid out of shape. Danil's utter determination to get Sapphire to laugh had been Mica's first clue that there was something more between them than friendship.

She wished she could share her worries for Danil with someone now, but Brin and the other two handmaids, Ruby and Alea, were just as busy following the princess's orders as she was. The other maids tended to keep Mica at arm's length anyway, as if they couldn't fully trust someone who could change her face. Once, Mica overheard Alea telling Ruby that half of all Mimics were thieves while they washed the huge windows in the princess's antechamber.

"They can just walk away with anything they want, and they'll never be caught," she said. "It isn't natural, what they do."

"I saw the last Mimic change her face once," Ruby said, lowering her voice to a whisper. "Gave me nightmares for a week."

"Aye," Alea said. "That's probably what she wanted."

"Or he," Ruby said with a shiver. "We don't even know what she really was."

Mica had slipped away without letting the women know she was there, but it made her less inclined to seek friendship with them. She hadn't fully appreciated what it would be like to live among so many non-Talents. The abilities were rare enough that people could get the wrong idea about them. And in this world, physical strengths mattered far less than political influence.

The Silver Palace nobles hardly paid attention to the Talents at all. Lady Amanta complained about how difficult it was to get a reliable Blur over a decadent meal of oysters and quail eggs, and Lord Fritz fretted about how a Muscle builder had failed to fix the satin curtains in his mother's sitting room. If any of them knew about the disappearances, they weren't nearly as concerned as they should be. Talents like Mica's family had fought and died to keep the empire safe. They had toiled on the front lines while these nobles flitted among the begonias in the conservatory.

Mica worried for her brothers and parents almost as much as she worried for Danil. The disappearances from the middle of the empire must mean Obsidian was growing bolder. And a bold enemy meant an increased risk of war. Mica assumed Master Kiev had deployed many spies in Jewel Harbor, but she couldn't help hoping that *she* would be the one to uncover the Obsidian agents and put an end to their schemes. Her prime suspect, Lord Caleb, remained elusive. If he had ever taken Jessamyn up on her offer of tea, it was while Mica was out on another assignment. He rarely attended the dancing lessons, which Mica watched from the balcony whenever she could, and when he did, he arrived late and left early. Despite his initial overtures of friendship, he made no further efforts to get closer to Mica.

Still, she gleaned hints about him from other conversations. He was from the Pebble Islands in the northwest corner of the empire, even farther away than Dwindlemire. He was not the heir to his family's noble seat, though Mica didn't know how many older siblings he had, or exactly how important his family was. And he was still a bachelor, which made him a favorite topic for the palace gossips.

"I swear Lord Caleb gets handsomer by the day," she heard a lady exclaim on the racquetball courts in the south garden one afternoon. The speaker, Lady Wendel, was taller than most men and almost as broad. "Bellina better seal that deal quickly, or someone else is going to swoop him up." There was a thwack as she hit the ball back to her opponent.

Mica knelt to adjust her shoes, as close to the two women as she could get. She was impersonating Lady Elana for a match against Lady Euphia on the next court. Her opponent showed precious little interest in the sport, and she was off on a lengthy refreshment break in the shaded portico beside the garden. Noble brothers Hugh and Hector Ivanson were playing a boisterous game on the only other court in the garden, and they paid no attention as Mica eavesdropped on the two ladies.

"*Scandalous,*" said the other one, who turned out to be Lady Amanta. Her long black hair, threaded with a touch of gray, was pulled back from her rather flat face. "*I* heard Lady Bellina still hasn't decided whether she can bear the Pebble Islands."

"He doesn't spend much time there anyway," Lady Wendel said. "She'll hardly miss a thing."

"True." Lady Amanta executed an elegant serve, her movements energetic for an older woman. "Lorna told me Bellina is worried about stepping on a certain pair of royal toes, though."

"The princess?" Lady Wendel whacked the ball back across the net. "I thought she wasn't interested in Caleb."

"Mysterious, isn't it?" Lady Amanta chuckled. "They're always so friendly with each other."

She stepped forward to return the volley, and the ball sailed away from the court. The two ladies paused as an attendant ran after it. Lady Euphia's simpering voice carried over the crunch of footsteps on the gravel ball courts, announcing her imminent return. Mica couldn't pretend to adjust her shoe for much longer.

"The Pebble Islands are too far away to be major players," Lady Wendel said. "I doubt Jessamyn would accept that match. Caleb isn't even the oldest son."

Amanta simply patted her hair with a gloved hand. "She does love to keep people guessing."

Lady Euphia emerged from the shaded portico where she had taken her tea, forcing Mica to return to her own game. But she caught Lady Wendel's final words: "The princess could do worse than Lord Caleb in the looks department."

When Mica reported the full conversation in the princess's antechamber later, Jessamyn dissolved into fits of laughter. "They're still gossiping about me and Caleb? Oh dear, that topic is *so* last season."

"He's not your suitor?" Mica asked casually.

"Lord Caleb is my dearest friend." Jessamyn wiped away tears of mirth. "He's an absolute darling, but I doubt very much that would be an advantageous match. I have several ladies in mind for Caleb, if Bellina doesn't succeed in snaring him. None of them deserve him, of course." Jessamyn suddenly fixed Mica with a shrewd look. "Why do you ask?"

"I'm just working out how all the pieces fit together," Mica said. "It'll help me do my job better." She frowned. She felt oddly relieved that Jessamyn and Caleb were not romantically involved.

"Well, the next job I have for you has nothing to do with lords or ladies, but it requires the *utmost* discretion." Jessamyn crooked a finger and lowered her voice to a whisper. "Can I trust you, Micathea Graydier?"

"Yes, Princess Jessamyn." Mica leaned toward her, hoping she might finally be sent to do something more exciting than listen to idle gossip. "I am here to serve the empire."

"Hmm." Jessamyn studied her, arching one of her magnificent eyebrows. "I certainly hope you are."

CHAPTER TEN

The task requiring the *utmost* discretion turned out to be picking up a long list of potions from the city.

"People talk whenever they see Brin or one of my Blurs in Potioners Alley," Princess Jessamyn said. "You must turn yourself into a stranger as soon as you leave the palace gates. I don't wish for the other ladies to learn all my secrets." She handed over the list of potions and shooed Mica out the door.

The mission may not be what Mica had expected, but she'd been waiting for an opportunity to see the city. She hadn't had time to venture out into Jewel Harbor since she arrived a few weeks ago. The Silver Palace was like a city unto itself, but she wanted to see more of the beating heart of the empire she had sworn to serve.

She adopted the face of a scullery maid as she hurried through the palace, then turned into a completely different woman as soon as she was out the door. She used a modified version of the cowherd's daughter from her regular rotation. That particular girl would be too timid in this chaotic place, and the mannerisms fit her look a little too well. For her new city woman look, Mica kept the same thick freckles but darkened her hair to the color of strong coffee. She adopted a more confident walk than the country girl would use, something between the rushing steps of a palace attendant and the high and mighty stride of a noble lady.

When she left the palace gates, the city noises rushed in around her like a tidal wave. The streets were even busier than when she arrived in the carriage, and this time she was knee-deep in the chaos. People strode about, jostling each other without apology or concern. Gone were the polite respect of the Academy and the sharp discipline of Stonefoss. In Jewel Harbor, no one looked where they were going. No one made eye contact with strangers. No one slowed down to really look at anything or anyone.

Mica was supposed to be impersonating a confident Jewel Harbor woman, but she couldn't help gawking. The city was magnificent. Above the packed streets, the buildings were decorated with sculptures, lattice windows, and tiles painted with intricate designs. The buildings nearest the palace were especially grand, though they too had given way before the ever-growing city's ravenous need for space. Little shops crammed into the alleyways and additions protruded from their roofs. Some of the buildings were connected with stone walkways crossing above the streets, while others leaned so close to each other that you could hop from one window to the next.

"So this is the Jewel of the Empire." Mica paused to stare at a stone walkway above the street that had shops built directly on top of it. It was a wonder the whole thing didn't fall onto the crowds below. "My brothers would never believe this."

Farther from the palace, the stone walkways gave way to rickety wooden bridges. The buildings were painted in a patchwork of colors, as if a different individual owned every room, each with their own ideas for how the outside of a building should appear. The array of rich details was dizzying, and Mica hardly knew where to look.

The people were just as colorful, coming from every island that made up the empire as well as lands much farther away. Their clothes were a myriad of fabrics and designs, ranging from the simple garb of sailors and servants to the opulent silks of merchants and courtesans. Their faces came in so many varieties that Mica found it impossible to catalogue them. It hardly seemed necessary for her to wear an impersonation at all. She would blend in here no matter how she looked. But there were eyes and ears everywhere in this city, and Jessamyn had demanded discretion.

Mica caught sight of a few pale Obsidian faces weaving through the crowds too. She followed an Obsidian man for a few blocks, his pale-white hair guiding her as effectively as a torch. When he arrived at the door of a many-storied tenement, a Jewel Harbor woman greeted him, shifting a baby to her hip so she could lean in for a kiss. Mica sighed. If the Talent kidnappers really were Impersonators, they wouldn't walk through the streets wearing their own faces. Plenty of ordinary Obsidian citizens lived here, she reminded herself. The empire and the nearby kingdom were not at war, even though relations were often tense.

The idea of Obsidian Impersonators acting as spies had been bothering her since Master Kiev's visit. The Obsidians enslaved their Talents, forcing them to live in camps and labor for the king, often under terrible conditions. The prosperity of their entire civilization was based on a horrific crime. But Impersonators could hide their abilities or disappear without a trace. How could they travel to the Windfast Empire as spies to do the king's bidding? That would make them complicit in the king's crimes against their fellow Talents.

Unlike in Obsidian, Windfast Talents were free to do as they wished. Blurs and Muscles were not required to serve in the army any more than Shields were required to be employed as bodyguards. They often fell into the careers that made the best use of their abilities, but the choice was important. Mica was tied to her assignment until she paid off the cost of her education, but she could have opted not to attend the Academy at all. When her debt was paid, she would be free to take up new employment.

As Mica wandered through the city with Jessamyn's potion list in her hand, she couldn't help wondering what it would be like if she had decided to make her fortune in Jewel Harbor instead of going to school. She may not have learned as much as she did at the Academy, but she wouldn't be stuck working for people who looked down on her because she wasn't a noble.

After taking a few wrong turns and stopping to ask for directions twice, she smelled the strange cocktail of odors she had noticed the day she arrived in Jewel Harbor: rosemary and sage, cedar and cinnamon, poppy, eucalyptus, incense. She followed her nose the rest of the way to Potioners Alley.

Shops lined the broad cobblestone lane, their windows displaying glittering bottles of multicolored potions. The scents issuing from them made Mica's head spin. She scanned the elaborate signs over the apothecary doorways, which promoted strange and fantastical potions guaranteed to cure ailments, improve looks, and temporarily enhance an ordinary person's speed and strength to Talent-like levels.

This street was as busy as any other, though the clientele came from a wealthier set, more likely to have attendants to hold their fine horses and coats made of imported silk and high-quality wool. Potions were not cheap by any standard, and Mica marveled that so many people in this city could afford them.

The shop Jessamyn sent her to wasn't the fanciest one. In fact, it looked almost shabby compared to the grand apothecary next to it. The sign above the window read Magic Q: Potioner Extraordinaire.

A tiny silver bell rang above the door as Mica pushed it open. Inside, long shelves held thousands of identical glass bottles, each one marked with a simple brushwork Q. Though the bottles were the same, the potions inside were different shades of red, from the faintest tint of pale rose all the way to a murky red-black goop. The shop appeared to be deserted.

"Hello?"

Mica walked down the first aisle, her steps ringing faintly through the room of glass. The red potions gave the shop an eerie quality, as if she were walking through a blood vessel. The light shining through the bottles from the window made her freckled skin glow red.

"Is anyone here?" Mica called, feeling unsettled. "I'm picking up an order for—"

"I'm here, I'm here. No need to shout."

A door at the back of the shop opened, and the potioner emerged. "Magic Q" wasn't at all what Mica expected. She had imagined a wild-haired old man, perhaps with a glass eye and grizzled features. Instead, a woman not much older than Mica strode down the aisle, wiping her hands on a stained smock.

"You're picking up?"

"Yes." Mica handed over the paper. "I need the potions on this list, please."

The woman scanned the list rapidly. She had sharp features, olive skin, and straight black hair cut to her chin in a razor line. "This is Princess Jessamyn's order."

"That's correct."

The woman looked Mica up and down. Her movements were crisp, her eyes intelligent. It was clear she didn't miss much.

"You must be the new Impersonator."

"How did you know?"

"The last one was terrible at voices. She sounded the same no matter what face she wore. Come on back. You can check the bottles before I pack everything up."

Mica followed the potioner out of the red-tinted room and into a much cozier workshop in the back. Daylight flooded through a high window, illuminating a sturdy wooden table covered in vials, chopping boards, and measuring spoons. Huge vats of liquid sat on the floor within easy reach of the worktable. Crates full of those identical bottles sat empty in one corner, and a shelf along the wall held groups of completed potions, each labeled in thin, curly handwriting. The space smelled like a well-used kitchen. It was quiet and surprisingly calming after the frantic streets.

"Are you *the* Magic Q?" Mica asked as the woman marched over to the shelf and began choosing bottles and moving them to an uncluttered corner of her worktable.

"It's Quinn. Magic Q is to attract the walk-ins. My real business is custom work."

"I'm Mica."

While Quinn selected the potions, Mica peeked at a small writing desk overflowing with notebooks and diagrams scrawled in that thin, curly handwriting. The lists of ingredients were incomprehensible to Mica, but it looked as though the potioner spent a lot of time improving on her craft.

"What do your potions do, if you don't mind me asking?"

"Anything you desire." Quinn glanced over her shoulder at Mica. "Or your employer desires. Let's see, this should be all of them." She set the final bottle on the table. "Go ahead and make sure they're full and sealed."

Mica picked up the bottles one by one, comparing them to the list Jessamyn had given her. She had no idea how to tell if the bottles contained the correct substances, but this clearly wasn't the first time Quinn had made potions for the princess.

"Iron Hair Strengthener . . . Ruby Rose Lip Tint . . . Alabaster Skin Ointment . . . These are beauty treatments. Why does she need expensive potions for that?"

Quinn barked a laugh. "That's easy for a Mimic to say."

"I mean she's already beautiful," Mica said. "She could use lard soap and paint her lips with berry juice, and she'd still attract every eye in the kingdom."

"You underestimate what my potions can accomplish," Quinn

said. "Princess Jessamyn looks relatively normal without my help. The extra sheen of the hair and glow of the skin does more than you'd think. I've no idea what you look like under that face, but I bet you use your power to clear your complexion and brighten your eyes sometimes too."

"I suppose." Mica had been trained to use looks to accomplish her goals, but she hadn't thought about how ordinary people did the same. "What's this one for?"

She held up a bottle labeled Burst. The liquid inside was the color of wine.

"It's a health tonic. That one gives an immediate energy boost." Quinn pointed to another bottle holding a creamy concoction, like chalk mixed with red dye. "And this one holds off illness. The princess is too busy to get sick."

"So this is why she has so much energy?" Mica said. "I was starting to think she was some sort of Blur-Muscle hybrid."

"In a way, she is." Quinn picked up the wine-red energy tonic. "This is three parts Blur, one part Muscle, plus a few secret ingredients of my own."

"I don't understand."

"I make all my potions out of Talent blood."

She said it so nonchalantly that Mica couldn't tell whether or not she was joking. She made her potions out of *blood*? The shop full of red bottles suddenly took on an even more ominous quality.

"Is . . . is that . . . legal?"

"I pay my suppliers well." Quinn glanced up and noticed the consternation on Mica's face. "No need to look so shocked. The Talents come to me. I'm not knocking them out in alleyways and draining them dry."

"You're saying Talents are selling their blood for you to use in potions?"

"That's right. It's powerful stuff."

"But . . . *why*?"

"Same reason people sell their hair, or their bodies, or their labor. People need to eat. Their children need to eat."

"Aren't there better ways for Talents to make money?"

"Sometimes there's work, and sometimes there isn't. People make do. Jewel Harbor is an expensive place to live."

Mica thought of the Mimic she had seen performing for coins in an alley when she arrived and how she had assumed he'd failed out of the Academy. Maybe there was more to it, especially if things were so bad that some Talents resorted to selling their blood.

"I didn't know it could be so hard here." She felt guilty for complaining about the Silver Palace, even to herself. She took a closer look at the potioner, who was probably five or six years older than her. "Have you always lived in Jewel Harbor?"

Quinn shook her head. "I came from Talon with nothing when I was twelve. Could have gotten myself into some real trouble, until another potioner took me in."

"And now you have your own shop?" Mica stared at her, fascinated. "And the princess trusts you to supply her secret beauty treatments? You must have worked really hard."

Quinn gave her a quick smile and began wrapping up the bottles in crinkly paper. "It's interesting work, and I get to develop my own products."

The light through the high window was fading. It would be dark soon. Mica wanted to linger in the shop and ask this woman more about her life in the city. She felt starved for company, for a sense of normalcy apart from the palace.

The potioner seemed to sense this as she tied up the package of potions and handed it to Mica. "The princess has been good to me, but she ran that last Mimic ragged. Make sure you get out on your own sometimes. If you come by another evening, I can show you this rooftop bar that's good for a quiet drink."

"I might take you up on that."

Quinn walked with Mica back through the rows of glittering bottles to the shop door.

"Be careful out there," she said. "Just because *I* won't steal your blood doesn't mean there aren't others who know how useful it can be."

CHAPTER ELEVEN

Mica's mind raced with this new information as she walked back up Potioners Alley with the heavy package under her arm. What if the Obsidians didn't want the Talents for their labor, but for their blood? If it could be used for cosmetic and healthful properties, what about lending non-Talented soldiers extra strength and speed in battle? Barrels of the stuff would be easier to smuggle out of the city than angry captives with supernatural abilities. She hoped she was wrong. If blood was all they wanted, Danil and the others could already be dead.

Whoever was behind the scheme would find plenty of victims around Jewel Harbor. She considered anew what it would be like to move to the city as a young Mimic if she hadn't gone to the Academy. She would have no room waiting for her at the Silver Palace. She would have no guaranteed employment. A friendly stranger could easily lure her in, perhaps only to buy her blood— or to drain it from her corpse and ship it back to Obsidian. She had to send word to Master Kiev right away.

Abruptly, she realized she had taken a wrong turn. She was walking down an unfamiliar alleyway, and it was getting darker. Shadows spread from every corner, changing the shapes of the buildings. She couldn't tell whether or not the walkway arching overhead was one she had seen on her way to Potioners Alley. The streets were less crowded at this hour, and the fading light made every stranger seem threatening, to be avoided rather than approached for help.

She was about to backtrack and ask Quinn for directions when rough voices rose nearby. A group of men was moving toward her, lurching as if drunk. Mica turned into a deserted alley to evade them, this one sheltered completely from the darkening sky. She assumed the body and face of a lean old soldier as a precaution, unfastening her skirt to reveal the loose trousers she wore underneath and flinging the skirt over her shoulder as a cloak. This impersonation wouldn't dissuade someone who wanted to steal her bundle of expensive potions, but it would keep away worse types of unwanted attention.

The group of men drew closer, laughing raucously. Mica hurried along the alley to where the path rounded a bend. From there she could see a lantern hanging above an archway at the far end, where the alley opened to a busier street. She started toward it, walking carefully to keep from making noise and drawing attention to herself. Another man, presumably another drunk, was sitting on a stoop halfway down the alley with his head resting on his knees, a parcel at his side. She skirted around him, unable to see his features in the darkness. He didn't look up.

"Oy, what you got there?" a man shouted as he came around the bend behind her.

Mica picked up her pace, moving faster toward the lighted archway. But the man wasn't speaking to her.

"You, on the stoop. You dead?"

"He's not dead," said another voice. "I reckon he's sloshed."

"*You're* sloshed, mate."

Boisterous laughter echoed down the alley. Mica was almost to the archway, but she paused to look back. The drunks—three of them—had surrounded the man, who still sat with his head on his knees. One of them kicked him, and he uttered a faint groan.

"Nice clothes you got there," said the ringleader. "You some lord?"

"You sick or something?" his companion slurred.

"What's in the parcel, eh?"

The third drunk reached for the bundle, and the seated man snatched it from the stoop so fast his hands blurred. He was a Talent! Why wasn't he using his supernatural speed to run away?

Mica hesitated, feeling torn. She shouldn't get involved. She was at the main street, and she could see the faint shimmer of the palace's silver dome in the distance. But then the lead drunk kicked the man on the stoop again, and indignation boiled through her. People didn't treat each other like that where she came from.

"You got any coin? Hey! I'm talking to you."

The bully took a swipe at the man's head, and he shot his hands up with impossible speed to block the attack. Yes, he had to be a Blur.

Mica made her choice. Nobody hurt Talents on her watch. She applied a few quick changes to her body, thickening her arms and stretching herself as tall as she could without making her legs too thin to use. She added a couple of grisly scars to the soldier's face and thickened the forehead so she looked like a real bruiser.

The final touch was modifying her voice. "Hey!" she shouted, adopting a deep growl reminiscent of Master Kiev. "Don't kick a man when he's down."

"Mind your own business, yeah?" one of the thieves called.

Mica knew she should just leave. She didn't need any trouble, and she was already late. But she couldn't turn away from the poor Blur. She may just be a princess's errand girl, but serving the empire included defending the weak.

"Go jump in the harbor, you cowards," she shouted.

The three drunks laughed, and the ringleader pitched toward her. "I reckon it's four against one."

"Three, ya fool," his companion muttered. "Jebson went home hours ago."

"Find your own payday," the leader shouted, undeterred. "This one's ours."

Mica advanced on her hidden spindly legs. Hopefully they'd interpret her slow steps as menacing. It was too late to stop now.

"I said," she growled, "go jump your cowardly behinds in the harbor before I haul you all before the emperor's justice."

The ringleader scoffed. "What's old Emperor Styl ever done for us? I ain't afraid of him."

His companion started to agree—until Mica got close enough for him to see her modified face. He blanched and started tugging on the ringleader's sleeve.

"Leave it, mate."

The third man took a closer look at her grisly face and backed away too. "Yeah, we don't need that kind of trouble."

The leader snarled at them and stumbled forward a few steps, muttering about weaklings. Then he focused on Mica, and the blood drained from his face. She must have done a better job on her impersonation than she thought.

"We was just messing with him." The ringleader lifted his hands. "No harm, aye?"

"Let's get another drink," said his friend.

The third nodded fervently. "A man's gotta drink to forget a face like that."

The would-be thieves lurched away and disappeared around the bend. Mica maintained a menacing stance until she was sure they had left the alley, then she returned her legs to a manageable thickness and knelt beside the man on the stoop. She was surprised he hadn't dashed off while his attackers were occupied. He wore a fine wool coat, and the parcel in his arms had torn open, revealing a bolt of expensive pearlescent silk. Some rich merchant who happened to be a Blur, perhaps?

"You'd better find somewhere else to sleep it off," she grunted, still using Master Kiev's voice. "Those thugs could—" She broke off as the man lifted his face. "Lord Caleb?"

"Who are you?" Caleb's voice was hoarse, and his skin was pallid. He wasn't drunk. He looked ill.

"What happened?" Mica said. "You look terrible."

"I don't know you, sir," Caleb said. His head drifted downward, as if it were slowly becoming too heavy for his body. There was no sign of the Blur speed Mica had seen when he blocked the kick. Had she imagined it?

"Please," he said, sounding as if every word was an effort, "could you . . . the palace?"

"I'll take you there." Mica looped Caleb's arm around her shoulder, wishing she had the strength of a Muscle as she hoisted him off the stoop. His body was feverish, and he was built more solidly than she expected. She struggled to support him while keeping the package of potions secure under her other arm. She had to leave his bundle of silk behind.

"Thank you, sir," Caleb muttered as they inched along. He didn't seem fully aware of his surroundings. He hadn't even blinked at the gruesome scars she wore on her face. She smoothed some of them away, resuming her usual soldier face.

"What were you doing in that alley?" she asked as she struggled along under his weight.

"Needed . . . help." Caleb's breathing sounded labored, and she was afraid he'd lose consciousness entirely. This might be her best chance to get answers. Though he was her lead suspect, she couldn't help hoping he wasn't involved in the disappearances.

"What did you need help with? Where have you been today?"

Caleb didn't answer. Suddenly he pitched forward, and Mica went down with him, landing halfway on top of him and scraping her knee roughly on the cobblestones. They were in a busier street now, but none of the passersby stopped to help.

"Caleb? Caleb!" she shook him, and he uttered a faint groan. She tried to haul him up, but her body was tired from holding impersonations all day. She couldn't move him.

His eyes drifted open, looking unfocused, and he mumbled something indistinct.

"What was that?"

"Ober," he whispered.

"You want me to take you to Lord Ober?"

Caleb's chin dipped into what could have been a nod or a faint. It sounded like a good idea to Mica. She'd deliver the incapacitated lord to his uncle's quarters, if she could get him up to the palace. Lord Ober would know what to do.

She tried to get Caleb on his feet again, but he didn't budge. She was aware of how vulnerable they were, falling down in the street where any thief could take advantage—or worse than a thief. Jewel Harbor had plenty of crime, and a mysterious Talent snatcher could be lurking nearby too.

"Caleb?" Mica slapped his cheek, eliciting another groan. "Stay with me a little longer. I need one more burst of . . ." Suddenly Mica remembered the package under her arm containing Jessamyn's potions. What had Quinn said about that wine-red tonic? It gave an immediate boost of energy.

Knowing she might lose her job for this, Mica undid the package and searched through the bottles, squinting to read the labels in the light from the nearest windows. She found the correct one and popped it open, trying not to think about how much it probably cost. Jessamyn had claimed Caleb was her dearest friend. They were about to test that notion.

She pried open Caleb's lips and poured in the wine-red potion. He swallowed reflexively. Once. Twice. Mica waited.

At first nothing happened. Then Caleb's eyes flew open, and his body shuddered violently. For a second, Mica was afraid she'd killed him. Then his eyes focused on her, and he lifted a hand as if to touch her face. He seemed to be breathing more easily. Not wanting to waste a minute of the tonic's effects, Mica hauled him to his feet again.

"Let's go, Lord Caleb. We're almost home."

Caleb was clearly confused, but he let her pull his arm around her shoulders and guide him onward. He was able to support his own weight now, and they managed the perilously slow walk back to the palace without another fall. He didn't speak to her, and Mica figured it would be better not to ask too many probing questions when she wasn't sure how aware the potion had made him. She was fairly certain he couldn't be an Obsidian Impersonator in disguise. She didn't know many Mimics who could hold their shape through near delirium. But that didn't mean he wasn't involved in the plot—and he was apparently hiding a Talent of his own.

When they reached the palace, she used her best Master Kiev voice to order a passing footman to lead her straight to Lord Ober's quarters in the west wing. Caleb lived in the west wing too, but she didn't want to leave him alone in his own rooms in this state.

Lord Ober answered the door himself, his face going ashen at the sight of his half-conscious nephew.

"I found him in an alley," Mica said. "Some thugs were using him as a punching bag."

"Come in quickly." Lord Ober wore a dressing gown, but his gray hair was neatly combed, as if he hadn't been to bed yet. There was a thick book, a burning candle, and a cup of tea on the table in his antechamber. He lit a few more candles as Mica guided Caleb to a low couch piled with cushions. "I must ask you to be quiet, as my wife is sleeping."

"Yes, sir," Mica said. "I'll be going if you—"

"Mimic," Caleb said faintly. "He's . . . Mimic."

"Is he?" Lord Ober looked at Mica with renewed interest.

"Thank you for bringing him here, sir. I don't know what I'd do without this fine young man. Won't you stay a minute?" He went to a side table to prepare two more cups of tea. "Do you impersonate for someone in the palace? I haven't seen this face before."

Mica hesitated. She didn't like giving up her go-to faces. She was surprised Caleb had noticed her ability. He must have seen her smoothing away the worst of those scars. She was about to claim Lady Bellina as her employer when Caleb lifted his head from the cushion to look at her.

"Micathea?"

She spun toward him. "How did you know?"

"I remember. From the cliff." Caleb shifted his elbows beneath him, propping himself up to look at her old soldier's features. She let them morph back into her own face. He watched the transition, eyes slightly glassy.

"Well, Caleb, you look as though you are recovering much faster than last time," Lord Ober said, approaching with the two cups of tea. He handed one to Mica, not looking remotely surprised to see a young woman where the old soldier had been, and gave the other to his nephew. "How are you feeling?"

"Like I could get up and dance," Caleb said, still holding Mica's gaze.

"Hmm." Lord Ober slipped a small potion bottle out of his pocket and held it up. "Do you want a dose then?"

"Oh, I gave him something already," Mica said quickly. She doubted it was a good idea to pump Caleb full of more potions than he needed. "I happened to have a health tonic, and he was in bad shape. I hope that was okay."

"You seem to have done him a world of good," Lord Ober said. "May I see this tonic?"

Mica set her package of potions on the table and extracted the half-empty bottle of Burst. Lord Ober examined the label closely then opened the potion and put a drop on his finger to taste.

"Exquisite," he said. "I'm not surprised this potion was more effective than the usual brew. You should procure more as soon as possible, Caleb, though I don't know this potioner's mark." He looked at Mica expectantly.

She hesitated, turning the warm porcelain teacup in her hands. She was supposed to be discreet about Quinn's shop, and she wasn't sure whether Lord Ober had connected her to the princess. But it sounded as though Caleb really needed the medicine Quinn could provide, and her new friend probably wouldn't say no to additional business.

"It's from Magic Q," Mica said. "She has a shop by the big apothecary in Potioners Alley."

"I've seen the place," Lord Ober said, examining the mark again. "Does the princess buy all her potions from this Magic Q?"

Mica's mouth opened.

"Oh, forgive me, Miss Micathea!" Lord Ober exclaimed before she could form a reply. "Where are my manners? You don't need to reveal your lady's secrets. As long as Caleb can get more of this fine health tonic, you needn't say another word."

Lord Ober ushered Mica into a chair and refilled her teacup. He seemed only mildly concerned his nephew had been found slumped over in an alley. This clearly wasn't the first time it had happened. She remembered Caleb had been ill during the Assignment Ceremony too. Mica was terribly curious about what, exactly, was wrong with the young lord. Lord Ober treated her cordially, as if she were a friend or advisor, but he didn't volunteer an explanation as he fussed over his nephew and rearranged his pillows.

Caleb himself said little. His condition seemed to be improving, and he even sat up to drink his own tea. His hair looked more tousled than usual, almost boyish. As he blinked at her over his cup, the idea that he was involved in the disappearances began to seem unlikely. But that open, curious face of his was hiding secrets. Maybe he hadn't been paying attention to her in order to ship her off to Obsidian—or drain her blood—but it seemed he was a Talent himself.

Eventually, Lord Ober bustled off to summon something to eat, leaving Caleb and Mica alone. She felt a little shy now. She had sort of saved his life. Did that mean they were friends? How much could she ask him?

Caleb smiled at her. "Are you going to say something or just stare at me?"

Mica started. "Are you a Blur?" she blurted out. *Smooth. Nice espionage work, Mica.*

Caleb sipped his tea calmly. "What makes you say that?"

"You moved very fast when those thugs kicked you."

"It was dark."

"That doesn't answer my question."

"I'd be showing off my speed at every opportunity if I were a Blur."

Mica frowned, aware he still hadn't really answered. "If you're not a Blur, then did you—never mind."

"What?" Caleb leaned toward her, and she got the sense that he somehow saw more than she meant to reveal in her face. "Go on, you might as well ask."

Mica spoke in a rush. "Did you drink a Blur's blood to get their speed?"

Caleb gaped at her for a minute. Then he burst out laughing, the same explosive sound that had made the nobles look up back at the dancing lesson.

"No, I didn't drink a Blur's blood," he said, his laugh seeming to shatter the tension that had lingered between them. "Any other questions?"

"Oh, well, if I can ask anything . . ." Mica shifted into a more comfortable position, feet curled beneath her. The idea that Caleb was the culprit seemed silly in the cozy confines of Lord Ober's sitting room. "I was wondering about that bolt of silk you were carrying. Was that for you, or is some lady going to be disappointed you lost her gift?"

Caleb grinned. "Maybe you can tell me. I bought the silk for Princess Jessamyn. She's been looking for that pearly shade for ages, and I happened to see it in the market down by the docks."

"Oh." Mica made her bottom lip grow and shrink as she considered this, until she realized Caleb was staring at the movement. She stopped. "You're good friends with the princess?"

"Jessamyn was kind to me when my father first sent me to Jewel Harbor to represent the Pebble Islands," Caleb said. "Some people call her calculating, but she has a good heart. She welcomed a homesick Pebble boy, even though there was little chance I'd ever have much political clout. And she also helped me understand that Emperor Styl isn't as scary as he seems."

"How old were you when you were sent here?" Mica asked.

"Eight."

"*Eight?*" Mica hadn't left home for the Academy until she was thirteen. "No wonder you were homesick."

"I understand the why of it better now," Caleb said. "Someone from my family has to represent our interests here."

"What about your uncle?"

"He's my mother's brother," Caleb said. "Not from the Pebble Islands at all. He represents Timbral, our nearest neighbor."

"I see." Mica looked around the antechamber, which was smaller than Jessamyn's and furnished mostly with bookshelves. Mica had never seen someone keep so many books in their own room. Lord Ober could fill half the Academy library with his collection alone. It was hard to believe that silly Lady Euphia also lived here.

"Do you miss the Pebble Islands?"

"All the time," Caleb said. "No matter how much time I spend in the capital, that will always be home. Everything I do here is to serve the Pebble Islands."

"Not the empire?"

Caleb paused, taking another sip of his tea. When he answered, his tone was careful, showing none of the boyish vulnerability she'd seen moments ago. "The Pebble Islands are a proud part of the empire. Serving them means serving Windfast."

Mica wasn't sure how to respond to that. Silence fell between them, and she regretted pushing him. As an Amber Islander, it was easier for her to think of her island and the empire as one and the same. Jewel Harbor was technically its own territory as the seat of the capital, but this crescent-shaped chunk of land was nearest to Amber Island, and the first emperor had been the Amber King long ago. She wondered if Caleb's family had been kings in their own right before the islands united. And there was still the matter of whether or not he was truly a Blur—and why he refused to admit it.

Lord Ober bustled back in, bringing a platter full of sandwiches. "You both must be starving," he said. "It's nearly midnight."

"What?" Mica leapt up. The walk back to the palace must have taken longer than she thought with the incapacitated lord in tow. "I need to report to the princess. Forgive me, Lord Ober, but I shouldn't have stayed this long."

"It's quite all right," Lord Ober said. "I do hope you'll stop by for tea another time. I am in your debt for helping my favorite nephew."

"It was nothing." Mica gathered her package of potions and dipped into a quick curtsy, not quite meeting Caleb's eye. "I hope you recover well, my lord."

"I hope I'll see you again soon," Caleb said, "in your form or another."

Mica curtsied again, not sure what to say.

Lord Ober accompanied her to the door. "I didn't have an opportunity to speak with you on our journey from the Academy, Miss Micathea, but Master Kiev spoke highly of you. Please let me know if I can help you with anything. Anything at all."

"Thank you, my lord," Mica said, wondering exactly how close he was to the old spymaster. "I'll keep that in mind."

"Good. Oh, and Miss Micathea?"

"Yes?"

"May I ask that you not mention my nephew's illness to anyone? He wishes to maintain his privacy in this matter."

"Even Princess Jessamyn? Aren't they friends?"

"I've no doubt he will tell her in his own time."

Mica didn't know how she was going to explain her late arrival without mentioning Caleb, but she supposed it wouldn't endanger the princess's schemes to keep this to herself. She could always claim she'd gotten lost.

"I won't tell her," Mica said at last. "You have my word." She made no promises about what she'd tell Master Kiev. He needed to know this secret, whether he was a friend of Lord Ober's or not.

"Thank you. I am always pleased to meet Impersonators, Miss Micathea. I hope we will speak again soon."

Mica ran all the way back to Jessamyn's chambers. She apologized for "dropping" the potion she'd used to revive Caleb and excused her tardiness by claiming she had gotten lost on her way home from the potioner's. She could see Jessamyn's respect for her slipping with every word.

"Why must these things happen to me?" the princess whined, tears glistening in her big brown eyes. "It's as if you don't even care about *my* feelings when you do such things."

"I'm sorry, Princess Jessamyn. It was my first time out of—"

"Do you think I want excuses? Honestly, it's not as if I ask for much." Jessamyn sniffed and patted her dark-red hair. "Now go put on your Lord Nobu face. Lord Riven is coming to see me, and he must believe he's not the only nobleman I've invited for a late beverage this evening."

Mica sighed and altered her features to resemble Lord Nobu's, adopting straight hair, dark eyes, and sallow skin. At least

Jessamyn wasn't going to fire her. Mica wasn't enthusiastic about her chances of making it alone in Jewel Harbor after speaking to Quinn, especially now that she knew people were out for Talent blood. She waited in the doorway until she saw Lord Riven approaching, then she gave her very best arrogant lord impersonation as she sauntered past him.

CHAPTER TWELVE

Mica had precious little time to explore her suspicions that the disappearing Talents were being used for their blood over the next week. Jessamyn was preparing to host a grand harbor cruise, and she kept all her attendants busier than ever. They spent more time building up anticipation for the event among the young lords and ladies than actually making the arrangements.

The princess didn't appear to be suffering from the loss of one vial of energy potion. She ran her life at the usual furious pace, skipping from dancing lesson to tea party to racquetball match to feast. She entertained noble visitors, called on them in their own chambers, and saw to it that the right people met even when she couldn't be there. Mica wondered if the nobles even wanted to socialize as often as the princess made them. Perhaps they were *all* sending hired Mimics to these events, running the Talents off their feet while they sipped ambrosia in their own quarters.

Mica kept a closer eye on Lord Ober after he asked her not to tell the princess about Caleb's mysterious illness despite their long friendship. She was supposed to watch out for uncharacteristic behavior in case any of the nobles had been replaced with

Obsidian Impersonators. But whenever she passed the two men in the palace corridors, Caleb looked healthier than ever and Lord Ober was his usual charming self. The latter had many friends among the nobility, and he got along well with the non-nobles too. She had seen him laughing with a group of Shield guards, and he'd even asked her about her children when she was impersonating a cook to listen in on a private dinner party. Such pleasantries were so rare from the nobles that she had gaped at him for a minute before giving a vague answer about the cook's darling little ones.

Though there was probably nothing sinister about the late-night encounter with Caleb and Ober, Mica included it in a report to Master Kiev anyway. She'd been taught at the Academy that she might never see how all the pieces fit together, but even the tiniest bead of information could prove essential.

The Blur messenger who carried her letters to Master Kiev didn't live too far from the palace. She snuck out to send her reports whenever she could steal time between tasks. The Blur, a young lad called Peet (gangly, with bright-red hair and a pointed chin), could make it to the Academy and back in a day.

"Master Kiev says to keep up the good work," he said when Mica went to see him a few days after the incident with Lord Caleb. He searched around his tiny flat for a tin of cookies to share with her. The bedsit was located on the fourth floor of a cramped tenement, and it only had room for a cot, a small table, and a handful of chairs. Still, if Peet was at home when Mica stopped by, he always offered her a cup of tea and whatever sweets he had on hand. "Oh, and here's a letter for you."

Mica glanced at the rolled scroll. Her name was inscribed on the outside in a dense handwriting that didn't belong to Master Kiev.

The letter was from Sapphire.

It took all of Mica's willpower to keep from ripping the scroll open right away. She was desperate for news of her friends. But she paused to ask Peet if the other Talents in Jewel Harbor were saying anything about the disappearances.

"I hear the Muscles at the docks don't go out alone anymore," Peet said. "I know a girl who pulls a ferry down there. She's thinking about moving out to Silverfell to live with her sister. And this is a five-foot-nothing lady who could pick up a horse and toss it one-handed."

"It's that bad?"

"Aye. People are going missing every few days."

"Every few *days*?"

She should have heard more about the disappearances up at the palace, if they were occurring so frequently. Wasn't that the whole point of stationing her at Jessamyn's side instead of out in the city?

"Do the ones who disappear have anything in common?"

"Just their Talent." Peet poured the tea and handed her a crumbling walnut cookie. "I heard about a Shield who works the furnaces in a smithy. He was seen having a pint at a pub over lunch one day, but he never came home for dinner."

"Was this near the docks too?"

"That one was, yeah. Then again, this Blur who has a regular message route clear over on the western side of the crescent went missing last week."

"Isn't the City Watch doing anything?"

Peet shrugged. "They said the fellow probably ran off for a drink somewhere and got lost."

Mica didn't understand. In Stonefoss there'd be outrage if people started vanishing. The authorities would take action. Yet she'd hardly heard a whisper about the problem from anyone except other Talents.

"Tell me something," Mica said. "Are all the missing people commoners?"

Peet thought for a moment, chewing on a walnut cookie. "All

the ones I've heard about," he said at last. "You think that's why no one cares?"

"It wouldn't surprise me," Mica said bitterly. The nobles in the Silver Palace couldn't be bothered with the troubles of working Talents. The elusive Emperor Styl hadn't done a thing about the disappearances. He didn't bother much with his daughter either, as far as she could tell. She'd had no idea when she swore to serve the empire that these were the kind of people whose rule she'd be protecting. She touched the scroll from Sapphire in her pocket, afraid of what she'd find inside.

"Well, I'd better get going," Peet said. "Gotta make it to Redbridge before dark."

"I have one more question," Mica said as she walked with him to the door. "Have you ever heard about Talents selling their blood to potioners?"

"Sure. I did it a few times before I started getting steady work from Kiev. You short on coin?"

"What? No," Mica said, surprised he was so casual about it. The practice must be more widespread than she realized. She was actually paid quite well, though she had precious little time to spend her salary. "How did the potioners find you?"

"I found them," the Blur said. "All you got to do is turn up to the bars around Potioners Alley and listen in on a few conversations. It's easy."

They stomped down the narrow stairs and parted ways at the bottom of Peet's building. She looked up at the young Talent, who was limbering up his gangly limbs for his run to the Academy.

"Thanks for your help, Peet. Be safe out there."

"May you thrive." And he was gone in a blur of motion.

Mica hoped Quinn had been serious about her offer of a drink, because she intended to take her up on it next time she went to Potioners Alley. She needed to find out more about those who dealt in Talent blood.

Mica pulled out the letter from Sapphire and read it as she walked back to the palace.

Dear Mica,

I wish I could write with happier news. Danil is still missing. I've searched every inch of Redbridge and the surrounding area a dozen times, but he's just . . . gone.

I'm leaving tomorrow for Winnow Island. Master Kiev convinced my assigned employer to take me on after all, even though I was supposed to report for duty over a month ago.

Mica paused. Had it really been over a month since she left the Academy? Time had flown by since she last saw her friends and family.

She continued reading.

Master Kiev says it's time to move on. I disagree, but there's nothing else I can do here.

Do you think you could talk to the princess about Danil? I'm sorry to ask it, but I feel completely powerless. Maybe you ended up in the palace for a reason.

I hope you're okay. I miss you.

Sapph

P.S. I saw Tiber Warson's mother the other day. She's as smug as ever.

Mica read the letter twice. It had none of Sapphire's usual verve. The sense of defeat in her cramped handwriting made rage simmer in the pit of Mica's stomach, and she struggled to keep her features from sliding out of place. She didn't understand why no one striking cared. The nobles were so terribly concerned with their parties and petty rivalries. Meanwhile, the Obsidian infiltrators were stealing the very best people in Windfast out from under their noses.

She read the letter again as she entered the palace gates, lingering on Sapphire's request. *Could* she talk to the princess about Danil? She wasn't sure how much power Jessamyn had outside the Silver Palace itself. Her complicated waltz of alliances and relationships seemed to have little to do with anyone apart from the nobility, even if she did care. Mica needed someone with real power, someone like Emperor Styl himself.

She snorted. She didn't have much chance of that. She still hadn't seen the emperor in person yet. He had a reputation for being as busy as Jessamyn, and Mica didn't think the princess herself saw much of her father. Neither one would listen to the likes of her.

"You're looking somber for such a fine day, Miss Micathea."

Mica looked up, realizing she had paused in the middle of the courtyard.

"Hello, Lord Ober."

"Out for a stroll?" He had a book under his arm, and a manservant with hair as gray as Ober's walked beside him, carrying a pitcher of chilled lemonade and two glasses.

"I'm just returning from an errand, my lord," Mica said.

"Care to join me for a beverage? My lady wife was supposed to meet me in the garden, but she has decided it's too warm out for her."

Mica hesitated, not wanting to miss her chance to gather information about the influential lord. But she had already been gone too long.

"I'm afraid the princess is expecting me."

"Ah well. I suppose it's just you and me for a drink then, Dak." Lord Ober clapped the gray-haired manservant on the back. "You've spent enough time on your feet today." He nodded politely. "Miss Micathea."

Mica watched the two men stroll off toward the garden

together. Why couldn't all the nobles treat their "inferiors" with such courtesy?

Speaking of servants, just then, Brin rushed through the palace gates behind Mica.

"You're not with her?" she exclaimed, wiping sweat-dampened hair back from her round forehead. "Oh dear, I thought I could run out for a moment. We'd better hurry!"

She seized Mica's arm and hauled her back toward the palace.

"Where were you—?"

"I had to check on my mother," Brin said. "She's ill, and I swear it gets harder every week to find time to see her."

"Could you ask the princess for time off?"

Brin gave a wild laugh. "You've met her, haven't you? She nearly took my head off last time I asked her for something. Just wait until she finally lets you impersonate her. None of us will ever get a moment's rest when she can be in two places at once again."

CHAPTER THIRTEEN

Mica had been in Jewel Harbor for six weeks before she was finally permitted to impersonate Princess Jessamyn herself.

"It requires trust to allow someone to act in your place," Jessamyn had said when Mica brought it up earlier. "Just because one is a good Impersonator doesn't mean one is a good actor. I shall decide when you're ready for the responsibility. The aftermath would be *exhausting* if you messed up."

Mica didn't argue, though she was eager for a chance to try out the princess's face. She had added the look to her nightly exercises, and she'd been studying Jessamyn's energetic mannerisms, her potion-softened skin, her bold eyebrows, and the particular sheen of her dark-red hair. She felt confident that she could do a good impression.

The princess finally decided to give her a chance the week before the harbor cruise. Mica would be allowed to assume the royal form to stand in at an official audience with Emperor Styl while Jessamyn attended a dance lesson, where she intended to set a few interpersonal dramas in motion.

Mica couldn't help feeling excited when she at last took the princess's shape and stood before the real thing.

"Hmm." Jessamyn walked all the way around her, studying her closely. "That's not horrible for a first attempt."

They were in the princess's large, gold-bedecked dressing room. Closets full of costly gowns and two towering cases for Jessamyn's jewels lined the walls. A standing mirror with three panels made it possible for the princess to admire herself from any angle, and there was a purple silk chaise longue where she could relax in the midst of dressing. Not that Mica had ever seen the princess actually relax.

Jessamyn began another circle around Mica, halting before she got far. "I must say, Micathea, your ear-work is not up to standard."

"I beg your pardon?"

"The ears. They're not right at all." Jessamyn pulled back her hair, offering a clearer view of her ears than Mica had seen so far. "Quickly now, see if you can't fix that."

Mica refrained from pointing out that she would be wearing her hair down today and twitched her ears until they settled into the correct shape.

"That will do for now." Jessamyn leaned in so she and Mica were nose to nose, perfect mirrors of each other. Or at least, Mica thought they were perfect.

"Can anything be done about those eyes?" Jessamyn said petulantly. "My goodness, you must think I'm positively manic."

Mica squinted, pulling back on some of the bright glint she'd added while Jessamyn kept up a running commentary. "Too far . . . no, that's not it either. Get rid of a little more of that yellow tint. It's a very specific brown."

Just how much time do you spend staring at yourself in a mirror, anyway?

"How's this?"

"I suppose that's as good as it's going to get." Jessamyn sighed. "Do practice harder in the future, Micathea."

The princess bustled over to a glass case where she kept an assortment of crowns and jeweled diadems. She unlocked it with a key she kept on a thin chain around her neck and pulled out a slim gold circlet set with a single emerald.

"Remember, you will not need to speak, unless it's to agree with my father or express sympathy to his supplicants. You are there to show the petitioners seeking the emperor's counsel how much their future ruler cares about their concerns. It is vital that they see you listening attentively, looking every inch the princess."

"May I ask a question?"

"You waste everyone's time when you turn one question into two."

Mica held in a sigh. "Why not go yourself to hear the people's concerns and send me to the dance lesson?"

Jessamyn burst out laughing. "Oh, Micathea, *Micathea*. You may be good at impersonating faces, but that does not mean you can imitate my dancing. Every lord or lady in attendance will know at once that it isn't me. They would be mortally offended if they knew they were dancing with my Impersonator." She was still chuckling as she ushered Mica over to a wardrobe bursting with multicolored silks to select an outfit for the audience. "Send you to the dance lesson. Imagine!"

Mica didn't feel that adequately answered her question. Who cared if the nobles were offended? Her dancing wasn't that bad! And she'd rather know that the future ruler of the Windfast Empire was actually listening to the citizens' concerns. She'd seen little evidence of it so far.

"Princess, I've heard Talents are being kidnapped," Mica blurted out before she could think better of it. "They're disappearing right from Jewel Harbor."

Jessamyn paused her scrutiny of the gown collection. Mica took that to mean she was listening and pressed on.

"Why isn't the emperor doing anything to find them? These

Talents are in danger, and no one in the palace is even talking about it."

Jessamyn hesitated for a split second before saying, "This is hardly the time, Micathea."

"But—"

She raised a hand sharply to cut her off. "Don't you have a job to do?"

At that moment, Ruby and Alea bustled in to help them finish dressing. They paused at the door, casting curious glances between the two identical princesses.

Jessamyn arched an eyebrow at Mica.

"Yes, Princess." She dropped into a curtsy, trying not to grind her teeth. "I am at your service."

As if she hadn't heard, Jessamyn spun to address her maids hovering in the doorway. "Well? What are you two waiting for? Fetch my dancing shoes."

An hour later, Mica processed into the imperial throne room in a regal green gown more beautiful than any she'd ever seen. Jessamyn's dark-red hair fell around her shoulders in soft waves, completely obscuring her perfectly rendered ears. The emerald on her diadem caught the light as she strode down the luxurious golden carpet stretching the length of the throne room.

Mica didn't know where to look first. Hundreds of people filled the room, but the vastness of the space made it impossible to concentrate on their faces. The white marble floor gleamed, and the walls were draped with the banners of every island and principality in the empire. Windows encircled the top of the walls just before stone gave way to the enormous silver dome. Mica felt a swoop of dizziness when she glanced up at its highest point. It was a wonder the whole thing didn't crash down on their heads.

She concentrated on imitating Jessamyn's walk, which was

somehow both stately and vigorous, as every eye in the immense room followed her progress. She curtsied deeply at the end of the golden carpet, then she looked at last upon Emperor Styl of Windfast.

He had a regal bearing and proud, cold features. Black hair, white skin, a thick, protruding jaw, and a high forehead. Though he remained seated, he was very tall, and he filled the massive throne easily. His face lacked the vitality Mica was used to from Jessamyn. He surveyed the throne room with a faint twist of his thin lips, as if it the place were full of insects and all the acknowledgment they deserved was a light sneer. Mica had never felt more intimidated.

"It is an honor to see you thrive, Your Imperial Majesty," she intoned.

"May you thrive, Princess Jessamyn Styldier."

The emperor's greeting was formal, his voice as clear as expensive crystal. Mica ascended the marble dais and took her place in the finely carved chair at his side, proud her hands remained steady.

A palace steward stepped forward to announce the proceedings. "People of Windfast, you may now bring your supplications before His Imperial Majesty Emperor Styl, and Her Highness Princess Jessamyn."

The emperor didn't look at Mica as the audience began, remaining utterly aloof. She recalled what Caleb had said about how Jessamyn helped him see that the emperor wasn't as scary as he seemed. She understood now why that was necessary. How did Jessamyn and her father interact when they were alone, *if* they were ever alone? As far as Mica could tell, they barely saw each other.

Imperial citizens were now lining up to make their entreaties. All were commoners, evidenced by their simple clothing and lack of attendants. The grandeur of the vast chamber made the supplicants look almost pitiful. One by one, they bowed before the emperor and shared tales of hardship: sons lost at sea, livestock lost to disease, limbs lost in accidents—which often led to lost jobs and homes. Mica couldn't help imagining her own family members being forced to prostrate themselves before the throne, bending their proud shoulders to beg for aid. The nobles enjoyed direct access to the emperor as perpetual guests of the Silver Palace, but these periodic audiences were the only chance most ordinary people had to speak to their ruler.

It's not fair. Mica's heart squeezed like a fist in her chest, and she fought to maintain a stiff, pretty mask. *It shouldn't be like this.*

As the supplicants made their requests, Emperor Styl offered words of encouragement and wisdom in that steady, crystalline voice. He helped where he could, offering jobs in the palace and settling interpersonal disputes, but too many supplicants went away looking defeated. Mica began to understand that no one resorted to audiences like this unless they were truly desperate, and sometimes it was too late for the emperor to help. She didn't think he meant to be cruel, despite his forbidding demeanor. Still, it was frustrating to see that even the emperor himself wasn't powerful enough to fix everything.

Whenever someone tried to argue with one of Emperor Styl's decisions, whether through tears or angry words, he didn't raise his voice or berate them for being disrespectful. Instead, he turned to Mica and said, "Do you agree, Princess Jessamyn?"

To which her answer, as Jessamyn had made her repeat over and over, was "Yes, Father. I believe you have made a wise decision."

Emperor Styl would nod, not quite meeting her eyes, and repeat his declaration to the aggrieved. When Jessamyn had explained this ritual, it sounded pointless to Mica, but now she saw how the people reacted to seeing the princess support her father's decisions. They would nod, draw themselves up, and retreat from the dais with quiet dignity. The disappointment seemed easier to take when the emperor sought a second opinion from the princess, as if the supplicants wanted most to be heard, even when they had an unsolvable problem.

By the time the audience drew to a close, Mica was answering with as much calm certainty as she could muster. "Yes, Father. I believe you have made a wise decision."

Then the very last person permitted to appeal that day marched down the long golden carpet. The squat little woman had soft eyes and gray at her temples. Mica recognized her.

"Your Imperial Majesties," Edwina said, bowing deeply. "I am Edwina, a freelance Impersonator from a small village two days north of Old Kings. I come to you seeking help for my husband Rufus. He has been missing for three weeks, and I-I'm afraid he has been abducted."

Mica's heart sank. She remembered Edwina's affectionate smile as she patted her sleeping husband on his paunchy belly that day in Lord Ober's carriage. Now she looked fragile, as if worry had eaten away at the bones inside her soft body.

"Go on, Madam," Emperor Styl said, his voice formal but not unkind. "Where was your husband last seen?"

"On his way to Jewel Harbor." Edwina's voice gathered strength as she continued. "He wanted to ask Lord Ober for more work. Times are hard, you see, and we have three little ones. But Lord Ober tells me he never arrived at all."

"Perhaps a highwayman—"

"Forgive me, Emperor Styl, but my husband served on the Imperial Army's Elite Impersonator division in his youth. No mere highwayman would trouble him."

Mica blinked in surprise, picturing the man's slouched shoulders and puffy face. It was difficult to imagine him as elite anything, much less in the army, which was rumored to use professional Impersonators as assassins—something they categorically denied.

"Have you spoken to the City Watch?" Emperor Styl asked Edwina.

"Yes. They tell me he probably found another woman." She swelled with indignation. "He would never. I can't believe it of my Rufus. And anyway, he's not the only one gone. There have been other Talents kidnapped without a trace."

Emperor Styl paused for a beat. "Madam, I assure you the City Watch—"

"They won't do anything!" she said. "He has served all his life. Why isn't the empire protecting its own?"

Emperor Styl rose to his feet so fast Mica jumped. His shadow seemed to fill the entire dais.

"I am afraid I agree that your husband has found another woman, Madam Edwina. I urge you to move on with your life."

Edwina took a step back, as if the emperor had slapped her.

"That's a cruel thing to say," she hissed, "but it doesn't explain the other Talents missing. Don't you care about them?"

Emperor Styl remained utterly calm in the face of Edwina's passion. "You must let it go and return home. Do you agree, Princess Jessamyn?"

Mica started. The squat little Impersonator looked at her, angry tears coursing down her round cheeks. Mica knew her line, but she couldn't bring herself to utter the words, not when she too had seen how little the nobles cared about Talents like Danil and Rufus. Jessamyn had barely acknowledged the issue when Mica brought it up earlier. She thought of Sapphire's letter, pressed beneath her pillow back in the princess's quarters. Perhaps she *had* been placed here for a reason.

"Do you agree, Princess Jessamyn?" the emperor repeated.

"No."

Emperor Styl's mouth stiffened, the only hint that he was surprised. Mica rushed on before he could stop her. "Father, I believe this woman's fears are founded. There is a danger to Talents. We should be doing more to find the missing and make sure no more innocents are taken."

Murmurs spread through the crowd, rippling like wind

over sand.

"And what do you propose, *daughter*?" Emperor Styl finally met her eyes. There was no shortage of vitality there now. He was furious. Worse, it suddenly dawned on Mica that the emperor knew she wasn't the real princess—had probably known it all along. And she had just contradicted him in front of the entire throne room.

She felt as if she'd just tumbled off the edge of a cliff—and she was still falling.

"W-We need to make sure the Talents are informed of the danger," Mica said. If she was going to lose her job—and possibly her head—she might as well get it all out now. "And we need to reassure them we're doing everything we can to s-stop these disappearances. They have to know we care about Talents and appreciate all the ways they help our empire thrive."

She pressed her hands into the intricately carved arms of the throne. The murmurs grew louder. She was going to throw up. She didn't dare look the emperor in the face—until his response made her gape at him in shock.

"My daughter is correct," Emperor Styl said smoothly. "Talents have worked since the youngest days of the empire to keep our islands unified. The service, discipline, and *obedience* of our Talents protect the Windfast Empire against all threats. It would be stupid to think we don't care."

Mica swore the emperor's eyes flickered to her at that, and she wished she could turn herself into a chair. Impersonation only went so far.

"We shall look into your husband's disappearance, Madam Edwina, and take steps to ensure no other Talents go missing. That is all we have time for today. May you thrive."

And Emperor Styl marched out of the throne room before anyone could so much as bow.

CHAPTER FOURTEEN

ica considered going straight to the harbor and boarding a ferry for Amber Island. Her brothers might tease her for not lasting long among the fancy ladies, but that was better than being beheaded by the emperor. She'd prefer either option to the lecture Jessamyn no doubt had in store for her.

"How bad is it going to be?" she asked Banner as they walked back along the east wing corridor. He had seen the whole thing from his post beside the dais.

"If I could transfer my impervious skin to you, I would."

Mica sighed. "I appreciate the sentiment."

She found herself looking forward to being sent home. Her parents would be happy to see her. She could catch up with friends she hadn't seen much since she went away to the Academy. She could finally get some fresh air and stroll slowly down streets that weren't packed with people. She wouldn't have to come running when a bell rang or attend yet another tea party in a stuffy silk dress.

She was enjoying the fantasy so much that she almost didn't react when Lord Caleb strode up the corridor and pulled her unceremoniously out of Banner's hearing.

"Can we talk, Jessa? I have a problem." Red lines marred his cheeks, and his waistcoat was wrinkled, as if he had been up all night, worrying and rubbing his face.

"What kind of problem?" she asked, careful to use Jessamyn's voice.

"It's about my—" Caleb stopped and looked closer at her. "You're Micathea. I beg your pardon. It was easier to tell with the last one."

Mica's eyes widened, and it was an effort to keep her impersonation intact. "How did you know this time?"

"It's the mouth." Caleb scrubbed a hand through his hair, seeming distracted. "Where's Jessamyn?"

"At the dancing lesson, last I heard."

"I just came from there. No matter."

"Wait," Mica put a hand on his arm before he could walk away. "Is there any way I can help?"

Caleb seemed to consider the offer seriously, studying her as if he could see right to her true face. But then he shook his head and removed her hand gently from his arm. He lingered for a beat too long, her hand in his, before releasing her.

"Forgive me for interrupting you."

And then he was gone, leaving Mica staring after him and wondering whether he'd blurred a bit as he left.

She was still trying to unravel the mystery of Lord Caleb when she returned to the princess's chambers to change out of Jessamyn's dress and face. What was his secret? If he was truly a Blur, it wasn't enough to explain how worried he had looked when he pulled "Jessamyn" aside. Talents occasionally appeared among the nobility, and it was no cause for distress. Whatever it was, he had been close to confiding in her. How had her mouth given her away? She made her lip grow and shrink in front of the mirror in the opulent dressing chamber, attempting to get the shape just right.

Suddenly, a crash came from the antechamber. Mica dropped automatically into a defensive stance as footsteps pounded across the outer room. She turned to the door with fists raised just as Princess Jessamyn hurled it open.

"Well!" she shrieked. "I hope you're proud of yourself for your little show, because you just undid *months* of work. I cannot believe you had the *gall* to contradict my dear father in front of his people, much less do it in such a spectacularly foolish and *unprofessional* manner."

Something in Mica snapped at the scathing tone. She took a step toward the raging princess, squaring her shoulders for a fight.

"Yes, I am proud of myself," she said. "Talents put their lives in danger every day for this empire while the nobles dance and gossip and throw stupid parties. People like Edwina and Rufus deserve to be taken care of after all they've done. Talents have been going missing for months. Obsidian has infiltrated the capital itself, and I am sick of everyone pretending it isn't happening."

"You're sick of it, are you?" Jessamyn's voice was suddenly so calm and quiet Mica was surprised she hadn't transformed into a different person. "You, who've been aware of the problem for what? A month? Did it ever occur to you, *Mimic*, that there might be a good *reason* we are not talking openly about it? Did it never occur to you that we might be trying to *solve* the problem when you bumbled in there and ran your mouth in front of everyone?"

"I—"

"Of course it didn't," Jessamyn said. "Because you think you're sooo superior, and you're the only one who cares, and aren't all these ladies so silly with their dresses and their tea parties."

Mica took a step back, exactly as Edwina had when the emperor rebuked her.

"We. Are. Looking. For. The. Missing. Talents." Jessamyn bit off each word. "The information you send to Master Kiev is help-ing." Mica opened her mouth, and the princess flung up a hand. "Yes, of course I know about your other mission. But what *you* don't know is that the perpetrator of these crimes is not Obsidian."

"You mean—?"

"Someone, most likely a member of this court, is kidnapping Talents and keeping them within the empire."

Mica's jaw dropped, growing a few extra inches for good measure, as the implications hit her.

"That is grotesque, Micathea. *Honestly.*" Jessamyn folded her arms and looked down her nose. "My father and I *were* hiding the fact that we're aware it is an inside conspiracy in order to increase our chances of actually catching the traitors."

"I'm sorry, Princess. I didn't know—"

"No, you didn't. But you had orders, which you directly disobeyed. Part of being an effective imperial spy is following directions even when you don't understand them." Jessamyn sighed. "It's a shame. I had such high hopes for you. It will be *so* much hassle to train your replacement."

"My . . . my replacement?"

Jessamyn dismissed her with a wave. "May you thrive, Micathea."

The princess strutted over to the mirrors and began combing out her hair, which she'd pulled into a thick braid over her shoul-der. She was wearing her riding clothes, Mica realized. She'd skipped a dance lesson to go riding? Why? And with whom?

It doesn't matter, she thought dully. She was fired. Master Kiev had been wrong. Her skills weren't adequate for the task of serving the princess after all—and now she knew that Jessamyn was much more in tune with what was happening around the empire than she realized. And she apparently knew more about Master Kiev's mysterious spy network than Mica did.

Shoulders sagging, Mica turned away from the princess and trudged across the thick carpet on the dressing room floor. The jewels and silk dresses seemed to mock her. She'd been too dismissive, unable to see that there was more going on beneath the glittering surfaces than she thought.

She got as far as the door before she realized she wasn't willing to give up yet. She turned around.

"Princess Jessamyn, please give me another chance. I'll make up for my mistake today. I can still help you."

Jessamyn didn't look away from the mirror. "And why would you want to do that?"

"I want to find the missing Talents," Mica said. "I think my friend Danil is with them, and my family are all Talents too." She thought about adding something about serving the empire, but she had a feeling Jessamyn would see the truth. She didn't have some vague patriotic motivation. This was personal. "Like you said, it'd take time to replace me. I'm afraid those Talents are being killed—or used for their blood. They may not have a lot of time."

Jessamyn put down her brush and fixed her bright, almost-manic eyes on Mica in the mirror. They were exactly the same height, and as their eyes met, Mica had the eerie sensation that only one of them was real, the other a mere shade. She wasn't sure which was which.

"I will give you another chance," Jessamyn said at last, "but only one."

Mica started to speak, but the princess raised an eyebrow, silencing her.

"I believe I can get out ahead of today's debacle. I shall make the Talent disappearances one of my little causes. That ought to keep everyone from taking my interest too seriously." She turned away from the mirror to face Mica. "Can you accept that my father and I really do care about our people, even if we do not announce every thought we've ever had about them from the dais?"

"Yes, Princess Jessamyn," Mica said quickly. "And thank you! I promise I'll do a better—"

Princess Jessamyn let out a longsuffering sigh. "Are you still here, Micathea? Run along. I have many important things to do."

CHAPTER FIFTEEN

Mica was surprisingly relieved to still have her assignment. She felt a renewed sense of purpose now that she knew the princess cared about the missing Talents—even though they were commoners. Jessamyn was certain the perpetrators weren't connected to Obsidian, though she declined to share her reasoning with Mica. This left them to grapple with why and how an imperial subject would do such a thing.

Despite her misstep in the throne room, Jessamyn allowed Mica to stand in for her frequently now. She attended an elaborate feast in the huge circular banquet hall, and it was an effort not to stuff herself with the decadent foods Jessamyn would have taken for granted. She visited an orphanage in the city and allowed the little girls to play with her dark-red hair. She even flirted with Lord Riven in the conservatory while Jessamyn was dancing cheek to cheek with Lord Dolan in the ballroom. *He* didn't notice anything different about her mouth.

The princess didn't usually share how all these carefully orchestrated moments contributed to her plans, but Mica began to pick up hints about what the princess was trying to accomplish. Sometimes they even talked about it.

"You see Lord Fritz and Lady Lorna over there?" Jessamyn whispered to Mica as they rode down to the harbor the morning of the long-awaited cruise. The two youthful nobles were riding knee to knee, and they kept glancing at each other and blushing whenever their eyes met.

"They look sweet together," Mica said.

"I know. It's too soon." Jessamyn's lip jutted out in a pout, which Mica studied carefully. "I'd better see if Bellina can claim a few extra dances with Fritz on the boat, keep him confused."

"Why? Fritz and Lorna seem like a good match."

Fritz had an endearing, boyish charm, and Lorna's buxom figure hid a wide-eyed innocent who loved animals and babies, no matter how fussy.

"They are," Jessamyn said. "But while Fritz has been safely oblivious to her interest, Lorna's father, the Lord of Silverfell, has been investing heavily in the merchants' guild. He's worried that if his daughter can't secure a marriage to Fritz, he's going to need an extra in with Lord Dolan as an alternative suitor for her. By the time our two lovebirds over there get together, I want Lorna's father to be fully committed to supporting the guild regardless."

"That's . . . complicated."

"In case you're worrying about how it affects your precious Talents," Jessamyn continued, "a stronger merchants' guild is good for the Muscles and Blurs who work on the ships, not to mention everyone who eats from their shipments."

"I know." Mica ground her teeth at the condescending tone. "I care about people besides Talents."

But Jessamyn had already spurred her horse ahead, squeezing in between Lorna and Fritz.

Shield guards held back the crowds as the princess and her entourage processed through the streets. Jessamyn had invited a select group to accompany her to the docks to review the final preparations for that evening's harbor cruise. It was essentially a floating party, where the nobles would take advantage of the cool sea breezes and the gentle current to enjoy a night of drinking and dancing on the water. The clear, sunny skies that morning raised their hopes that the late-summer weather would be just right for a leisurely turn about the harbor.

Mica was impersonating Brin today, wearing her frizzy hair and frantic expression. The maid had taken ill thanks to the stress of planning the event. She'd been involved in so many of the preparations that Jessamyn needed Mica to speak to the various vendors as the handmaid to make sure everything was in order. The real Brin, with flushed cheeks and glassy eyes, had explained the details to Mica from her bed.

"You *must* make sure the evening goes smoothly," she had pleaded, clutching Mica's hand. "The princess will be terribly upset if it isn't perfect."

"I'm sure it'll be—"

"And don't let anyone overcharge you. It'll come out of my pay if she isn't satisfied."

"I'll take care of it." Mica extracted herself from Brin's feverish grip. "You focus on getting better."

The sea air rang with the shouts of dockworkers when their party arrived at the pier. Muscles were unloading cargo from a huge trading ship at the first mooring, the wooden dock creaking and groaning under their feet. Some sailors handed elaborately woven carpets from the ship's deck to be loaded onto a wagon on the dock, while others rolled barrels full of Timbral wine past the princess's entourage, not pausing to bow for the lords and ladies.

Mica and the others dismounted amidst the quayside chaos and walked past the trade ship to a pleasure barge floating at the next mooring. The vessel had a wide deck and shallow draft. A flat-topped cabin occupied the center, with a wooden bar running alongside it, where revelers could rest their drinks. A mast with a crow's nest rose above that, built to provide views of the harbor, not to support a sail. The barge relied on oars for movement rather than the vagaries of the wind. A few workers were up in the crow's nest now, stringing lights from the mast. Others were hanging banners over the sides, transforming the barge into a large colorful bird perched on the water. Several smaller boats waited nearby, younger birds in plainer colors, ready to transport the Shield guards and additional refreshments.

Mica worked to confirm that all the arrangements would go as planned while the princess showed her chosen nobles (Ladies Lorna and Elana, Lord Fritz, and the brothers Hugh and Hector) around the barge. Jessamyn had explained that the whole point of this morning's excursion was to make these five feel as if they were part of her inner circle. She fully expected them to brag about it at the party, which would in turn make the rest of the nobles even more eager to get into her good graces.

While the princess was thus occupied, Mica spoke to the restaurateur from the northern tip of the crescent who had been hired to cater the harbor cruise, the musicians who would provide the entertainment, and the captain of the barge. The captain was a thin man of Obsidian origin who wore his long, pale hair pulled back in a ponytail. He seemed unsettled when he spoke to Mica, and she wondered if she'd executed Brin's frazzled mannerisms a little too well.

"Everything is ready for tonight," the captain said, twisting his pale hands together so the blue veins stood out on the backs. "You know I won't fail you."

"I just have to make sure everything is perfect for the princess."

"It will be. You will never forget this night."

"Good. Now, I must find the sommelier. Where *is* that man?" Mica hurried off, smoothing her skirt anxiously over Brin's hips.

She found her way belowdecks, where rows of benches awaited the arrival of the oarsmen. Circles of light spilled in from the oarlocks, illuminating the cramped hold in patches. She found the barrels of wine and liquor that had been ordered for the cruise, but the sommelier was nowhere to be seen. As she turned to leave, a pair of men stomped down the ladder.

"Sorry, miss," said the first (beefy arms, brown skin, jowls). "We're here to move these barrels topside."

"I'll get out of your way." Mica paused as the men moved forward. The second man, who had a long, crooked nose, was leaner and weaker-looking than the first, but both of them lifted fat wine barrels under each arm without straining. Muscles then.

"Excuse me," Mica said. "Do you live around the docks?"

The beefy man dipped his head, revealing a thinning patch in his dark hair. "Aye, miss."

"Have you heard anything about fellow Talents going missing around here?"

The two Muscles exchanged looks. "We've heard a whisper or two."

"Do you know anything about the victims? Who they might have spoken to before they disappeared? Or if they had any enemies."

The man with the crooked nose frowned, tightening chapped lips. "Why does a lady's maid such as yourself want to know?"

"The princess cares," Mica said. "Can we leave it at that?"

The Muscles looked at each other again. "Official story is the Talents disappear without a trace," the beefy man said at last. "But that ain't true. Some people have heard screams."

"What do you mean?"

"They won't say where, but word is there's a street in the warehouse district where people hear strange noises. Anyone tries to report it, and they get a visit from the City Watch." The man spat on the ground, making his jowls jiggle. "My mate got told the place has been investigated already and he should stop causing trouble."

"Aye," said the other man, "but the screams don't stop."

Hardly daring to breathe, Mica said, "Do you know where the warehouse is?"

They didn't. Dozens of warehouses lined the waterfront, and they could only give her a vague idea of where the noises had been heard. Nevertheless, it was a solid lead.

"What about these visits from the City Watch?" Mica said. "Is it a specific officer?"

"I saw him once," said the beefy man. "*Once*, after he warned my mate to let it go. Then I never saw him again."

An Impersonator then. But how did he or she know to show up when people reported hearing noises from that particular street? Perhaps he was a real City Watchman who adopted different faces to deliver his threats. She wouldn't put it past the noble conspirator to have lackeys among local law enforcement.

Mica thanked the Muscles for the information and climbed back out of the hold to rejoin her party, an extra spring in her step. This might be a breakthrough. She could begin searching warehouses that night, when most of the nobility would be busy on the harbor cruise. It was the perfect opportunity.

Unfortunately, Jessamyn had other plans.

"I need you to come on the cruise tonight," she said as they paraded back to the palace so the ladies could dress.

"You said I'd have the evening off."

"I'm not sure how you expect to save anyone if you're not actually doing your job, Micathea."

"I have a lead." Mica abandoned Brin's frazzled voice for a moment. "I wasn't going to sit around and—"

"Your social life bores me," Jessamyn said. "I have more important things for you to do tonight."

A vein pulsed in Mica's temple. Why had she thought her job would be easier now that she and the princess were working toward the same goal?

"As you wish." She resigned herself to yet another night listening in on the nobility while she refilled their wine goblets. "I'm sure Brin will let me wear the dress she got for tonight."

"You won't be going as Brin," Jessamyn said impatiently. "I

daresay she'll rally. In fact, I might gift her a potion from Magic Q to get her through the evening. She has *so* been looking forward to the festivities." Jessamyn's eyes went a little dewy, as if she could hardly believe how generous she was to her employees. But when she looked back at Mica, her gaze was sharp. "This cruise is one beautiful woman short of a real party. I need you to play that Obsidian lovely you showed me on your first day."

Mica blinked. "The Obsidian—"

"You'll be a visiting lady seeking better relationships with our fair empire. You just arrived in Jewel Harbor today, and I decided to invite you along on our little gathering."

"You *want* people to see you encouraging better relationships with Obsidian?"

"It's not about that. Keep up, Micathea. I wish for a disruption this evening. Several of the women believe they will be the prettiest one at the party—apart from me, obviously." She nodded to where Lady Lorna and Lady Elana rode side by side ahead of them. Both ladies were drawing eyes, not just from the lords in their company, but from passersby on the crowded street.

"*You* must be more gorgeous than all of them, while remaining unattainable." Jessamyn's eyes blazed with some of her famous manic energy. "Enchant our lords and confound our ladies without presenting a real possibility for a future match. It will be utterly devastating."

Mica was beginning to see where she was going with this. One of Jessamyn's greatest sources of power was the fact that she hadn't chosen a consort yet. She worked hard to keep several lords believing they had a chance with her, and she wasn't afraid to use passion and longing to wheedle assurances of support out of her suitors. It made sense that she'd use the allure of a stranger to disrupt her rivals too.

"Do you want me to target anyone in particular?"

"Your presence alone will be enough for my purposes." Jessamyn gave a wicked grin. "Oh, this will be fun! You'd best sort out a name and story for yourself. You know Obsidian well, correct?"

Jessamyn didn't wait for Mica's nod before spurring her horse forward to speak with her noble guests. In fact, Mica had spent more time studying the Obsidian political system than her own. She could easily come up with a suitable identity that wouldn't give her away.

More importantly, Mica might be able to gather information tonight that didn't involve petty jealousies. She'd play the exotic seductress, but she'd also observe whether anyone saw fit to approach an Obsidian lady for reasons that had nothing to do with her beauty.

Mica still couldn't shake the suspicion that the Obsidian King had a hand in the Talent disappearances, despite Jessamyn's belief that a Windfast noble was behind it all. Who else but the King of Obsidian would need so many Talents, dead or alive? Perhaps rooting out nefarious alliances was exactly what Jessamyn intended. It would be like the princess not to share her entire plan with the person tasked with carrying it out.

Mica would have to investigate the warehouses on the waterfront another day. Tonight, she had a party to attend.

CHAPTER SIXTEEN

J essamyn lent Mica a dress she hadn't worn yet to show off her Obsidian beauty. The gown was pearly white and gossamer thin, making her look as if she were wearing a swath of moonlight. The bare-shouldered cut was less formal than the gowns the ladies usually wore to social events at the palace, and a royal-blue mantle would protect her from the crisp night air. Mica's moonbeam hair fell loose over the mantle in a shimmering curtain. She adjusted the length a few times, finally settling on tresses long enough to brush her backside—which had been rounded and shaped for maximum allure.

As a final touch, Jessamyn gave Mica a dazzling sapphire necklace to wear for the night. No sooner had the heavy gems settled on her chest than the princess changed her mind and ordered her to remove it.

"You're supposed to look like a glamorous noble lady, not a queen." She rummaged through her jewelry boxes. "Hmm, that was a gift from Lady Elana . . . she'd recognize it . . . that was my mother's . . . that one's just *dreadful*." Jessamyn paused and studied Mica for a moment. "It's better without jewelry. Now hurry up and put on those shoes with the crystals."

Jessamyn herself donned a regal shade of carmine sure to stand out against the blues of the sea, and before long they were sweeping out of the palace doors to a golden carriage waiting to carry them back to the docks. The sun was sinking toward the horizon, and most of the lords and ladies had already gone on ahead. They would arrive last—and in style.

Banner opened the carriage door for them, his freshly polished boots shining.

"My princess. My lady." He offered a smart bow to each of them then glanced back toward the palace doors. "Where is Miss Brin?"

"She wasn't feeling up for the cruise," Jessamyn said. "Can you imagine?"

Banner frowned. "She was quite excited."

"She doesn't care at all about inconveniencing me," Jessamyn said petulantly. "Go on then. We mustn't keep our guests waiting."

Banner handed them into the carriage, casting an approving eye over Mica's new face, and strode away to take his seat by the driver. Mica was left alone, facing Princess Jessamyn across the royal carriage.

"Now then, you must get into character," the princess said. "I won't tolerate any slips tonight."

As the carriage rolled out of the palace gates and bounced down toward the harbor, Jessamyn grilled Mica about her life as an Obsidian lady named Rowena. Mica had taken classes at the Academy on how to develop safe background stories for her impersonations. The key was to include as much truth as possible and never ever to break character. Even so, it was strange to speak with the princess so directly. Jessamyn usually flung orders at her while she did several other things at the same time. Mica didn't think they had ever sat face to face for a conversation before—real or not.

"Do tell me more about your estate, Lady Rowena." Jessamyn

leaned forward and touched her arm, as if they were sharing a secret. "I've heard *such* lovely things about the southern coastal regions."

"It's beautiful," Mica answered in an Obsidian accent, low and musical. "The rocks around the South Bay are volcanic, and the sand is as black as coal."

"I could read that in a book. Tell me how it *feels* to walk along one of those beaches."

Mica did her best to describe a place where she'd never been as if it were her home. Then the princess pelted her with questions about her family and her role in the Obsidian King's court. She'd endured similar examinations at the Academy, and by the time they neared the docks, she felt confident in her impersonation. Jessamyn seemed thrilled with the game of it all.

"I hope you enjoy the cruise, Lady Rowena," Jessamyn said. "You've *never* seen Jewel Harbor like this."

"How far will we be sailing?"

"It's not about the *sailing*." Jessamyn gestured out the window, where the water was coming into view. "We'll do a circle between the arms of the crescent, first staying close to our own waterfront and then looping around past the shores of Old Kings. We'll dine on the most exquisite food and drink you've ever encountered. And the company! I can't *wait* to introduce you to some of the lords." Jessamyn's laugh seemed to fill the whole carriage. "We make them handsome in the empire."

The evening was taking on a surreal quality. Mica had played many noblewomen since arriving at the Silver Palace. She knew people treated them differently than regular women, making way for them and taking pains to ensure they were happy. But she hadn't ever spent time with Princess Jessamyn in a noble guise. She was getting the full blast of Jessamyn's charm.

The carriage stopped, and the princess didn't wait for Banner before opening the door and leaping out.

"Here we are. Ah! Isn't it gorgeous?"

She took Mica's hand and pulled her across the dock to the party barge. It was transformed in the twilight. Tiny lanterns strung from silk cords trailed from the low railing all the way up to the crow's nest. The colorful banners fluttered in the breeze, making the barge look as if it could take off at any moment and fly into the setting sun.

A row of uniformed Shields saluted as Jessamyn and Mica crossed the gangway to the waiting vessel. As soon as they were aboard, the Shields dispersed to the smaller boats to escort the party barge into the harbor.

The noble guests were gathered on the wide stern deck, lounging on linen-covered cushions around low tables. Many already had goblets in hand, which they raised to greet the princess as they showered her with compliments.

"Your gown!"

"Your hair!"

"You look stunning."

"Gorgeous. Absolutely gorgeous."

Jessamyn hurried to introduce her companion. "You *must* meet my new friend Lady Rowena of Obsidian," she trilled. "We're going to show her true Windfast hospitality tonight. Oh, Lady Wendel, I love your dress. You must tell me where you got that fine wool. Lord Nobu, won't you be a dear and fetch me a drink? Come along, Lady Rowena, we must watch the sunset from the bow."

Mica let the princess pull her forward, every eye following them. Mica's carefully constructed beauty drew looks of admiration and jealousy as intended, but that was only part of what ensnared the attention of the guests. Mostly it was the princess herself. Jessamyn seemed to have a magic orbit of energy and glamour, one she could invite a select few to share. This was her talent, her power. She made her friends and admirers feel special. And tonight, at least, Mica felt it too.

They took up a position in the bow as the barge cast off. The deck swayed beneath their feet, and the lights swung from the mast as they glided across the harbor, evidence of the oarsmen working hard in the hidden bowels of the vessel. The scent of salt and damp wood soon replaced the cloying odors of the over-crowded capital, and the rush of water softened the city noises.

The silver dome of the palace glowed as daylight crept from the city, leaving behind streaks of purple and indigo and gold. The shifting colors transformed Jewel Harbor from a busy, over-whelming mess into a thing of splendor. Mica didn't need to pretend to be awed. She had lived in Jewel Harbor for months now, but Jessamyn was right: she had never seen it like this before.

Lights had begun to come on along the waterfront, making the city glitter like a gem, when the princess's voice startled Mica out of her reverie.

"I'll leave you here, Lady Rowena." Jessamyn pressed her hand as if they shared a special friendship. "I do hope you enjoy yourself." Then she waltzed away in a whirl of carmine to clink glasses with Lady Ingrid, leaving Mica alone.

The evening was warm still, and Mica removed her royal-blue mantle to feel the breeze on her bare shoulders. Well-dressed servants began to circulate with wine and trays of food in bite-size portions: fresh oysters, tiny pieces of toast piled with peppers and baby shrimp, delicate cakes topped with seashells made of spun sugar. The nobles lounged around the decks, expertly juggling drinks and delicacies as they admired the view of their city from the harbor.

Mica couldn't help noticing the other boats sailing beyond the protective ring of their escort vessels. Sailors in worn trousers stared at the feasting nobles as if they were mythical creatures, and Mica felt the urge to call out that she wasn't really one of them.

"Lady Rowena, it is a pleasure to make your acquaintance."

Mica turned to find Lord Dolan bowing deeply before her.

The nobleman, who was known for his influence with the merchants' guild, had small, close-set eyes and wispy hair, which he parted straight down the middle. He was among Jessamyn's more persistent suitors.

"My name is Lord Dolan. I have traveled in your fair lands before."

Mica dipped her head in the Obsidian fashion, her hair falling forward over her bare shoulders. "Did you enjoy your visit, my lord?"

"Indeed. The food is superb." He raised his drink, which was nearly empty, in a toast. "I must say it's impossible to get proper Obsidian cuisine in Jewel Harbor."

"Such a shame."

"My lady." Young Lord Fritz shouldered in beside Dolan. "Princess Jessamyn suggested that you might wish to have some of the interesting features of our coastline pointed out."

"That would be—"

"I can do that for you, my lady," Dolan interrupted.

"It's no trouble at all," Fritz said earnestly. He pointed across the water to where the outline of Old Kings was visible against the star-strewn sky. "Do you see that hill rising above the eastern shore? That's the ruins of the old Amber Kingdom. The bones of ancient kings can still be found in a crypt dating back three centuries."

"It's actually *four* centuries," Lord Dolan said, giving the younger lord a dismissive sneer. "At least tell the lady the correct information."

The two lords jostled each other as they pointed out more landmarks for "Lady Rowena." Mica made polite noises in response, though the two lords paid little attention to whether or not she was actually interested in all the things they wanted to tell her.

"An Amber King was the one to unite the Windfast islands against our Obsidian foes," Lord Fritz said. A blush stained his boyish cheeks. "Begging your pardon, Lady Rowena. I'm not saying you're a foe."

"It's quite all right," Mica said graciously. "Tell me more about this Amber King."

"He was a Talent, they say," Fritz said. "A Shield who couldn't be killed. But he wanted to protect the other nations too."

"You don't really believe that," Lord Dolan scoffed. "He was a Muscle. I'm certain of it. That was back in the days when kings rode into battle and physical strength carried more weight."

"No, I'm sure he was a Shield."

Mica happened to glance over her shoulder as the two lords argued over ancient history. Lady Lorna had her eyes fixed on Lord Fritz. A faint frown creased her forehead as he fawned over the beautiful newcomer. Many of the guests were stealing glances at Mica too. Jessamyn had left her at a prominent location, as if she was on display for the crowd milling around the forward deck. Mica felt a little uneasy with so many eyes on her. She hoped her impersonation would hold up under such intense scrutiny.

Lord Dolan had taken over the lecture again. "The Talent strain stopped appearing in our imperial line roughly four generations ago . . ."

Mica caught a glimpse of the Obsidian captain of the party barge watching her from across the deck, twisting his blue-veined hands. He seemed confused, as if he couldn't imagine what a lady from his homeland would be doing here. Hopefully, he wouldn't ask too many questions about "Lady Rowena's" origins.

". . . and that was when my family took over the merchants' guild. We've been running it ever since." Lord Dolan had switched to a different history: his own. "We are always interested in trade relationships with lands near and far."

Mica murmured something noncommittal so as not to get Dolan's hopes up about a new trade partnership with her fictional noble family.

The night grew darker, and there was talk of dancing. The hired musicians clambered up to sit on the flat roof of the cabin so they'd be out of the way and struck up a simpler tune than the usual elaborate courtly dances. The nobles quickly partnered up, using the forward deck as a dance floor. Those who didn't want to participate retired to the lounge area in the stern.

Lords Fritz and Dolan argued over who would have the first dance with Lady Rowena, but before they could settle the dispute, Lord Riven swooped in to take her arm. He introduced himself and guided her onto the small dance floor with an imperious air. Envious eyes followed their every step.

Mica had been practicing her dancing, and she didn't mess up too badly despite the audience. She was nimble on her feet, and —as she had told Jessamyn—she was a fast learner. She was beginning to think she needn't have spent so much time on her origin story, though. Lord Riven spent the whole dance talking about himself: his hunting trips, his extensive holdings on Amber Island (which happened to include Redbridge), his skill with the sword, his fine collection of horses. He wore his mask of lordly arrogance so thick it was impossible to tell how much was his actual personality and how much was a role he had decided to play. Mica suspected he didn't even like women much, but he was a powerful man who wanted to make an even more powerful match, ideally one that came with a seat on the imperial dais.

Mica couldn't predict if Jessamyn would end up taking Riven as her consort. She'd have to pick one of her suitors eventually, but her mask was even harder to see through than his. Mica still hadn't figured out which of the lords the princess actually liked. Well, apart from Lord Caleb.

She hadn't seen the Pebble Islands lord since right after the fiasco with the emperor. In the midst of being fired and rehired, Mica hadn't forgotten her encounter with Caleb in the corridor. She assumed he had later found Jessamyn and told her about whatever had been troubling him, but the impression of that brief moment had lingered. He had looked at her and recognized her for who she was. She couldn't help thinking about him after that.

And about how handsome he is . . .

Mica stamped down on the thought, even as she peeked over Lord Riven's shoulder to see if she could spot Caleb. She couldn't deny she was attracted to him, but the nobles were strictly off limits, especially those who were hiding things. She wouldn't jeopardize her mission for a man, no matter how appealing.

Lady Bellina appeared to be looking for Lord Caleb too, standing on her toes and peering over the crowd of dancing couples. Her golden curls were especially bouncy today, and she wore a blue dress that matched her eyes exactly. Mica noticed Lord Nobu sneaking glances at her. Perhaps he'd be a better match for the curly-haired lady. Bellina may be pretty, but Mica had never seen Caleb looking at her with anything more than courtesy.

The song ended, and Lord Riven executed a perfect bow, not quite meeting her eyes. "Thank you for the dance, Lady Rowena."

"I was pleased to hear so much about your accomplishments," she said dryly. "Truly, you are magnificent."

Lord Riven coughed, his mask slipping to reveal a hint of confusion, and he handed her off to Lord Fritz. The boyish blond twirled Mica around until he caught sight of Lady Lorna's face, at which point he sheepishly handed her off to Lord Hugh, the younger of the two Ivanson brothers, who happened to be standing nearby. Hugh was so shy that he could barely look at her as they waltzed stiffly around the deck. As soon as the song was done, he handed her over to Lord Dolan.

Dolan had been drinking deeply while waiting for his turn to dance with the beautiful Obsidian guest. His breath was sour, and his hands around her waist felt damp through the gossamer gown. He kept her for two dances, holding her a little too tight and a little too close. Mica maintained a polite mask, trying not to allow revulsion to show on her disguised features.

When a third song began, Dolan still didn't let her go. His sweaty hands slipped further down her back, grasping, groping. Mica wanted to wrench away, maybe jab him in the kidneys for good measure. An Obsidian lady probably wouldn't handle the scenario the way a soldier's daughter from Stonefoss would, though.

How do these ladies deal with boorish behavior without breaking decorum? Am I supposed to put up with this?

Mica struggled to create distance between them without blowing her cover, but Dolan refused to relinquish an inch no matter how much she squirmed. His breath was hot on her neck, rattling her composure.

Then a familiar square hand tapped him on the shoulder.

"May I cut in?"

It was Caleb.

Dolan narrowed his small eyes, looking as if he wanted to say no. Mica seized the opportunity to twist loose from his grasp, abandoning decorum altogether. She offered Caleb her hand, and then they were spinning away from Dolan, weaving through the other couples toward the opposite side of the dance floor. Mica took in deep breaths of night air, relief flooding her senses like fog rolling off the sea.

"I hope you don't mind me stepping in, my lady," Caleb said as they broke through the crowd near the portside railing. "Lord Dolan can be overeager. Would you like to take a break from dancing?"

"No, I'll dance with you," Mica said, perhaps a bit too quickly. "If you wish."

"Of course, my lady."

Caleb adjusted his hand on her waist, where it had tangled in her long tresses, and they swayed in a small circle at the edge of the crowd. He wasn't an especially smooth dancer, and it occurred to Mica that he always arrived at the lessons late and left early. He must not like dancing at all, yet he had intervened when he saw Lord Dolan making Lady Rowena uncomfortable. Mica beamed up at him for that, making good use of her perfect mouth and otherworldly green eyes.

He blinked and cleared his throat. "How . . . how do you like Jewel Harbor so far, my lady?"

"It's lovely," Mica said, enjoying the effect the dazzling smile had. "I miss my estate on the South Bay, of course."

"Oh?"

"It has a wonderful view of the beach. The black sand stretches for miles, and it feels like sugar under your toes."

"I'd like to see that one day."

"Have you never been to Obsidian before?"

"No, my lady."

As she told him more about her "homeland," Mica couldn't help admiring the details of Caleb's square face, the way the breeze stirred his hair around his slightly pointed ears, the way he looked at her as if he was really listening. She knew this dance wouldn't have been proper between them in her normal, non-noble body. Did he find her current ethereal form as alluring as some of the other lords did? She felt an unpleasant twinge at the thought, almost as if she were jealous of Lady Rowena for this dance.

That's a ridiculous thing to feel.

Against her better judgment, Mica tightened her grip on Caleb's hand and moved a little closer, as if proving to herself that her feelings wouldn't get in the way of her mission. She could dance close to him without getting flustered.

You're a professional, she told herself, even as her heart beat like a drum against her ribs. *And don't forget he's keeping secrets too.*

"Tell me, Lord Caleb," she said huskily, gazing up at him through her enhanced lashes. "What's your favorite thing about Jewel Harbor?"

Caleb's eyes widened, as if he was surprised at the question, or maybe at the intimacy of her tone.

"It's like the Windfast Empire in miniature," he said after a long pause. "People from every island with their different traditions and experiences live in one chaotic city. You get a hint of what every part of the empire is like."

"Except the parts that aren't chaotic," Mica said.

Caleb chuckled. "That's true. You don't get the same sense of space as in the rolling countryside or on the windswept cliff tops." His arm curled a little tighter around her waist, tangling in her hair again, and he looked down at her blandly. "Like in Gullton, for example."

Mica's eyes flew up to meet his, just in time to catch a triumphant twinkle in their depths. He *knew*! How did the bastard keep figuring out her disguises?

"Gullton."

"Yes, Lady Rowena. Gullton."

Mica scowled at him, an expression she definitely hadn't planned on using with this face. His shoulders began to shake with silent laughter beneath her arm, and she abandoned any remaining pretense.

"How do you always know?" she hissed.

"You called me by name."

"Someone could have told it to me."

"I know," Caleb said, "but you're also a complete stranger who appeared out of nowhere at Jessamyn's side. The others were too captivated by your beauty to notice anything odd about that."

Mica raised an eyebrow. "You're not captivated by my beauty?"

"I didn't say that."

They were still dancing in a little circle by the portside rail. His arms were warm around her body, holding back the night air. Mica knew she should excuse herself. He was a lord, and now he knew she was just the Impersonator. Hadn't Jessamyn told her the nobles would be offended if they realized they were dancing with her? But Caleb obviously didn't care. If anything, his expression softened as he looked down at her.

"Show me your real eyes," he said, so quietly the words were almost carried away on the wind.

Nerves stirred in Mica's stomach, her breathing becoming shallow. So much for not getting flustered. She shifted her irises slowly, allowing golden brown to permeate the unnatural green until they were her own hazel. Caleb watched her, and she swore his pulse quickened beneath her hand.

"You . . . you didn't answer my question," she said.

Caleb cleared his throat, as if mastering himself. "It's possible I've mentioned Gullton to a number of strangers who could be Impersonators," he said. "This is the first time it actually worked."

Mica burst out laughing, dipping her head to his shoulder to muffle the sound.

"There are several new palace employees who think I'm obsessed with the town of Gullton."

Mica giggled, imagining him dropping hints at random cooks and guards in an effort to catch her out. She squeezed his hand a little tighter.

"Ahem," came a polite cough.

Mica pulled back from Caleb, suddenly aware that they had been chuckling in each other's arms as if they were the only two people on deck. Jessamyn was waiting beside them, eyes flashing angrily.

"You lost this, Lady Rowena." The princess held out the royal-blue mantle with a pointed look at Mica's bare shoulders. "I wouldn't want you to be cold."

"You are too kind, Princess Jessamyn."

Mica changed her eyes back to the appropriate color for the impersonation as she stepped away from her dance partner and slung the mantle over her shoulders.

Jessamyn leaned in, as if to kiss Lady Rowena on the cheek. "Don't you have work to do?" she hissed.

Mica was confused at the reproach in her tone. Wasn't this exactly what Jessamyn had told her to do? Make the ladies jealous by taking up the lords' attention? On the other hand, Bellina wasn't even watching her dance with Caleb, too busy chatting animatedly with Lord Nobu over by the bar.

"Excuse me, my lord. My lady." Mica dipped into a quick curtsy, not daring to meet Caleb's eyes, and hurried away from him and Jessamyn. She made her way to the less crowded stern and leaned on the railing, head spinning slightly.

The breeze cooled her cheeks and helped to clear her mind. What had she been *doing*? That would have been the perfect time to probe Caleb for information about his mysterious illness and his Blur speed. Instead, she had clutched his hand and pressed against his body, unable to keep from getting closer to him.

And it had upset the princess. Mica winced. She didn't want to get in the way if there was more between Jessamyn and Caleb than she let on. Still, if the princess wanted to use her as a pawn in her games, it would help if she told her the rules.

"You're quite popular this evening, Lady Rowena. I wasn't sure I'd get a turn to talk with you."

Mica checked to make sure all her features were in the correct shapes as Lady Wendel strode up beside her. She'd been drinking tea with Lord Fritz and Lady Lorna at the low tables, but they were so absorbed in conversation that they didn't seem to notice her departure.

The noblewoman towered over Mica as she offered her hand. "I'm Lady Wendel of Pegasus Island."

"A pleasure."

"I love your dress," Lady Wendel said, examining it closely. "Wherever did you get the silk? It's practically transparent."

Mica couldn't tell if that was a compliment or not. "It was a gift from a friend at court."

"What else are the ladies wearing at the Obsidian Court this season?" Lady Wendel leaned on the railing beside her, just a little too close. "And how do they feel about wool?"

Mica and Wendel discussed materials for winter gowns as they sailed through the night. The coast alongside them was darker here, where the busy districts of the city gave way to quieter residences. They were almost to the southernmost tip of the crescent. Soon they'd turn around and cruise back along the Amber Coast. Mica contemplated how to sneak away to investigate the warehouse district when they returned. She wasn't especially excited about sharing the carriage back to the palace with Jessamyn.

She was about to return to the busier part of the ship to continue with her task when she noticed something moving in the water. She leaned over the railing, squinting at what appeared to be a small rowboat. There were people inside, but they didn't have a single light among them. Strange. Why would someone be out here without so much as a torch? Mica looked around for their escorts, but the boats full of Shields seemed to have fallen behind. She felt a jolt of alarm.

Then a spark flared to life on the little rowboat, followed by a sputtering flame. The flame lifted, illuminating the shaft of an arrow and a bow clutched in a ghostly pale hand.

"Look out!" Mica shouted as the flaming arrow shot through the air and landed in the center of the barge.

CHAPTER SEVENTEEN

M ica hit the deck, pulling Lady Wendel down with her. She smelled a whiff of smoke, a hint of sulfur. Then an explosion erupted atop the cabin.

Burning wood flew across the barge, one piece smashing directly into Lord Fritz's face as he jumped up to shield Lady Lorna. Screams split the night air. A blazing fire raged across the center of the boat, and flames crept up the mast.

The smoke spreading across the deck wasn't enough to obscure the figures scaling the side of the barge and climbing aboard, figures with pale hair and paler skin. The knives in their fists caught the light from the inferno.

"It's an Obsidian attack!" someone screeched as the first lord fell with a blade in his belly. It was Hugh, the shy lord Mica had danced with earlier. The attackers swarmed among the revelers, cutting down any who stood in their way.

Mica knew she had to get to Jessamyn. Her duty first and foremost was to defend the empire and its future ruler. She scrambled to her knees, gathering up her silk skirts and tying a quick knot to keep them out of her way. Suddenly, an iron grip closed around her wrist.

"*You!*" Lady Wendel shrieked. "You planned this, you Obsidian witch!"

"I'm not—let go of me." Mica tried to pull out of the larger woman's grasp. People were running around them. Lord Dolan waved his fists drunkenly, not discriminating between friend and foe.

"I knew there was something strange about you!" Lady Wendel tried to grab Mica by her long hair, remarkably ferocious in the face of danger.

"I don't have time for this." Mica delivered a swift jab to Lady Wendel's nose, knocking her back. She twisted out of the noble-woman's grip and landed a second strike to her face. It didn't knock the larger woman out, but she closed her eyes long enough for Mica to squeeze her own features back onto her face and escape. This wasn't a good time to look Obsidian.

She discarded her mantle again, her pearly-white dress quickly becoming smudged beyond recognition, and looked around for a weapon. Why hadn't she thought to wear an ankle knife? There was no sign of the Shield guards who were supposed to be sailing alongside them in smaller boats. A few injured noblemen and servants crawled across the stern deck, none of them armed either. Mica snatched up a discarded wine glass and cracked it on the deck to create a jagged edge. It would have to do.

The bulk of the fighting raged on the narrow decks bordering the burning cabin. The Obsidian attackers were attempting to charge the foredeck, where most of the nobles were gathered. The nobility seemed to be making a decent stand against the surprise attack. *Someone* had to be armed up there.

Mica couldn't see the brilliant carmine of Jessamyn's gown from here. She approached the burning cabin, hoping to find a way through—or over—the flames while the attackers were busy on the side decks. Heat scorched her cheeks, the thickening smoke making her eyes water. The mast groaned ominously, flames reaching all the way to the crow's nest now.

Suddenly, Mica remembered the oarsmen below. The Muscles had been confined in that cramped hold while the nobles drank and danced above them. They should be able to break out without any trouble, but she couldn't see any of them in the chaos on deck. Were they still down there?

Mica didn't hesitate. She kicked open the cabin door, nearly breaking a toe through her flimsy dancing slippers, and released a billow of smoke. The trapdoor to the hold was closed, not a Muscle in sight. Knowing she only had a few minutes before the cabin collapsed, she held her breath, rushed to the trapdoor, and climbed into the bowels of the boat.

The hold was lit with a dim red glare. Mica reached the bottom of the ladder just in time to see the pale-haired barge captain standing up from the writhing form of a Muscle oarsman, a vial of potion clutched in his hand. The rest of the Talents in the hold were already dead.

As the final oarsman shuddered and breathed his last, the Obsidian captain saw Mica. Their eyes met over the bodies of his victims. Then he hurled the vial across the hold.

Mica dodged, and the vial shattered against the ladder. The wood smoked and hissed as the potion spread down it, eating straight through the rungs. The captain was already moving, scrambling over the fallen Muscles toward Mica, who leapt back and crashed into the bulkhead.

The man was on her a second later. His blue-veined hands closed around her throat.

"I got you, Windfast scum." He sneered with bloodless lips, his breath hot on her face.

Mica struggled against him, trying to pry his fingers away from her windpipe with her left hand, wishing for the strength of a Muscle. She still had the broken glass in her right hand, but if she killed this man, they'd never know how the Obsidians had managed this attack. She was a spy first and foremost, and she needed information. She felt remarkably calm as she identified a spot where she could jab her shard of glass without severing the man's jugular.

One . . . two . . . She attacked—or tried to.

But her hands felt heavy, and her limbs refused to obey. She fumbled with the shard of glass. Why was it so hard to get a good grip? The hold was growing dark, hazy. She had waited too long. She couldn't lose consciousness yet!

She tried to stab with the makeshift weapon again, no longer caring whether she killed the man or not, but her actions were clumsy, her strength fleeting.

Movement danced across her vision, pale-white hair, sneering lips, the eyes of death. Then a flash of carmine.

Suddenly, there was a terrific crack, and the captain released his grip on her throat. Mica slumped against the bulkhead. Smoky air rushed into her lungs. She gasped, struggling to raise her shard of glass before her assailant could grab her again.

Then a second crack sounded through the hold, and the captain's eyes went utterly blank. Crimson lines trickled down his forehead, and he collapsed in front of her, blood matting the back of his skull.

Princess Jessamyn stood above him, a cast-iron teapot in her hands.

"Princess!" Mica choked out.

"Well, get up," she said calmly. "We have to go."

Mica scrambled after Jessamyn, pausing long enough to ascertain that the Obsidian captain was dead. They would get no information from him.

They scaled the half-ruined ladder and ran out of the burning cabin, eyes watering from the smoke. Chaos reigned on deck. The nobles had broken through the Obsidian attackers on the starboard side, and they were fighting across the stern now, using whatever weapons they could find. Few had come to the harbor cruise with so much as a belt knife or decorative sword.

Lord Caleb led the noblemen's defense, armed with a stringed instrument from the quartet. He swung it like a club, making a musical crunch every time it connected with an Obsidian skull. Lord Fritz fought at his side with a jeweled dagger, a nasty cut marring his youthful good looks. Lord Dolan was still flailing about with his fists, bellowing curses.

"Best stay out of their way," Jessamyn said, crouching by the low drinks tables in the stern, the teapot still clutched in her hand. Her eyes blazed in the light from the burning cabin.

"Where are the Shields?" Mica said. "They should be here by now."

Shouts were coming from the water beyond the barge, as if the boats full of Shield bodyguards had also been attacked. They were much farther away than they were supposed to be, leaving the party barge vulnerable.

The nobles were fighting back now, though. The Obsidian attackers didn't fare as well after losing the element of surprise. They were outnumbered, and as far as Mica could tell, none of them were Talents. Other ships in the harbor had heard the commotion and seen the flames roaring into the sky, and they were speeding to their aid, powered by Muscle and Blur oarsmen.

A sharp whistle cut through the shouts, and the Obsidians began to slip away, leaping off the sides of the barge and swimming for the dark shore of Amber Island. The noblemen cheered as their attackers began to disappear into the night.

Caleb used the tattered string instrument to knock the last of the Obsidians off the barge. He turned and caught sight of Mica and Jessamyn crouching behind the tables. A look of pure relief crossed his face, echoing Mica's own feelings. He had a rip in his silk waistcoat, but he appeared to be uninjured. He beckoned for them to join him by the railing.

But as Mica stood up, there was a horrific screeching sound.

The burning crow's nest snapped off the top of the mast and fell. As it slammed through the blazing roof of the cabin, the mast splintered. People screamed as sharp pieces of wood hurtled across the deck like javelins.

Mica watched in horror as a jagged beam shot straight for Caleb at the railing.

He'll move. He's fast. He'll Blur out of the way.

The thoughts came in an instant. He was fast. He would be okay.

But Caleb didn't move fast enough. He barely had time to take a step before the beam thudded straight into his body.

And stopped.

Mica stared. The wood had struck the dead center of his sternum, where it should have punched into his heart. But instead the end had splintered from the force of hitting Caleb's skin.

Caleb's impervious skin.

What in the Windfast?

The noise continued around them, cries of distress, of confusion. Caleb blinked at the heavy piece of wood that should have speared straight through his body, looking almost as surprised as Mica felt. *Almost.*

Caleb looked up and met Mica's eyes for one blazing moment. Pandemonium raged around them as the people on the boat called out to each other, not realizing what had happened. Or what *hadn't* happened.

He should be dead. I don't understand.

Caleb was still pinned to the side of the boat. The weight of half the mast pressed the thick beam against his chest. He wrapped both hands around it and shoved. It didn't budge. He looked around, slightly panicked, as if afraid the others would see. He pushed harder, the wood groaning.

Mica hurried forward to help. Before she reached him, he suddenly blinked and lifted aside the beam as if it were no more than a bundle of sticks.

He's a Muscle now too? What is going on?

Mica halted in front of him. "You want to explain—?"

"Later," Caleb said hoarsely. "Are you okay? Where's Jessa?"

Mica looked around. The nobles were beginning to pick themselves up, or crouch over the fallen. The crackling flames didn't drown out the cries of the injured. There was no sign of the princess.

"She was right behind me."

"Come on." Caleb grabbed Mica's hand and pulled her through the smoke, still offering no explanation for the impossible feats she had just witnessed. No one was both unnaturally strong *and* impervious to injury. No one. It just wasn't how Talents worked.

They found the princess in the bow, overseeing the evacuation from the barge. Other ships in the harbor had come to their aid, and the revelers were being ferried to safety on an assortment of fishing boats.

Caleb released a sigh. "I thought for sure they were here to kidnap her."

"Me too," Mica said. "What do you think they were after?"

"I don't know. Maybe they wanted to show they can reach us in the heart of the empire."

Mica wished Jessamyn hadn't killed the captain of the barge. They might have been able to get him to talk. On the other hand, he might have choked Mica to death if she hadn't. The princess had saved her life.

Jessamyn was clearly in her element as she directed the evacuation. "Hurry along now. We may not stay afloat for much longer. Don't push, Lady Bellina. There is space for everyone." She had disposed of her iron teapot in favor of a burning brand taken from the wreckage of the party barge, the torchlight flickering over her red hair like a fiery crown. The look suited her.

The Shield bodyguards arrived at last. The Obsidians had attacked their boats too, keeping them busy while they assaulted the party barge. Their clothes were ripped from knife slashes, but they were otherwise uninjured. Jessamyn waved off Banner's apologies and ordered him to check the burning hold for survivors. Only a Shield could enter it safely now.

When Jessamyn spotted Mica and Caleb, her eyes immediately went to their clasped hands. They released each other at the same time.

"I cannot believe someone had the nerve to ruin my harbor cruise," the princess said as they joined her. "Poor Brin has been planning it for months, and now no one will even talk about how delicious the food was or how perfect the decorations looked. And you've ruined my dress, Micathea. How inconsiderate of you."

Mica didn't bother to apologize, too busy thinking about what Jessamyn had just said. Brin had worked so hard to plan the harbor cruise. Brin, who had arranged for the Shield guards to be on separate boats from the nobility. Brin, who had been so excited to attend the cruise—right up until she fell so ill even Magic Q's potions couldn't help her rally.

Mica remembered what the Obsidian captain had said to her when she wore Brin's face. "*You know I won't fail you. You will never forget this night.*"

Mica sighed. Brin would be gone by the time they returned to the Silver Palace. The only question was how long it had been since she was replaced by an Obsidian Impersonator. Perhaps she had been one all along.

Speaking of secret Talents . . .

Caleb took up a post at Jessamyn's side and remained there throughout the rescue operation. The princess refused to leave until all the injured were cared for. Caleb seemed determined to serve as the princess's bodyguard while her Shield was busy, something none of the other lords emulated. He caught Mica's eye once or twice but showed no further signs of remarkable speed or strength.

No one else seemed to have noticed the anomaly. A few of the nobles complimented Caleb on his fighting as they disembarked, though. He acknowledged their praise, offering no explanation for why he had escaped unscathed.

"Those Obsidian cowards were no match for you," Lady Wendel said, her words a bit muffled thanks to a bloody nose.

Mica chose that moment to slip away and examine the fallen attackers in case Lady Wendel recognized her clothes and realized who had punched her. There were only three Obsidian bodies apart from the captain. Two had died of their injuries. The final one had been wounded in the leg, and he'd been poisoned when he couldn't escape. It was impossible to tell if he had taken the poison himself or if one of his comrades had forced it on him. The men wore humble clothes, as if they were sailors or farmers, their faces even paler in death. Mica rifled through their pockets, but they carried no identifying papers. They didn't even have any money on them, which struck her as odd. She couldn't tell if they had been paid in Obsidian crowns or Windfast marks. Whoever had hired them was extremely careful.

But what was their goal? The injured and deceased nobles had already been removed from the barge, and Mica didn't yet know how many casualties there had been. Were the Obsidians simply trying to kill as many nobles as possible? Or maybe they had taken something?

Banner returned from the hold, his clothes blackened and smoking.

"No survivors," he said shortly. "The Obsidian captain had this."

He handed Mica an unmarked vial, similar to the one the captain had thrown at her. It was empty.

"This must be what he used on the oarsmen."

Mica pocketed the vial, feeling a pang of sadness for the Muscles who had helped her earlier that day. Once again, simple

Talents had been the victims of schemes that had nothing to do with them.

"I think it was Brin," she said, watching Banner for a reaction. It had never been clear to her whether he returned Brin's affections. For all she knew, that infatuation could have been part of an impersonation all along.

Banner's eyebrows drooped as he considered the accusation. "She did oversee most of the arrangements for the cruise. It is possible."

"Do you know where her mother lives?" Mica asked, remembering the handmaid's mother's illness. "Maybe someone was threatening her."

"Brin's mother died last year," Banner said. "I sat with her at the memorial."

"Oh."

Little more needed to be said after that. Mica and Banner rejoined Jessamyn and Caleb and climbed into one of the rowboats sent to their rescue. They were the last to leave the vessel. No sooner had they disembarked than the party barge sank at last into the harbor, hissing and burbling as the fire was quenched.

"I am not paying for that," Jessamyn said primly.

They were welcomed aboard a squid-fishing vessel and ushered into the cramped cabin, where the crew hurried to drape blankets smelling of fish guts around their shoulders. Jessamyn wore her blanket as if it were a fur mantle, holding court with regal poise as the sailors and nobles fussed over her. In the confusion, Mica managed to pull Caleb aside and bring her mouth close to his ear.

"*Now* will you answer my questions?"

Apparently expecting this, Caleb led her back out to the deck where they couldn't be overheard. They had quite the escort now. Every sailboat and fishing vessel within a mile had gathered to chaperon their return to the city. Some of the nobles were continuing the party with their rescuers. Mica spotted Lord Riven swigging rum with the sailors on a flat-bottomed barge not far from their fishing boat, no doubt bragging about his performance during the fight.

Caleb strode to port and put both hands on the railing, as if bracing himself for Mica's questions.

"Go ahead."

"What *are* you?"

Caleb snorted. "And you wonder why I don't talk about it."

"You're impervious," Mica said. "You lifted that beam as if it weighed nothing, so you're a Muscle. And I'm sure I saw you moving super-fast before, meaning you're a Blur too!"

"I told you I'm not a Blur."

Mica folded her arms, her fish-scented blanket slipping off her shoulders. "Can you Mimic too?"

"I don't know. That's why I wanted to know so much about how impersonation works, how it feels."

"So what'd you do? Kidnap some Talents and steal their abilities? Maybe you drained them dry in your warehouse?"

"Of course not." Caleb turned to face her. "I don't *know* how I got this way. Believe me, I wish I understood it."

The weariness and resignation in his eyes gave her pause.

"Have you always been like this?"

"Since I was a kid." He ran a hand through his hair, ash from the burnt ship sifting onto his shoulder. "I started noticing it when I was six or seven, which is normal for Talents. But there's nothing normal about this. I can't control any of the things I do."

Mica wanted to believe him. His face was as kind and open as it had seemed back on the cliff top in Gullton. But that open face had obscured a huge secret.

"Why have you been hiding your abilities?" she asked.

Caleb tapped his fingers on the railing, taking his time before answering. But she knew he was going to answer. There was little use in hiding things from her now.

"My family was embarrassed," he said at last. "They thought having faulty offspring would reflect poorly on them." He shook his head, as if brushing away an old injury. "Now, keeping it quiet is easier than trying to explain." He glanced down at her. "Otherwise, people accuse you of drinking the blood of Talents."

She winced. "I'm sorry about that."

"It's all right, Mica."

Caleb caught her gaze and held it. Her skin tingled under his stare. How could he always make her feel so . . . *seen*? And this was the first time he'd called her Mica.

She adjusted the blanket looped around her elbows, attempting to recapture the conversation. "So you thought understanding impersonation would help? That's why you were asking me so many questions."

"You can control every inch of your body." Caleb looked her up and down, and Mica felt a blush creeping through her. "I can never predict when one of the abilities will manifest. They've saved my neck a few times, like you saw today, but sometimes I try to use one of the Talents, and it doesn't come through for me." Caleb pulled up the edge of his shirt, revealing a nasty scar across his abdomen. "That's from when I was young and stupid and picked a fight with the wrong person."

Mica reached out to touch the scar, feeling the rough lines with her fingertips. His skin was warm beneath her hands, and she distinctly heard his breath catch at her touch. Then he dropped his shirt with a glance at the boats around them. With so many blazing lights, it wouldn't be hard for someone to see them.

Caleb leaned on the railing, and when he spoke again his voice was brisk. "So now you know about my curse, making you one of the few."

"I wouldn't call it a curse," Mica said. "I can't tell you how many times I've wished my ability came with speed or strength." She thought of when she received her assignment, how she feared she hadn't been sent to Obsidian because she wasn't good enough at fighting. Blur speed would help with that. And if she had been strong enough to overpower her Obsidian attacker, she could have held him for information instead of nearly being choked to death.

"You don't understand," Caleb said. "It is a curse when you can't guarantee whether the ability will show up in any given scenario. It's inconvenient if you suddenly use Blur speed without realizing people are watching, but think about being in a fight where there's a possibility you can take a hit without injury. When there's a fifty-fifty chance the blade won't go in at all, it's a tempting gamble. Or think if you see someone in trouble and try to use your super strength to save them, but the power doesn't come and you have to watch them—" He broke off, not needing to complete the sentence, and looked out at the lights on the water.

There was a story there—a painful one. Mica rested a hand on Caleb's arm. They were well past the point of propriety by now anyway.

His skin was hot to the touch, much hotter than it had been a moment ago.

"You're feverish."

"And that's the other problem with my little bursts of power." Caleb looked down at her again. His eyes had gone a little glassy.

"You get sick afterwards," Mica said. "That night I found you—"

"Correct. Uncle Ober theorizes that I'm not supposed to be a Talent, so anything I do burns through a ton of energy at once. My body can't handle it."

Mica frowned. Something about that didn't quite add up, but she wasn't sure why.

"I'll probably be fairly useless shortly," Caleb said. "Can I trust you to—?"

"I'll make sure you get home safely."

Caleb smiled softly. "Thank you. I meant to ask if I can trust you not to mention this to anyone, even in your official reports?"

Mica hesitated. This was the sort of thing she should relay to Master Kiev, especially since she'd already named Lord Caleb as a suspect in the Talent disappearances. She wanted to trust Caleb more than ever, but nothing he had said tonight absolved him of suspicion. It would be a betrayal of her duties not to say something.

"Why don't you want anyone to know?" Mica said. "You could be something new—a fifth Talent. Maybe people at the Academy could help you."

"My uncle thinks—whoa, I'm getting a little lightheaded." Caleb slid down to sit on the deck, and Mica remembered how she'd found him on that stoop, flitting in and out of consciousness. "He thinks . . ."

Caleb trailed off, eyelids flickering, and Mica never learned what his uncle thought. She wasn't convinced Ober's attempts to help Caleb self-medicate with energy potions were good enough anyway. He needed help from a real expert.

"Let's talk it over when you're well," she said. "I won't say anything until then."

Caleb mumbled something incoherent as his head dropped onto his knees. Mica settled in beside him, pressing her arm against his as the boat glided back toward the city.

CHAPTER EIGHTEEN

The palace was already on alert when they returned a few hours after midnight. Emperor Styl oversaw the crisis from the throne room with the severity of a thunderstorm. He kept his Blurs running around delivering orders almost as quickly as he could write them. He deployed both the City Watch and the Old Kings garrison to search for the attackers, who seemed to have vanished after escaping the barge.

Meanwhile, the nobles were working themselves into a frenzy, especially when they learned that five of their number, two lords, one lady, and two servants, had died in the attack. Jessamyn spent a sleepless night calming the fears of the survivors and urging them not to blow the incident out of proportion. But rumors spread through the city like spilt wine, and by daybreak, half of Jewel Harbor believed the empire was at war.

Mica spent the small hours of the morning interviewing the maids, Alea and Ruby, about Brin. The handmaid was indeed missing from her sickbed.

"She's been busy," Alea said. "But we all are." She looked Mica up and down. "Maybe if you pulled your weight and helped with the cleaning more often . . ."

Mica resisted the urge to remind Alea that she was not, in fact, a maid. "Has she met with anyone strange?"

"Not sure what counts as strange by *your* standards."

Mica was too tired to address the implication, just wanting to get through the interviews. But Ruby wasn't much more help than Alea.

"I've barely seen her in the past few weeks," Ruby said. "I swear I could go days without so much as passing her in the corridor."

"Doesn't that strike you as odd?"

"Her mother is ill," Ruby whispered, scandalized. "Show a little heart."

"How long has her mother been ill?"

Ruby pursed her lips. "Since this winter, I'm sure."

"She ought to be more considerate, really," Alea put in. "*We've* got mothers too."

In the end, the others had simply been too busy with the princess's usual tasks to shed much light on how Brin had orchestrated the attack. But if she'd been using her mother's illness to excuse her absences since the winter, Mica had probably never met the real Brin at all.

As the sun rose over Jewel Harbor, Jessamyn enlisted Mica's help containing the outrage among the nobility. She sent her to reassure the ladies who'd been on the boat that the culprits would soon be found. Mica hurried from sitting room to sitting room in the north wing while Jessamyn worked her way through the east, taking full advantage of her ability to be in two places at once. Mica wanted to check in with Peet and see if he'd heard anything from Master Kiev, but she didn't have a chance until the afternoon when the princess was called to her father's private chambers for a rare meeting. Mica hadn't yet figured out how close Jessamyn and her father were, and the emperor remained an enigma. Still, word traveled quickly that he had summoned his daughter, so

Mica was able to suspend her impersonation duties and sneak away.

Peet had spent the morning darting around the city, collecting information for his own reports. The Blur was in communication with many of the spies in Master Kiev's network, and they had all been blindsided by the attack on the nobles.

"We keep tabs on Obsidians in the city," Peet explained to Mica as he offered her some grapes from a wooden bowl. "Most are just trying to live their lives. I can't see what they'd gain by stirring up trouble."

"People up at the palace are already talking about reopening hostilities."

Peet grimaced. "I got a feeling it'll get worse before it gets better."

The prospect of conflict with Obsidian made Mica even more nervous for her family than the disappearances. Talent soldiers were always the ones on the front lines. She hoped it wouldn't come to that.

"Did Master Kiev reply to my last report?"

Peet shook his head and popped a grape into his mouth. "He was off traveling last time I was at the Academy."

"Traveling where?"

"No one seemed to know."

Mica stilled. "He hasn't been back to the Academy since your last visit, and no one knows where he is?"

"I wouldn't worry about Master Kiev," Peet said. "That man's a legend, you know."

"Has he ever been gone for this long before?"

Peet shrugged. "He has responsibilities all over the empire."

Mica was almost afraid to voice her suspicions. Whoever was kidnapping Talents wouldn't go so far as to capture the Head of the Impersonator Academy himself, would they?

"Can you tell me more about Master Kiev's responsibilities?"

she said. "He's a spymaster, but he hasn't really explained how it all works."

"That's kind of the point," Peet said. "People don't take kindly to the idea that Mimics might be spying on them right here in the empire. They know we send spies off to foreign lands, but it's not a good idea to shout about the ones we keep on the home front."

"So the spymasters hide in plain sight as Masters of the Impersonator Academy and gather information on what's happening in the empire?"

"Some of the Masters might be ordinary teachers, mind," Peet said. "I don't know who's involved. Master Kiev is the only person I report to."

"And he reports to Emperor Styl?"

"And Princess Jessamyn." Peet grinned. "Her Ladyship is very intelligent, you know. And brave. She'll make a good empress."

Mica pictured Jessamyn standing above the Obsidian captain with a bloodied cast-iron teapot.

"I think you may be right."

———

Mica wasn't gone from the palace long, but it looked as though a tornado had ripped through the princess's chambers in her absence. Dresses and shoes were scattered over the couches, and their cushions tumbled across the floor. Jessamyn was dashing around like mad while Alea tried to do up the ties on her midnight-blue gown.

"There you are, Micathea! My father has called a public audience to address the crisis." She shoved a slate-gray dress into Mica's arms. "I've just learned Lady Ingrid is too shaken from last night's events to attend. I need you to come as her and support everything my father and I say."

"Isn't that—?"

"I don't have time for your questions." Jessamyn crammed a

silver diadem onto her own head. She looked as though she was running on pure manic energy despite her long night. Mica spied a bottle of Quinn's potion on the table.

"You can either redeem yourself for your last mistake or get out of my sight at once."

In answer, Mica's hair turned jet black and her features became hawkish and severe. "I'm at your service."

Jessamyn explained the situation as they hurried up to the throne room accompanied by three other Shield guards in addition to Banner. Word had spread at Blur speed that Obsidian operatives had infiltrated the capital and killed several of the most powerful men and women in the empire. Their home islands wanted justice.

"Our aim is to prevent outright anarchy," Jessamyn said as they reached the throne room doors. Angry voices rumbled within. "Can you remember that, Micathea?"

Mica dipped into a stiff curtsy, imitating Lady Ingrid's proud bearing perfectly. "Yes, Princess."

The Shields heaved open the doors, and Jessamyn stormed into the fray.

Almost every noble in the palace was assembled beneath the silver dome. They had brought along every Shield guard in their employment, and a few had hired extra Muscles too. It was utter pandemonium. The nobles chattered to each other in tight knots or shouted out their opinions, trying to be heard above the crowd. It was impossible to pick out individual words, and almost as difficult to see over the throng.

Jessamyn and Mica pushed their way toward the dais, following the golden carpet stretching up the center of the throne room. Emperor Styl stood tall before his ornate chair, his jaw tensing so hard it looked as if it had been carved from marble. His folded his thick arms over his chest as he listened to two nobles argue themselves hoarse at the front of the room.

Mica recognized one of them as Hector Ivanson, the brother

of Lord Hugh, who had died in the fighting. The other was Lady Velvet, Lord Fritz's mother. She clung to her son's arm as if for support, but her thin mouth was set in a stubborn line. Lord Fritz himself tugged at the bandage on his face, looking slightly dazed.

"This was an act of war!" Lord Hector shouted, half to the emperor and half to the room at large, as Mica and Jessamyn reached the front of the crowd. "We must march on the Obsidians at once!"

"We do not yet know whether their king ordered the attack," Emperor Styl said calmly.

"Who else would do it?" The bereaved noble's chest heaved with emotion. "I must have vengeance!"

"How do you know it was even an Obsidian plot?" said Lady Velvet. "This could have been an inside job. I wouldn't be surprised if we can trace it back to the highest powers in the land!"

"Honestly," Jessamyn muttered to Mica. "She thinks my father ordered this? He'd never put me in danger." She gave Mica a shove. "Say that."

Mica barely had time to grasp what was happening before she stumbled forward and blurted out, "I hope you're not seriously accusing His Imperial Majesty of arranging this disaster, Lady Velvet, especially when his own daughter was in danger last night."

"Lady Ingrid is right," someone else said. "Emperor Styl would never hurt Princess Jessamyn."

A few others murmured their agreement. Mica glanced at Jessamyn but didn't receive so much as an approving nod from the princess. Emperor Styl's face remained impassive too, neither confirming nor denying the sentiment. Mica couldn't figure out what she was missing about his relationship with his daughter. He was the least affectionate father she had ever met—and she had grown up on a military base.

Lady Velvet seemed appeased, but Lord Hector looked about wildly. "I demand vengeance!"

Lord Ober stepped out of the crowd and put a hand on his shoulder. "Easy there, my lord." He looked up at the stone-faced emperor. "I agree with Lady Ingrid that this was not some imperial conspiracy. However, I wish to know what will be done. My nephew went on that harbor cruise in good faith." He turned so that his voice carried throughout the throne room. "Timbral and the Pebble Islands have always supported the empire, and this is the thanks we get?"

"I hear Lord Caleb was injured and can't even get out of bed!" someone called out. "Who will answer for that?"

Angry mutters spread through the crowd. Lord Ober raised his hand, and those nearest to him fell silent to listen.

"We of the nobility live in the Silver Palace in order to represent the interests of our individual homelands," Lord Ober said. "If the people of the islands see their representatives being put in danger, they will question whether they are truly being heard."

"They're not just in danger," shouted Lord Hector. "My brother's body is even now beginning to rot!"

"This is true," Lord Ober said. "If these deaths are not avenged by the very empire that exists to protect them, who's to say what else the Obsidians will be allowed to do?"

"Hear! Hear!"

The conversations around the throne room were dying down as more of the nobles listened to what Lord Ober had to say. He had natural charisma, helped by his distinguished yet approachable face. He drew people in, whereas the emperor's forbidding alabaster visage held them off.

"The Windfast Empire is only as good as its ability to protect us," Lord Ober said. "The emperor must show the islands that we will not accept such blatant acts of aggression against us."

"Lord Ober speaks the truth!" The nobles surged forward, nearly pushing Mica onto the steps of the dais. A space remained clear around Jessamyn, her silver diadem shining as bright as a star.

"If the emperor won't act, we're better off on our own," came another voice.

"Maybe we are anyway!"

Emperor Styl gazed at Lord Ober, his grim features unreadable, as the crowd began to turn in the Timbral lord's favor. Mica didn't understand why the emperor wasn't saying anything. Shouldn't he use that clear, powerful voice of his to calm the crowds?

Mica pushed her way back toward the princess as the angry murmurs gathered momentum. "They're not suggesting—?"

"Unfortunately, they are." Jessamyn was studying the nobles around her as carefully as if she were a Mimic preparing to impersonate them. "Lord Ober isn't wrong. The Windfast is a delicate construct."

Mica couldn't believe the nobles were speaking so openly about being better off without the empire in front of Emperor Styl himself. Wasn't that treasonous? It would be for the likes of her. Every day she spent in the Silver Palace, Mica understood less about how the empire worked at the highest levels. The lords must think themselves powerful indeed to speak so freely before their ruler.

Lord Ober advanced, stopping just short of ascending the steps of Emperor Styl's dais. The nobles who supported him edged closer too. The Shield guards tensed, as if preparing to throw their bodies in front of their employers. That wasn't a good sign.

Lord Ober took a deep breath, as if inhaling the support of the crowd, and said, "I call upon the Emperor of Windfast to consider military action against the Obsidian Kingdom."

Shouts erupted across the hall, both for and against Lord Ober's proposition. The demand sounded far weightier coming from him than from the distraught Lord Hector, who still called for vengeance.

For one terrible moment, Mica imagined all four of her brothers marching to war.

Then Emperor Styl gave Jessamyn a nod so subtle Mica would have missed it if she hadn't been watching for his reaction.

The princess stepped forward. "My lords and ladies," she said. "I understand your concerns about what happened last night. However, I believe this talk of military action should go no further. I have new information I must share."

Jessamyn climbed up to the dais so everyone could see and hear her. Her winsome features contrasted perfectly with her father's stark face, her beauty drawing every eye.

"The King of Obsidian did not order the attack," Jessamyn said. "My own handmaiden, Brin Tarndier, orchestrated the whole thing. I fired her yesterday, you see. The little thing was just too stressful to have around. She became distraught upon losing her job. She threw a screaming tantrum in the middle of my sitting room and broke my very favorite vase from Silverfell."

Jessamyn gave a petulant sniff, and Mica could almost picture the scene herself, even though she knew it was a fabrication.

"Brin happened to have contacts in the criminal underbelly of this city. She shared the details of our cruise with petty criminals, inviting them to steal our jewels. That some were of Obsidian extract has no bearing on what occurred. I personally saw a few Windfast scoundrels among our assailants."

Murmurs spread through the crowd at that. Mica knew this was her cue.

"It's true!" she called in Lady Ingrid's voice. "I was wearing a precious necklace that was snatched right off me by a Windfast man."

This time Jessamyn gave a faint nod of approval.

"We all had a scare out on that boat," the princess continued. "We should focus on the criminals, not on turning this into an international incident. Let us not allow it to provoke us to reck-lessness."

Despite having led the charge earlier, Lord Ober didn't argue with the princess. He put a hand on Lord Hector's shoulder and spoke soothingly to him, apparently satisfied with her account. Without Lord Ober's backing, the push for war crumbled fast.

Mica wondered if Caleb would have agreed with his uncle's position if he'd been here. She hated the Obsidians as much as anyone, but she didn't want to risk her entire family over a couple of dead nobles. She trusted that the princess was doing the right thing.

When Mica turned back to Jessamyn, she caught her sharing a look of understanding with her father. Their silent communica-tion was subtle, a twitch of thin lips here, an arched eyebrow there, but it had the texture of a secret code. Mica was beginning to suspect that the apparent distance between the two was yet another mask. Styl and Jessamyn must have planned out the ebb and flow of the audience together. Where he was stone, she was velvet. He was a storm cloud, and she was a ray of sunlight. They were playing a game of their own making—and this time they had won.

As the chatter in the hall turned more and more in Jessamyn's favor, Emperor Styl stepped in to seal the victory.

"We take the official position that a disgruntled former servant was responsible for this tragedy," he declared in that clear, ringing voice. "We shall be more careful of future hires. Now, let us put aside all talk of retaliation and focus on ridding our city of the criminals who would commit such act of cowardice for jewels."

Mica maintained Lady Ingrid's appearance as she and the princess left the throne room not long after. She caught sight of

Lord Ober outside the doors, surrounded by an animated group of lords and ladies.

"Crisis averted for now," Jessamyn said as soon as she and Mica were out of earshot of the other nobles. The Shield guards kept their distance, giving them space to talk.

"You don't really think this was about jewelry theft, do you?" Mica asked.

"No, but don't you lecture me about lying," Jessamyn said. "If we ever go to war with Obsidian, it must be for the right reasons. We cannot allow them to provoke—"

"I think you did the right thing, Princess," Mica said. "The lie was necessary."

Jessamyn looked over at her, fiddling with a strand of dark-red hair. Then she nodded, as if Mica had passed a test. Or maybe Jessamyn was the one who needed to pass.

"I'm surprised Lord Ober was so vehement," Mica said as they strode down the corridor, their footsteps echoing in time with one another. Although the emperor, with Jessamyn's help, had shot down Lord Ober's proposal to immediately strike back at Obsidian, the Timbral lord had gained admirers for advocating a tougher response to the provocation.

"I'm not," Jessamyn said. "This isn't the first time he has taken an aggressive position, or an unpopular one. Plenty of people admire him for his willingness to oppose the majority."

"He's powerful, isn't he?"

"He grows more so by the day. Generally, I think he's quite levelheaded." Jessamyn quirked an eyebrow. "It's not bad to encourage the occasional dissenting voice, you know."

"But does he usually argue for *war*?" Mica asked. "That's where striking back at Obsidian would lead."

"No . . . That was new."

"Hmm." Mica had been taught to keep an eye out for sudden changes in a person's behavior or positions in case they'd been replaced. She had missed it with Brin, and she didn't intend to make the same mistake twice.

"I can look into Lord Ober more, if you like," she said. "Maybe he has been—"

"The situation is too delicate right now," Jessamyn said. "I can't be seen making overtly political moves after taking a strong stance on this issue. I don't want you snooping around him right now."

"What about Caleb?"

"*Lord* Caleb has a great deal of respect for his uncle," Jessamyn said. "I'll discuss it with him, but in the meantime, it's best if we encourage everyone to calm down." She adjusted the diadem on her head. "Perhaps it's time we had another ball."

They walked in silence as Mica thought over what Jessamyn had told her. She appreciated that the princess was taking the time to answer her questions. Mica and Jessamyn seemed to have turned a corner back in the hold of that barge. Escaping death had brought them closer together. As much as Mica hated to admit it, she was coming to respect the princess.

"You called the Windfast a delicate construct earlier," she said. "What did you mean by that, if you don't mind me asking?"

"The imperial family walks a careful line with the nobility we invite to live in the Silver Palace," Jessamyn said. "Many are the sons and daughters of governors who would otherwise be kings and queens of their territory. They send them to us to make sure their loyalty to the empire serves them in the long run." She looked over at Mica. "They also send their Talents to serve in the Imperial Army with the understanding that their territories will be protected in return. People from the different lands may have unique customs, but they are united as imperial citizens."

They reached the princess's quarters, pausing so Banner could unlock the doors.

"Imagine if every island kept every Talent born on their shores," Jessamyn went on. "They could build their own little armies. The larger islands might try to take over the small ones. They would all look out only for their own interests. Their people would lose the benefits they have come to enjoy under imperial trade agreements. And that's the best-case scenario."

Jessamyn crossed her sitting room to the large window. Jewel Harbor spread before her, glittering in the afternoon sunlight.

Mica stepped up beside her. "And what's the worst-case scenario?"

"Obsidian," Jessamyn said, still looking down upon her city. "They nearly destroyed us before. We survive *only* because we have put aside our differences to work together as a single unit. We are stronger together. That is why my father and I must keep the nobles engaged here at court. If the Windfast islands fight amongst themselves or go separate ways, it will only be a matter of time before the King of Obsidian swallows us up one by one."

CHAPTER NINETEEN

J essamyn encouraged everyone to return to normal after the harbor cruise disaster. She had explained to Mica that she couldn't be seen as being too political.

"People want their princesses to be pretty and well dressed and charming. It makes them uncomfortable when princesses have opinions and influence too. Don't get me wrong. I rather enjoy being enchanting, but I have to wield my diplomatic clout carefully."

"The emperor isn't exactly pretty," Mica muttered, slightly louder than she intended.

"Of course not, Micathea. Pay attention. People want their male leaders to be strong and stern and forbidding. *I* didn't make the rules."

After stepping out to avert the crisis, Jessamyn turned more vigorously than ever to dancing and matchmaking and party planning. She arranged romantic rendezvous with three different lords, and each left the trysts looking a little starry-eyed, though none would say exactly what he had or hadn't done with the princess. Mica was finally coming to understand the purpose of all this frivolity. It gave the nobles something to whisper about besides Jessamyn's efficient shutdown of a potentially disastrous military action.

Even so, no one could ignore what had happened on the cruise. Many nobles hired extra Shield bodyguards and Muscles to look out for them. Being surrounded by half a dozen extra retainers would no longer be worth the inconvenience eventually, but the Talents did good business in the meantime.

Mica herself slipped into the guises of various nobles and their servants to find out what people were talking about behind closed doors, flitting from face to face faster than ever before. Her primary aim was to figure out if one of the nobles had specifically been targeted during the harbor cruise attack, or if something had been stolen. They still didn't know what their attackers had been trying to accomplish—and if they had succeeded. If the primary goal had indeed been to provoke a war, the perpetrators would likely try again.

Jessamyn wanted Mica to unravel the mystery of the attack, but that left her with little time to investigate the problem closest to her heart: Danil's disappearance. The longer he was gone, the less likely it became that he was alive. She still hadn't been able to search the warehouse district where screaming had been heard—screaming the City Watch had been so quick to dismiss.

Mica feared the missing Talents would be forgotten. Sapphire hadn't written her any more letters, and it had been far too long since she'd heard from Master Kiev. She felt blinded without more information or instructions, and she became more and more convinced that Master Kiev himself had been taken.

She became so convinced, in fact, that she experienced a real shock when she stopped by Peet's place one morning and Master Kiev himself was sitting in the small flat, eating sugared almonds with the young Blur.

"Master Kiev! What are you doing here?"

"Good afternoon, Micathea. Would you care for a sugared almond?"

Mica gaped at him. "I've been worried about you."

"Why is that?"

"I haven't heard from you in weeks!"

"That is the nature of our work," Master Kiev said, his deep voice calm. "Some Impersonators spend years as sleeper agents, simply going about their lives until they are needed. You've only been here for a few months."

"But so much has happened." Mica pulled up a stool and accepted the tin of almonds Peet handed her. "Did you get my report about the harbor cruise?"

"Alas, that is why I am here. I am meeting with my contacts in the city in an effort to get to the bottom of this." Master Kiev rubbed a hand over his face, which looked thinner than ever. "We believe the Obsidian King ordered the attack to stir up conflict, though we are not yet sure why. I may need to pay a visit to his court myself."

"You're going to Obsidian?" Mica exchanged glances with Peet, who was drumming his fingers on his knobby knees. "But what about the missing Talents?"

Master Kiev sighed heavily. "I must focus on the larger threat right now."

"But—"

"It gives me no pleasure to neglect the investigation into the disappearances," Master Kiev said. "But there are forces at play that could endanger every Talent in the empire, not only those currently missing."

Mica stared at him, the sugared almonds forgotten in her hand. She understood why Master Kiev and Jessamyn wanted to focus on a potential Obsidian threat, but they had been her primary hopes for Danil and the others. They cared about the Talents, commoners though they were, and they had taken steps to tackle the problem. But if they focused their political influence and network of spies on uncovering Obsidian conspirators, who was left to search for the Talents? Weren't they the ones who were so convinced the kidnappers were *not* Obsidian?

"I must go," Master Kiev said, joints popping as he stood. "My ship leaves in a few hours, and I have more people to see."

"Sir," Mica said. "I want to keep looking for the Talents."

"Your duty as an Imperial Impersonator—"

"I meant in my own time," Mica said quickly. "I won't disobey orders."

Master Kiev studied her in that guarded way of his, and she did her best to hide her apprehension. She didn't want to be alone in this task. But she remembered what she and Sapphire used to say. "Don't fall apart, or at least make it look like you're not." She met his gaze without fear.

"Please. We can't abandon them."

"Very well," he said at last. "I hope you learn something, but take care for your own safety. I don't want you putting yourself in dangerous situations."

"I'll be invisible, just like you taught me."

Master Kiev nodded. Then he popped the last of the almonds into his mouth and turned to the door, assuming a pale, pinched face she had never seen before.

"It may be some time before you hear from me again. Continue sending your reports to Redbridge. May you thrive, Micathea."

"May you thrive, Master Kiev."

It wasn't until Mica was almost back to the palace that she realized she had forgotten to tell Master Kiev about Lord Caleb's mysterious abilities. She had seen little of Caleb since that night on the boat, though that hadn't stopped her from mulling over what he had told her—and thinking about him in general. She considered trying to catch Master Kiev before he departed the city to discuss it, but Jessamyn ordered her to the gardens to play a racquetball tournament in her place. By the time the final match ended, it was too late.

Dealing with the fallout from the harbor cruise kept her busier than ever, but Mica seized her chance to make progress on her own investigation when Jessamyn sent her to Magic Q to pick up a new batch of potions. The princess had exhausted her supply faster than usual after so many late nights spent entertaining.

"Ask Quinn if she recognizes that vial of potion the Obsidian boat captain was carrying," Jessamyn said. "It's one of our only clues."

"I'll see what she can tell me." Mica pocketed the vial, already thinking about the other questions the potioner might be able to answer.

"Run along now." Jessamyn flapped her hands impatiently. "I won't need you again today."

Mica paused at the tapestry leading to the servants' corridor. "What are you doing tonight?"

"I don't have to give you my entire schedule." Jessamyn rolled her eyes to the ceiling. "Some people can be so presumptuous."

Mica didn't bother to argue. She changed out of the dress she'd worn to a luncheon as Lady Elana in record time, her excitement building. It was still a few hours before dark, meaning she'd have the entire evening off. She hadn't had such a good opportunity to pursue her own investigation since she arrived in Jewel Harbor. She intended to make the most of it.

Soon Mica was hurrying out of the palace, wearing a brown Mimic's skirt over trousers, a white blouse, and the city-woman face she had donned the first time she met Magic Q: black-coffee hair, thick freckles, confident stride.

On her way to the potioner's, she stopped at a shop Banner had recommended to purchase a pair of knives that could be worn beneath a skirt or a sleeve. She never wanted to find herself armed only with broken glass again.

The knives she selected were exquisite. The blades, forged

from the lightest steel she'd ever felt, were no longer than her hands, with curved, leather-wrapped handles that would be easy to grip for a quick slash. She knew better than to get into an extended fight if she could help it. She needed weapons that would get her out of a tough spot just long enough for her to disappear. At the urging of the shopkeeper, she chose sheaths made from buttery leather that could be attached to her leg or arm. The blades would lie flush against her skin, barely noticeable until she needed them.

The purchase total came to more money than Mica had spent in the rest of her life combined. She was paid quite well for her job as Jessamyn's Impersonator, but she'd barely had time to spend any of her salary. She had certainly never expected to own such fine weapons. Her brothers would be jealous.

As she counted the glittering Windfast marks into the shopkeeper's hand, she thought about what her brothers might be up to. Aden and Emir were nearing the age when they would be considered for commission as officers. Aden fully intended to rise as far as he could through the military ranks. He had a knack for leadership, and the members of his company looked up to him in much the same way that his younger siblings always had. Emir was a quieter sort, and Mica couldn't picture him commanding a battalion. She wondered what it would be like for him to work in Jewel Harbor as a civilian, carrying messages alongside Peet and the other city Blurs. She wouldn't mind having family closer. Of course, Wills and Rees would get into as much trouble as a couple of young men with impervious skin could if *they* ever came to the big city. They were better off with the discipline the army provided.

Mica pushed down a wave of homesickness. It would be nice to have her brothers around, but she didn't want them anywhere near Jewel Harbor while Talents were disappearing. She still had work to do.

She strapped the knives to her legs before leaving the shop.

The next time she found herself with an enemy's hands wrapped around her throat, she would be ready.

Daylight was fading fast by the time she arrived at Magic Q's. She found Quinn in the front of the shop this time, taking inventory of her rows of shimmering red bottles.

"Hello again," Mica said. "I've come for the same order."

Quinn glanced at her, sharp eyes taking note of the face Mica wore.

"Still here, eh? You haven't gotten tired of her drama?"

"The princess isn't so bad," Mica said.

"You must be tougher than I gave you credit for." Quinn took the list Mica offered. "Anything new on here?"

"I don't think so," Mica said. "She wants a few extra bottles of that energy tonic."

"Hmm, I hope I have enough left." Quinn pursed her lips and looked closer at the inventory list in her hand. "I've been doing brisk business with that one."

"Did Lord Ober end up ordering some from you?"

Quinn looked up sharply. "How did you know?"

"I told him about your skills." Mica didn't mention that Lord Ober himself wasn't the one actually consuming the tonic. She still hadn't breathed a word of Caleb's secret to anyone.

"I guess I have you to thank for my good fortune then," Quinn said. "He has become one of my best customers."

"You make a good product," Mica said. "That's all on you."

"Perhaps." Quinn glanced at the window, where darkness was falling. "It's almost closing time. Let me buy you that drink I mentioned to say thank you."

"I'd like that." Mica planned to explore the warehouse district tonight too, but she'd been hoping Quinn would be a good source of information on the potioner community. Maybe she'd even meet some of Quinn's Talent suppliers. She grinned. "I could use a night off."

"It's settled then."

Quinn tidied up a few papers in her workroom while Mica checked that the new potions were fully sealed and bundled them up to carry on her back. She'd have to be careful of the package this evening. She may be well paid, but these potions were still worth more money than she had in the world.

After locking up the shop, Quinn took Mica to a rooftop bar not far from Potioners Alley. Lanterns were beginning to come on all over the city, dulling the light of the stars. They climbed a rickety staircase through an overcrowded tenement building that was only a little nicer than the one where Peet lived. The large rooftop was filled with scuffed wooden furniture and illuminated by candles on the tables. Assorted patrons occupied about half the tables, chatting quietly over beers and chilled wine. The bar felt removed from the usual chaos of Jewel Harbor, and the sounds of the city were muted. Mica could almost imagine they were in a country pub if not for the view of the Silver Palace in the distance.

A group of men raised their glasses to Quinn as she passed their table. She didn't acknowledge them with so much as a nod.

"Potioners," she said to Mica. "Two years ago, they wouldn't even make eye contact with me, the two-faced bastards."

"Why not?"

"They don't like anyone from outside the city. Thought I was some island yokel until I started making a name for myself." Quinn jerked her head toward the far corner of the roof, hair swinging around her chin. "Grab us a table while I get the drinks."

Mica chose a table near the low wall surrounding the rooftop, studying the group of potioners out of the corner of her eye. They wore well-cut clothes of quality linen and wool, too humble for the nobles in the palace but more expensive than anything her brothers would wear on leave. At least one of the potioners was a Talent, a Shield who was casually running his hand through the flame of the candle on their table. His impervious skin must come in handy when dealing with bubbling cauldrons.

Quinn soon joined her, juggling a pitcher of chilled wine filled with slices of fruit and two heavy glass tumblers. The potioner poured a glass for each of them and raised hers.

"To striking good business!"

The chilled wine was sweet on Mica's tongue, but she was careful to swallow only a tiny bit. She needed to be alert later tonight.

"How did you end up becoming a potioner?" she asked her companion. "You mentioned before that one took you in when you came to Jewel Harbor. Is that how you learned?"

"I could already do a few things before then," Quinn said. "I'd learned the basic potions back home. I experimented a lot and came up with some new recipes I thought were pretty special. Wasn't enough to make it in the big city."

"You seem to be doing fine," Mica said. Quinn had both the princess and one of the more powerful lords in the city as her dedicated customers.

"Now, yes, but it was difficult." She ran a finger around the rim of her glass tumbler. "I was selling potions out of clay mugs from a cart at first. You have to be pretty desperate to buy a potion from a barefoot kid with a cart. But my concoctions worked well, and an older potioner heard about me. He was starting to think about retirement, and he needed an apprentice who could eventually take over his business. He's the one who taught me to use Talent blood in my mixes."

"Not every potioner does that?"

"Correct. It still makes some people queasy."

Mica looked into her drink, the bloodred liquid shimmering in the candlelight. *She* certainly felt uncomfortable with the notion, even though both Quinn and Peet had assured her the Talents gave their blood voluntarily.

"Could you drink the blood of a Talent directly to get their ability?"

"No." Quinn shuddered. "What a morbid suggestion."

Mica blinked. "You're the one who uses—never mind. The blood potions can make someone a Talent temporarily, right?"

"Sort of," Quinn said. "A potion gives an extra burst of strength or speed or protection, but it doesn't turn the person into a Talent. Once they use up the energy, for lack of a better word, it's gone."

"Does it drain the person?" Mica asked. "Like if someone uses a speed potion, do they wind up sick or exhausted afterwards?"

Quinn shook her head. "They're feeding purely off the potion, so it shouldn't affect them otherwise. Think about the princess using all those energy potions. You don't see her sleeping them off later, do you?"

"I guess not." Mica frowned at the apple slices floating in her glass. It didn't sound as though potions could fully explain Caleb's uncontrollable bursts of Talent, whether he was drinking them intentionally or not.

"Is it possible to give a person more than one Talent-like ability at a time?"

Quinn tapped her fingers on her glass. "Maybe for a few seconds. No one has come up with one that works effectively for a sustained period of time. Imagine if you could make someone strong, fast, and impervious to injury all at once. They'd be unstoppable."

Mica could imagine it all too well. Muscles, Blurs, and Shields had to work together on the battlefield, requiring strict discipline and devotion to a common goal. She could only imagine what would happen if a single soldier could use all three abilities—never mind if they could change their shape at the same time.

But what if someone had figured it out? What if someone was using the blood of the missing Talents to confer multiple abilities at once? They could create the most unstoppable army the world had ever seen. Mica took a huge gulp of her chilled wine, attempting to wash away the image of her brothers facing such an army. She choked as a piece of fruit caught in her throat. *So much for staying alert.*

"What about Mimics?" Mica said when she could breathe again. "Can a potion allow someone to impersonate?"

"That's generally considered too dangerous," Quinn said. "Just because someone swallows a potion doesn't mean they can control their features or contort them safely."

"Makes sense," Mica said. "I went to school for that—and I was born with the ability."

"Exactly." Quinn grabbed the pitcher and topped up both of their glasses. "Shields, on the other hand, require no control whatsoever. That woman over there made her fortune selling Impervious Brew, which protects you even if you're fast asleep." She gestured toward a merry little lady with silver hair and spidery wrinkles around her eyes. "Speed and strength are somewhere in between. If you take one of those potions recklessly, you could hurt yourself or someone else."

Mica nodded, thinking of how risky it was for Caleb to never know when he would suddenly have too much of a good thing. Not that she was supposed to be thinking about Caleb.

"Those potions are still safer than enabling true impersonation, right?"

"Correct."

"So you don't buy Mimic blood at all?"

"Oh, I can still use it," Quinn said. "It's especially helpful in cosmetics and the like. I can brew potions that'll change someone's eye color or complexion without them having to control anything. Mind you, that can go horribly wrong if the mix isn't perfect."

Mica had a brief vision of someone's skin sagging like her old woman impersonation. She shuddered.

"Why do you ask?" Quinn leaned forward, the candlelight flickering in her dark eyes. "Are you interested in selling?"

"No, it's not that." Mica hesitated. Now that Master Kiev and the princess were occupied with Obsidian, the investigation was up to her. Quinn had been a useful source so far. Mica hoped she could trust her.

"Have you heard about the Talents going missing?" she said at last. "I thought it could have something to do with their blood."

Quinn sat back, frowning slightly, and Mica worried she'd offended her. She hurried to clarify. "I'm sure no upstanding potioner—"

Quinn raised a hand, cutting her off. "I'd be careful about asking too many questions."

"What? Why?"

"This is a big city but a small island."

"What does that mean?"

Quinn's sharp gaze darted around the rooftop. "I mean you're not the first person to ask around about the Talent disappearances." She raised her glass to her lips and spoke into it. "See that man by the bar, talking to the lady?"

Mica glanced over discreetly. The man was red-faced and round, with mousy brown hair plastered onto a sweaty forehead. He was laughing loudly with a full-lipped woman wearing a corset to buoy her ample figure.

"What about him?"

"He's on the City Watch. I hear they get hostile when people show too much interest in missing Talents."

"I've heard about the City Watch telling people to keep quiet too," Mica said, remembering what the Muscle oarsman had said about a Watchman intimidating his friend into not mentioning the warehouse by the docks. "They're involved somehow."

"Look, I'd leave it alone if I were you," Quinn said. "It's not worth getting into trouble."

"What kind of trouble?"

Quinn didn't answer. She poured them each another glass, but Mica felt the atmosphere between them chilling. She feared she'd lost Quinn as a source entirely.

Then she remembered the vial in her pocket. She pulled out the unmarked bottle and passed it over the table.

"I don't suppose you know which potioners use bottles like this, do you? This one didn't have a label."

Quinn studied the vial in the candlelight.

"These are common," she said. "You can find this size and shape in half the shops on Potioners Alley." She pulled the stopper and sniffed carefully. Her eyes widened at whatever the residual smell told her. "That was a pretty nasty potion, though. Where did you get this?"

"It's a long story."

"Like I said, you could find hundreds of bottles like it. They make them right here in Jewel Harbor. Sorry I couldn't be more help."

"You've already helped me a lot," Mica said. She could now be fairly certain the Obsidian barge captain had purchased his poisons right here in the city. If only she knew whose money he had used.

The rooftop bar was becoming crowded, and Mica and Quinn had to lean in closer to hear each other talk. They moved on to safer topics, mostly speaking about their families back home. Quinn's parents had been salt miners back on Talon, though both had passed away since she moved to Jewel Harbor to make her fortune. Mica didn't go into detail about her own background, employing the vague method of small talk that had actually been taught in classes at the Academy. It was amazing how long you could carry on a conversation without saying anything at all.

Clouds had begun to gather overhead, further obscuring the stars. The air had a heavy, expectant feeling that signaled an approaching rainstorm. Mica occasionally lifted her tumbler to her lips, but she didn't drink any more chilled wine, feeling a sense of expectation that had little to do with the weather.

She kept an eye on the City Watchman over by the bar. When he finally drained his glass and waved to the barman to pay his tab, she stood.

"Thank you for the drink, Quinn, but I'd better get going."

"Sure. Looks like it'll rain soon anyway." Quinn reached for Mica's abandoned drink, apparently intent on unwinding that evening regardless of the weather or company. "Good luck with the little cyclone up at the palace. And look out for yourself. Seriously, you don't want the wrong people to hear you asking questions."

"I appreciate the warning." Mica grinned. "They won't even know it was me."

CHAPTER TWENTY

M ica followed the City Watchman and the corseted lady down the rickety staircase through the tenement building. She paused on a landing to unfasten her skirt and sling it over her shoulder alongside the package of potions. She assumed her mischievous lad face before continuing down the stairs.

She followed the pair at a distance, adopting the loose saunter of a young man with one too many drinks in his belly. It was late, and the crowds in the street were thinning. Mica was afraid the watchman would simply take his companion home to bed, until they cut through a shadowy alley and the lady shed her corset and skirt. Her sagging bosom became rippling muscle, and the full lips receded, adding definition to a lantern jaw. The Impersonator shrugged on a uniform jacket, and by the time the pair emerged from the alley, the woman had transformed into a second member of the City Watch.

Mica quickly checked her own features, making sure they were nothing like her real appearance or the city-woman face she'd worn in the bar. Fellow Mimics tended to be good at spotting impersonations. With luck, those men wouldn't see her at all tonight.

She crept along behind them, keeping her stance loose despite her eagerness to finally uncover the truth. She didn't know the city too well yet, but she recognized where they were heading: the warehouse district near the docks.

They reached the convoluted warren of alleys and grim walls. Many of the warehouse buildings looked identical, and Mica had to pay close attention to the twists and turns so she could find her way back. Learning the route was no easy task. After one too many turns, she began to fear the watchmen were leading her in a circle. Her heart raced, and she struggled to maintain her impersonation. Had they figured out they were being followed?

She saw precious few people apart from her quarry among the warehouses. The streets were as quiet as they ever got in Jewel Harbor. Most of the workers had long since gone home for the night, and dawn was still hours away. If she was seen, those watchmen may not believe her drunken lad impersonation this far from the nearest pub. Mica was about to switch her face again when she heard the first scream.

The sound came from up ahead of the two watchmen, eerily muffled in the darkness. The mousy-haired man said something to his lantern-jawed companion, and they turned down a side street between a pair of hulking warehouses made of dull red brick. This had to be the place.

The scream came again, louder this time. Anger simmered inside Mica at the sound, quickly approaching a boil. She peeked around the corner of the brick building, fists clenched to keep from drawing one of her new knives. Any light reflecting off the steel was sure to give her away. She stayed in the shadows as the pair halted in front of a warehouse door. Keys jangled faintly. The men glanced around to make sure they were alone before opening the door and going inside. Mica kept hidden until the lock clicked.

As soon as they were gone, she emerged to survey the warehouse. It was one of the larger ones on this street, connected to the smaller building next to it by a wooden walkway. The windows were boarded up, making it look abandoned. Mica circled around, checking the boarded-up windows for weak points, but the place was as secure as a seaside fortress in wartime. Someone definitely didn't want anyone else to know what was going on inside.

She studied the adjacent buildings, hoping she might find a way to the rooftops. Most were in shambles, except for the smaller building connected to the warehouse with a walkway. It was just as carefully boarded up as the larger one, but the walkway itself appeared to be open to the air.

Another scream rang out, making Mica jump. How could no one have reported this place by now? Either the rest of the warehouses on this block were abandoned, or the corruption in the City Watch went even deeper than she thought.

She considered the walkway connecting the redbrick warehouses for a moment more. Then she backtracked to a warehouse that wasn't boarded up, a gray stone monstrosity situated next to the smaller of the two redbrick buildings. She climbed through a broken window and picked through the rubble and dust until she found a stairwell. A few minutes later, she emerged on the rooftop of the gray stone structure.

Clouds hung low in the sky, obscuring the moon and making it difficult to see. The air felt damp and thick, as if the rainstorm was hovering directly over the city now, waiting for the right moment to break loose. Mica's heart pounded as she looked over the edge of the roof at the smaller of the two boarded-up buildings. The gap between the roofs wasn't too wide. She should be able to make it.

"Here goes nothing."

She took a deep breath and jumped. The impact jarred her teeth, and the clatter of her feet on the rooftop sounded far too loud. She hurried across the expanse and crouched beneath the low border wall on the opposite side, hoping it would shield her from view of the tall redbrick building. Thankfully, the boarded-up windows meant she had a decent chance of not being seen.

She crouched on the roof for a few tense minutes, listening to the noises rising from the two connected buildings. Voices murmured, too soft to make out. Scraping sounds came from the room directly under her feet, as if furniture was being moved. Every so often, she heard a faint scream from the larger building across the walkway. As far as Mica could tell, that was where most of the activity was taking place.

Suddenly, the scraping noises beneath her stopped. Mica held her breath. A door creaked open, then slammed, and footsteps crossed the wooden walkway to the other warehouse. Another door opened and shut. Mica strained to hear the click of a lock, but it didn't come. As far as she could tell, the doors leading to the walkway were not secured.

It's now or never.

Leaving behind her package of potions, she climbed over the wall and slung herself down onto the walkway. She landed catlike on the boards and hurried to the door of the smaller warehouse. She pulled it open a crack, listening for movement inside. Nothing. She slipped inside and pulled the door shut behind her.

The room was as empty as it sounded. The things she'd heard being moved were wooden boxes. Trails of grime and dust showed that some of the boxes had recently been pushed out of their original positions. Mica took a quick look inside a few, all too aware of the multiple doors leading in and out of this room. She moved carefully, leaving as little evidence as possible of her presence, as she filed away any clues. Adrenaline thundered through her, but she couldn't help grinning. *This* was the kind of spy work she had expected to do after the Academy.

The boxes contained an assortment of tools she wouldn't be surprised to find in an apothecary: measuring cups, glass bottles of various shapes and sizes, scalpels and other knives suitable for chopping ingredients into tiny pieces.

A few more bowls and pans, and this could be a kitchen supply room.

Burlap sacks were piled in a corner, the smells wafting from them hinting at herbs and spices. Mica opened one, releasing the aroma of rosemary into the air. So far everything here supported her theory that someone was making potions. But one ingredient was still missing. One liquid ingredient.

She listened at the doors surrounding the room full of boxes, but there didn't seem to be much activity in this building. Most of the action must be happening in the larger warehouse across the walkway. Could that be where the missing Talents were being kept? At least some of them were still alive, if the screaming was any indication.

She frowned. *It has been a few minutes since I last heard any—*

Suddenly, the storm broke over the warehouse with a violent thunderclap. The rush of water drowned out every other sound except the thunder. She'd no longer be able to hear anyone coming.

Just what I need.

Mica crouched beside the sack of spices, considering her options. Officially, she was supposed to observe and report, not take action. Now that she knew the location of the warehouse, she could send in the authorities to stop whatever was going on here. But at least some of the authorities were in on it. What if the entire City Watch already knew what was happening here? They wouldn't help her.

Then the scream came again, so loud and desperate that it cut through the drumbeat of the rain, before abruptly stopping. Mica made her decision. She drew one of her knives and crept back to the door. The rain made it difficult to hear any activity across the way, but she couldn't wait any longer. She yanked open the door and darted across the walkway, the downpour drenching her in seconds, then she slipped through the other door, entering the large warehouse at last.

She found herself on a catwalk high above a vast space crammed with wooden crates. The position was exposed, and she had to dive behind a stack of barrels a dozen feet away to avoid being spotted at once. An acrid smell far worse than anything in Potioners Alley filled the warehouse. The air felt sickly, and Mica's damp clothes quickly became uncomfortable in the too-warm space.

Despite the rain thundering on the rooftop, she could hear a lot more now that she was inside the main building. She heard people—more than she expected—moving around below her, coughing and shuffling, groaning. And she heard angry voices rising from the far side of the warehouse.

"—told you two not to be seen together."

"Relax. I wasn't wearing my real face."

"I don't care." The voice was gravelly, as if the speaker had spent far too much time shouting. "You're a sorry excuse for a Mimic."

"Just because I didn't go to some fancy academy—"

"Be happy you didn't. Otherwise, you'd be out there in a crate with the more valuable Talents."

Mica couldn't hear a response. She pictured the lantern-jawed member of the City Watch struggling not to talk back to the man who was berating him. She risked sticking her head out from her hiding place for a peek at the warehouse floor, which was filled with large wooden crates. The missing Talents were imprisoned inside the things? Had she found them at last?

The two City Watchmen stood in an aisle running through the center of the crates, but Mica couldn't see the man they were talking to. There appeared to be a cleared-out space that stretched from the aisle to the wall left of Mica's current position. She began to edge around the catwalk, hoping to get a look at what was inside it.

Then the unseen man spoke again in that gravelly bark,

which sounded vaguely familiar. "I'm done with this one for now. Put her back and bring me that big fellow. The Mimic."

Mica froze, watching in horror as the two watchmen dragged a young woman out of the cleared area and down the aisle. Blood dripped down her arms, and her face was covered in bruises. Mica couldn't tell what kind of ability the young woman had, but she didn't look as though she was in any condition to use it. White-hot rage blazed through her at the sight. How dare they treat someone like this, Talent or not?

The men made no effort to be gentle with the girl, not slowing down even as she struggled to get her feet underneath her. It took all of Mica's willpower to keep from leaping down and attempting to free the woman then and there. But if there were Talents in all these crates, she couldn't afford to be rash. She needed backup.

Observe and report, she told herself. *You're a spy, not a hero.*

Mica stayed hidden as the watchmen shoved the girl into one of the crates and locked it up. She stayed hidden as they moved toward another crate almost directly below her spot on the catwalk. She could probably drop right on top of them from here, but that wouldn't get her the information she needed to stop this operation. She stayed hidden as they fiddled with the lock, already calculating how soon she could return with reinforcements. She could get out the way she came in and disappear without anyone ever knowing she had been there.

Mica knew that was the wisest course of action, and so she stayed hidden—until the men opened the crate and dragged Danil out onto the floor.

CHAPTER TWENTY-ONE

M ica didn't have time to talk herself out of it. The moment she recognized Danil's curly hair and saw the pallor in his formerly rosy cheeks, she leapt into action.

She drew her twin blades and dropped from the catwalk onto the Impersonator watchman. Her knives sliced deep into his shoulders, forcing him to drop his grip on Danil.

"What the—Where'd you come from?"

The man flailed and swung his fists, the surprise attack not enough to take him out of action, as Mica clung to his back like a bat. His hair changed color rapidly then began receding into his scalp.

"Get him off me!"

Mica hung on tighter.

The mousy-haired watchman gaped at the spectacle, momentarily loosening his hold on Danil's bound arms. Mica's friend wasn't as weak or disoriented as she had feared. He suddenly lengthened and thinned his hands to slip free of his bonds and rolled away from his captor. The man cursed and tackled him.

Mica lost sight of Danil and the other watchman as her own opponent changed tactics, pitching back into the nearest crate and crushing her against the rough wood. Mica gasped as pain exploded in her back. The watchman staggered sideways and slammed her against another crate, the crash reverberating through the warehouse. Mica dug her knives deeper into his shoulders, using them like claws to keep from being thrown off his back. Blood gushed over her hands. She could feel him weakening. But not soon enough. He slammed her back again, and one of her ribs cracked, sending a flash of agony through her.

She couldn't hold on much longer. She clenched her teeth and twisted her knives even deeper. The Watchman shuddered violently, his hair going pure white and then black as jet. Then he collapsed to the ground.

Mica landed on top of the body, pain lancing through her side. She couldn't pause to examine her injury. She yanked her blades free, noticing as she did that the watchman's face had changed one last time in death, becoming uglier and more ordinary. The lantern jaw had slumped into a weak chin, and the hair had gone thin and gray. She turned away from the Mimic's body, trying to shake the impression that she had just killed two people instead of one. One was enough.

Danil was on his knees with his big hands around the mousy-haired watchman's throat. He was squeezing with all his strength, his eyes shot through with pure terror. The enemy was already dead.

Mica grabbed his arm.

"Danil! It's done. We have to go."

Danil didn't move, his eyes still wild with fear and shock, sweat and dirt matting his curly hair.

Shouts came from the other side of the warehouse. The place was far from empty, and they had made a lot of noise. They had seconds before they were discovered.

"Danil, it's me." Mica shifted to her own face and stuck it close to Danil's. "It's Mica. You can let go now."

He blinked at her, his eyes slowly clearing, and at last his grip loosened. He dropped his former jailer's body and shuffled back, staying on the ground himself. That was when Mica noticed that his leg now ended a few inches below his knee.

Horror rose in her chest, but she clamped down hard on it. They weren't out of danger yet.

"They're coming closer."

Danil looked up at her, his face bloodless. "Go without me."

"Not a chance." She looked around at the grisly scene, an idea coming to her. "I need you to trust me."

She squeezed her jaw into a lantern shape, adopting the chosen features of the man she had just killed. She took his City Watch jacket and then rolled his corpse into Danil's crate and slammed it shut. She grabbed Danil's arm and twisted it behind his back just as half a dozen guards charged around a corner into their aisle.

"Quickly!" Mica shouted in the watchman's voice. "The sneak who attacked us is wounded. Catch him before he escapes!" She shuffled through the pool of blood on the floor, trying to hide the trail that led straight to the crate. Danil helped as much as he could while making it look as if he was struggling against her.

The guards started toward them. "The prisoner—"

"I've got him," Mica barked. "He's getting away. Move your striking feet!"

Four of the men ran off, but the last two remained behind. Mica bit back a curse as the pair headed up the aisle toward them. She and Danil couldn't take both with their injuries.

"How do we know you're really Benson?" asked one of the guards (thin-faced with straw-blond hair and plain clothes).

Mica gave an impatient snort and changed her face to that of the full-lipped woman she'd followed out of the rooftop bar.

"Happy?"

The guards came nearer. "We'd better put the prisoner back until—"

"He's still needed." Mica changed back to the lantern-jawed watchman's face. It would all be over if the guards looked inside Danil's crate and found the body. "You don't want to make *him* angry, do you?"

The guards exchanged glances, and Mica prayed she'd guessed right about the fear their gravel-voiced employer instilled. He had certainly sounded like the angry type.

"I guess not," said the thin-faced blond after a minute. "I've made that mistake before."

The pair reached them, eying the blood spreading across the aisle and the mousy-haired dead man. Mica hoped they'd be too distracted to notice that Benson had shrunk a foot since they last saw him. The second guard, who was young and swarthy, knelt to attend to the strangled watchman.

The thin-faced blond took Danil's other arm. "I'll help you with this one."

Mica had no choice but to accept. She and the guard dragged Danil down the aisle, struggling to support his weight. How soon before the thin-faced guard realized she wasn't nearly as strong as Benson had been?

"Who attacked you?" he asked.

"Young lad," Mica said. "Jumped me from the catwalk."

"How'd he find us?"

Mica grunted noncommittally, and the other man gave her an odd look. She wondered if Benson was normally more talkative than this.

"His Lordship won't like it when he hears about this," said the guard. "He has been so careful."

Mica's breath caught.

"Have you seen His Lordship lately?" she asked. *Say his name. Say his name. Say his name.*

The thin man snorted. "Do I look like I go to the pub with him?"

They were almost to the cleared space Mica had seen from the catwalk, where that poor woman had been made to scream. This might be her only chance to find out who was pulling the strings. She needed something more to go on.

"Who else do you think knows about this place? If that attacker got in . . ." She trailed off, hoping it would encourage the guard to keep talking.

"Didn't I say how careful he is? I reckon His Lordship's own nephew doesn't know what he's up to."

Mica stumbled. It couldn't be Lord Ober. He wasn't the only lord at court with a nephew. On the other hand, he *was* powerful enough to pull this off, and Mica had personally seen him show an interest in both potions and Talents. But she had thought he respected Talents, even though many of the other nobles took them for granted. She didn't want it to be him.

Fortunately, the thin-faced man hadn't noticed her stumble, seeming to think that their prisoner had tried to jerk away. He gave Danil a rough shake.

"Doesn't matter, does it?" he said. "With that spoilt princess making noise up at the palace, I reckon he'll ship the whole operation off to his own island. It was going to happen anyway."

"When will he ship—?"

"It's about time!"

They had reached the cleared space at the center of the warehouse, where the owner of the gravelly voice was waiting for them by a table spread with shiny metal instruments. The space was a grotesque imitation of Quinn's workshop, with vials of liquid, piles of finely chopped ingredients, and stacks of books and parchment. A second table dripped with blood, and beside it was a shelf with a row of jars containing human body parts. Mica tore her eyes away from the gruesome display to concentrate on the man responsible.

He was old, with thick, white eyebrows and a horribly scarred face, as if he'd been splashed over and over again with hot oil.

Mica recognized him. She had bumped into him in a crowded inn back in Gullton, not ten feet away from Lord Ober.

The man's piercing blue gaze flickered across her as if it were a tongue of flame.

"That is not Benson."

CHAPTER TWENTY-TWO

Mica released her grip on Danil and hurled herself into the old man without a thought. He was only a little bigger than she was, and she managed to shove him backward into the table full of metal instruments. They hit the ground hard, the instruments crashing down around them with a riotous clatter. Mica almost dropped her impersonation as the impact jarred her injured ribs.

"Grab him, you idiot!" the old man shouted at the thin-faced guard.

Before he could reach her, Mica lurched over to the shelves, snatched up a jar holding a floating eyeball, and chucked it at the guard. He shrieked as the glass broke, and the eyeball slithered down the side of his face. Danil wrenched out of his grip, teetering on one foot.

The thin guard scraped frantically at the putrid liquid drenching his clothes, no longer paying attention to his prisoner. But the old potioner was getting up, reaching for his vials of poison. They couldn't fight that.

"Let's get out of here!" Mica pulled Danil's arm over her shoulder and hauled him toward the front of the warehouse.

They hobbled down the aisle as fast as they could. Rattling noises came from the crates, weak voices asking what was going on out there. Behind them, the old potioner shouted for more guards, his gravel voice poisoned with pure rage.

"The others," Danil grunted as he struggled along on his surviving foot. "We have to save them."

"We'll come back for them." Mica couldn't slow down. They were almost to the door. "And we'll bring the whole striking Imperial Army with us."

Danil didn't argue. Footsteps pounded as more guards converged on them from the corners of the warehouse, where they'd been searching for the intruder. *Too many.* They were too close.

The locked door loomed ahead of them.

"Brace yourself!" Mica shouted, and she and Danil threw themselves at the door.

It burst open under their combined weight, and they tumbled out into the pouring rain, Mica barely keeping her friend from pitching into the mud.

"Keep moving," she said. "Just a little bit farther."

They rushed away from the warehouse, taking frequent turns through the warren-like district to throw off their pursuers. Shouts chased them through the dark. Every second, Mica was sure they would be caught. Still, she noted the twists and turns, adding them to her mental map so she could find the warehouse later. She was going to rip that gruesome operation wide open.

Eventually, the rain drowned out the sounds of pursuit. They continued on through the muddy streets, not daring to slow down. They were almost to a main road, but Mica couldn't tell if they were still being followed. They needed to disappear.

She pulled her friend into a darkened doorway.

"Can you impersonate? We can't outrun them forever."

"I think so," Danil said. "But my leg won't—"

"I know." Limbs could be stretched and thickened into a

whole host of shapes, but they couldn't be replaced. Their pursuers would be looking for a one-legged person. Mica thought for a moment, still holding off the paralyzing horror at what had been done to her friend. There would be time for that later.

"Do that small, chubby lady." She ripped off her cloak and fastened it around Danil's waist as he shrunk into a much shorter and rounder woman. The skirt fell all the way to the ground. "That'll cover it well enough."

Mica changed into her lean old soldier form, threw away the bloodied City Watch coat, and looped her arm around Danil's waist. With luck, they'd look like an ordinary couple out for a midnight stroll. In the rain. She winced. No time to do better than that now.

They limped out to the main road, joining the late-night traffic and doing their best to look inconspicuous. Most passersby kept their heads down anyway, those who weren't swaying drunkenly. Mica steered Danil toward the palace, trying not to glance back too often to see if they were being followed.

As the fear of being caught faded, she began to feel the pain in her cracked rib more intensely. She bit back a groan, knowing Danil was in far worse shape than she was. She wished she had something to give him.

She stopped. *The potions!* She had left the package of potions from Quinn's shop on top of the smaller warehouse. Dare she go back for it? She was less worried about the cost than about the potions causing problems for Quinn. What were the chances they'd be discovered tonight?

As if in answer, the rain fell harder than ever, making it difficult to see more than a few feet ahead. Mica doubted anyone would be searching the top of the warehouse roof tonight. Besides, if Mica had anything to say about it, they'd be tearing the place to the ground by sunrise. She hoped Lord Ober, if he was really behind all this, was ready for the wrath of the Talents.

Mica held onto that wrath as she and Danil struggled through the dark. It kept her pointed toward her destination, even as the adrenaline of their narrow escape wore off. She was beginning to shake, and not just from the anger and the cold and the pain in her rib. Over and over again, she felt the thud as she landed on Benson's back, the hot rush of blood over her hands, her blades twisting deeper. She had never killed a man before. She was supposed to stop bad guys by sneaking around and gathering information on them, not by ripping into them with steel claws. Mica wondered if Jessamyn had felt this way when she killed that Obsidian captain to save her life.

"Mica," Danil said, perhaps sensing her tremors. "You did the right thing. They were monsters."

"I know," Mica said shortly. But she squeezed her friend a little tighter, her lean arms around his soft shoulders. "We're almost there."

She couldn't take Danil directly to the palace in case his presence tipped off "His Lordship," so she brought him to Peet's flat, resuming her own form as she knocked. The Blur was at the door an instant later. He ushered them in without question and helped her settle Danil on his bed.

"I'm glad you caught me here," Peet said as he dug through a pile of clothes on his floor for something Mica could wear that wasn't covered in blood and mud. "I only just returned from visiting Edwina at her inn."

The young Talent held out a shirt, trousers, and a plain red coat. Mica turned herself back into a man briefly so she could change her clothes in the tiny room.

"I know where Edwina's husband is," she said as she tugged the shirt over her head. "Along with all the other Talents."

"Not all of them," Danil said, lifting his head from the bed.

"What do you mean?"

"They shipped people out sometimes. After they finished."

"Finished what?"

Danil's face went dark. "You'd better hurry, Mica. They need to be stopped before they move anyone else."

"The princess will help us." She put on the red coat. "Will you be okay here for a little while?"

"I'll look after him," Peet said. "Maybe I'll make us a midnight snack."

"Thank you, Peet." Mica paused at the door. "Before I go, Danil, did you ever hear who was behind . . . everything you went through?"

"There was a lord, a powerful one, I think." Danil propped himself up on his elbows to speak to her, rainwater still dripping from his curls. "They were always careful not to say his name. I can identify a few of the guards, though, and the potioner is called Haddell. I'll never forget that as long as I live."

A tense silence beat between them. Mica felt horror bubbling within her again at what her kind, merry friend had endured. Horror—and rage.

"We'll stop him," Mica said. "I'll be back as soon as I can."

Mica ran the rest of the way to the palace, wearing Peet's face and red hair as well as his clothes until she got to the gates, where she turned into her favorite scullery maid. She tried to keep out of sight anyway. It was late to be running through the palace corridors, and she couldn't afford to be stopped and questioned. The rain had washed the blood from her hands, but she felt as if everyone she passed could see it on her, see right through her. She pushed away the distress and focused on the rage.

Mica reverted to her own face when she reached Jessamyn's chambers. Banner must have seen the urgency in her expression because he stepped out of her way as she ripped open the small door set in the larger one and burst into the sitting room.

"Princess Jes—"

Lord Ober was standing in the princess's chambers.

Mica swallowed everything she had been about to say as she met the lord's eyes. He nodded at her, looking as pleasant as ever. Jessamyn leapt up from her couch, her eyes igniting.

"Can't you see I'm busy, Micathea?" she hissed. Then in a much more jovial voice: "You must excuse her, my lords. I've no doubt there's a perfectly good explanation for this boorish intrusion, which I will hear *later*."

"It's no trouble at all," Lord Ober said. "Far be it from me to get in the way of an Imperial Impersonator. Go right ahead and say what needs to be said, Miss Micathea." He smiled kindly at her. Mica had a sudden urge to slice off that fine specimen of a nose.

Every part of her was screaming to confront Lord Ober, but she couldn't do it like this. She had no proof the warehouse was his. All she had to go on was the brief reference to a nephew and his interest in Talents. Danil had claimed the name of the nefarious mastermind had never been said aloud. The guards and the old potioner must have been all too aware that one of the Talents could escape. She had to be careful here, even though it meant holding back her fury.

"Forgive me, it can wait." Mica dropped into a deep curtsy, pasting on a calm mask. As she stood, she realized Lord Caleb was standing over by the window, watching her with a slightly bemused expression. That was why Jessamyn had said *lords* plural. Mica couldn't help looking Caleb over, trying to gauge how much he knew. Was his mysterious ability connected to a mad potioner who kept eyeballs in jars?

Jessamyn cleared her throat, forcing Mica to turn away from the young lord. The princess jerked her head toward the tapestry on the far wall, and Mica had no choice but to cross the antechamber and enter the servants' corridor. She immediately pressed her ear to the door to listen to the discussion on the other side.

"I hope your Impersonator is serving you well, my princess," Lord Ober was saying. "She came highly recommended."

"She has disappointed me less than some."

Lord Ober laughed, the rich sound all too similar to his nephew's laugh.

"I believe we've covered everything," Lord Ober said. "I'm glad we will be unified on this matter."

"I am as well, my lord," Jessamyn said. "The empire is stronger when we work together."

No, it's not! Don't trust him!

"Agreed. I shall take my leave now, Princess." Heavy footsteps moved toward the outer door. "I look forward to seeing you at the feast."

Hurry up, you conniving traitor. Mica put her hand on the door-knob, getting ready to rush back in.

Then Caleb's voice filtered through the door. It sounded as if he was still over by the window. "I wish to visit with the princess a little longer, Uncle Ober."

"Of course. I'll leave you young people to it," Lord Ober said warmly. "May you thrive."

Mica heard the outer door close. She hesitated for only a second longer as she debated about whether to wait for Caleb to leave. That guard back at the warehouse had said His Lordship's nephew didn't know about his schemes. It was time to find out for sure.

She opened the door and flung back the tapestry. Caleb was looking right at it, as if expecting her. A smile broke across his face as she entered. She wondered if he'd stayed behind just to see her. She had no time to untangle *that* thought as Jessamyn advanced toward her.

The princess was not smiling. "Excuse me, Micathea. I didn't call—"

"It's an emergency," Mica said. "Princess, I found the missing Talents. They're being tortured and experimented on. I rescued one of them. He'll tell you more." She took a deep breath and looked straight at Caleb. "But I think Lord Ober is behind it."

Both of them stared at her for a moment in shocked silence.

"Have you taken leave of your *senses?*" Jessamyn said at last.

"I followed two members of the City Watch to a warehouse not far from the docks. I heard screaming and saw a young woman with her arms covered in blood. There's this vile old potioner, and—"

"That does *not* explain why you would accuse—"

"Excuse me, Jessa." Caleb held up a hand, interrupting the princess's rebuke. He fixed Mica with a steady gaze. "Where is this warehouse?"

Mica gave the location and described the two redbrick warehouses side by side, one big and one small—

"Connected by a wooden walkway?" Caleb finished for her.

"That's right." Mica could hardly breathe. He couldn't have known about it, could he? About the blood and the crates and the screams. Her fingers twitched toward the curved knife strapped to her thigh.

"It belongs to my uncle," Caleb said. "The warehouse. I haven't been there in years, though. It used to store the wine he imports from Timbral Island."

"Not anymore," Mica said. "It's evil, what he's doing in there."

Caleb sat down slowly, as if the truth was settling on him, pressing him down. He truly hadn't known, hadn't expected his uncle to be a monster. Mica felt a pang of sympathy for him. She herself was disappointed Lord Ober wasn't as good to Talents as he pretended. She couldn't imagine how his nephew must feel.

Suddenly, there was a terrific crash, and glass shattered across the floor. Mica whirled around. Jessamyn had smashed a crystal vase, a new one given to her just last week by one of her suitors.

"The nerve of that man!" The princess stomped across the chamber, looking for more things to throw. "Lord Ober came here tonight to talk about friendship and how we should work together for the good of Windfast. He dared ask me to be his ally while running this abhorrent scheme behind my back?" A porcelain teapot soared through the air, followed by two cups, their saucers, and the sugar bowl. It was a wonder the noise didn't wake the entire palace.

"That's why he was here?" Mica asked, staying well back from the flying crockery.

"He is about to propose that my father mobilize our armies for a series of war games," Jessamyn said. "He only wants such a grand move to shore up his influence, of course, but he had just about convinced me that a show of force would remind Obsidian we won't be intimidated. He thought he could neutralize me as an opposing voice." She reached for a decorative iron bowl, which looked heavy enough to crack open her floor.

"Princess!" Mica said. "Perhaps you should stop throwing things until—"

"I'll throw whatever I please!" Jessamyn snapped, but she put the iron bowl back where it belonged. "Fine, fine."

"Can you send in soldiers to free the Talents?" Mica said. "They might move them after tonight, and then we'll never catch them. And we have to arrest Lord Ober."

"Hold on, I'm thinking." Jessamyn paced, the shards on the floor crunching with every step.

Mica looked over at Caleb again. His hands were clasped before him, and he sat as still as if he were meditating. Though he was clearly troubled by the revelation of his uncle's schemes, Mica felt weak-kneed with relief that he hadn't known about them. She'd wanted him to be as good and kind as he seemed.

As though he sensed her watching, he looked up to meet her eyes, his gaze steady despite the turmoil within.

They watched each other, caught in a moment of pure stillness as Jessamyn raged nearby. Mica's heart beat a painful rhythm in her chest. And in that still moment, she knew with crystalline certainty that her feelings for Caleb went far beyond physical attraction. *You're in trouble now, Mica.*

The princess stopped trampling glass into her floor and put her hands on her hips.

"Lord Ober is too powerful," she announced. "I cannot simply arrest him."

"What?" Mica tore her eyes away from Caleb to stare at the princess. "I don't understand."

"Yes, well, that's why you're not in charge here, Micathea. Our relationships with the nobility of the islands are more tenuous than you may realize. Those who live here and participate in palace life with all its trappings remain invested in the politics of the empire." She waved her hand at the window. The lights of Jewel Harbor below them appeared faint through the veil of rain. "As long as the rulers of the islands have a chance to influence the emperor and perhaps marry a princess or the scion of a more powerful island, they are willing to play this game. If we start sending in imperial soldiers and arresting lords after they disagree with me publicly, they'll move out faster than you can say harbor cruise." The princess looked at Caleb now, and the fire in her eyes softened. "We can't expect the ruling families of the islands to send us their sons and daughters and uncles if we might throw them in a cell at the slightest provocation."

Mica hardly thought that warehouse counted as a *slight* provocation. "But what he's doing—"

"Is despicable," Jessamyn said. "But he must be dealt with carefully. Lord Ober is smart enough to cover his tracks. He can always claim he had no idea what was happening on his property. I think we need to dismantle this warehouse project quietly. We can't afford the tension among the nobles right now."

"Why not?"

"Because we are on the verge of war, Micathea."

"What?"

"War," Jessamyn repeated. "Haven't you been paying attention? Impersonator spies in Obsidian have picked up on increased military activity. We fear the Obsidian King may make another bid for the islands. We cannot be divided if and when he does."

Mica didn't know what to say to that. A tiny part of her wondered which Impersonator had successfully brought the threat to light. She felt an irrational certainty that it had been Tiber Warson. But war was far more serious than her petty rivalry with her old schoolmate. War meant her brothers on the front lines. War meant people dying, Talents and ordinary folk alike. War meant bigger enemies than even Lord Ober.

"Is that why we were attacked on the boat?"

"As far as I can determine, that was an act of terrorism designed to provoke us to act prematurely," Jessamyn said. "We didn't fall for it, but Lord Ober took advantage of the incident to establish himself as the warning voice against Obsidian. It has certainly won him additional friends. No doubt he seeks to usurp my influence with my father too." She frowned at the broken crystal and porcelain all over her floor as if she had no idea where it came from. "No matter. Take me to the Talent you rescued. We must discuss how best to liberate the rest without drawing the wrong kind of attention."

"I'll do it," Caleb said quietly.

"Pardon?"

He stood. "I will lead the action against this warehouse operation. That way you'll keep your hands clean, Jessa. It will be seen as a family affair, not an imperial one, if I put an end to his . . . experimentation."

Jessamyn tapped a finger against her red lips for moment. "Are you sure? I know you and your uncle are close."

"Not as close as I thought." Caleb glanced over at Mica and then back at the princess. "But you are right: the empire is stronger when the governing families of the islands are united."

Pity shone in Jessamyn's eyes as she looked at her friend. But she gave a sharp nod. "Very well. Micathea will help you. Go now, and don't tell me too many details."

"What about Lord Ober?" Mica said.

Jessamyn smiled and patted her hair. "After we cut his little scheme out from under him, I think he'll find I'm less of an ally than he thought. I believe I shall pay a visit to my father."

CHAPTER TWENTY-THREE

As they walked back to Peet's flat, Caleb asked Mica to describe what she had seen in detail, especially the boarded-up windows of the warehouse, the old potioner, and the guards. He looked up when she described how she had jumped onto Benson and clawed her knives deep into his body.

"Are you hurt?" he asked gently.

She looked away. "My rib is cracked, but I'm fine."

Caleb made a sudden movement, as if he was about to take her hand. But he pulled back, a shadow falling over his eyes.

It occurred to her as they were climbing the rickety staircase to Peet's flat that she was leading Caleb straight to the only proof of his uncle's treachery. She had been taught to suspect everyone at the Academy, and he could still be in cahoots with Lord Ober. But Mica trusted Caleb out of an instinct that went far deeper than any classroom lesson, one she couldn't begin to explain.

Peet flung open the door at the first knock. He inspected the stairwell carefully, looking for eavesdroppers or perhaps checking to see if anyone else was with them before ushering them in to see Danil.

"He was asleep before the door closed behind you," Peet said.

"I went out to get some food and a potion for the pain. I know a fellow who knows a fellow." Mica noticed he had picked up a wider array of food than usual in the few minutes he had been out, completely filling the small table. Peet blushed when she asked about it. "I thought Her Highness might be with you."

"Well, Danil looks like he needs the sustenance," Mica said. "Thanks for looking after him."

"Anything for a fellow Talent."

Mica touched Danil's shoulder, which was thinner than it used to be, thinking of all those happy afternoons he had spent trying to make her and Sapphire laugh. It was painful to see him so frail. She wished she could let him sleep, but they had work to do. She shook him gently.

Danil came awake at once, bolting upright, his hands reaching for Mica's throat. Caleb and Peet were there so fast they knocked into other as they each tried to stop him from choking her.

"It's fine," Mica said. "Danil, it's me. You're safe, remember?"

"Sorry." Danil sat back, and the aggression and tension, which were so unlike him, faded away. He rubbed his eyes with his large fists, and Mica glimpsed a shadow of her old friend.

She motioned to the other two men that it was safe to stand back. Peet was looking curiously at Caleb. He must have seen how fast the young nobleman moved. Mica asked the Blur to fix them all some tea before he could start asking too many questions.

She pulled up a chair beside Danil while Caleb watched from a respectful distance.

"We need to talk to you about the warehouse," she began.

Danil grabbed her hand, his skin feeling slightly feverish. "Is Sapphire with you?"

"She had to go to Winnow Island, but she has been worried sick about you."

"I hope she doesn't think I took off because of what we . . ."

"Don't be silly. She just wants you to be safe," Mica said firmly. "Now, why don't you tell us what happened, and then we can see about getting you two back together."

Danil hesitated. His gaze was haunted, and Mica feared he'd never again be the gentle giant she remembered. He looked past her, suspicion in his pallid features.

"Who's he?"

"This is Lord Caleb. He's here to help us."

"Is he a Talent?"

"Even better." Mica gestured for Caleb to pull up a chair. "He's a friend."

Peet handed around strong cups of tea, and Danil recounted what he had been through over the past few months, ever since he got knocked on the head by someone whose face he hadn't seen and woke up tied to the back of a horse halfway to Jewel Harbor. He had been thrown into a crate in the warehouse and pulled out every few days for the potioner with the scarred face to poke and prod. The old man had taken blood, hair, saliva, even toe nails. He had forced Danil to perform impersonation after impersonation, sometimes under the influence of different potions.

"What was he trying to do?"

"I think he wanted me to be stronger," Danil said. "It was almost as if he was trying to turn me into a Muscle."

Mica and Caleb exchanged tense glances.

"Did it work?"

"Not on me," Danil said. "I think he had some successes, if what I heard from the other prisoners is true."

"You talked to them?"

"We could speak to each other through the crates, but we had to be careful that the guards didn't catch us. Anytime one of us appeared to manifest a second Talent, they got shipped away. But when I didn't get any stronger than a normal fellow my size, the potioner started using me for parts."

He pointed at his leg, which now ended midway down his calf. Peet had cleaned and bandaged it for him while Mica was at the palace. It made her feel sick that this had been done to her friend—and most likely to others.

"Do you know why he did . . . that?"

Danil shook his head. "I heard him say once that bones are the new blood. Does that make any sense to you?"

"Some Potioners use Talent blood in their concoctions," Mica said. "Maybe he has figured out that bones work better."

Peet shuddered, wrapping his arms tight around his gangly frame. "I doubt many people want to sell their bones, no matter how hungry they get."

"I agree," Mica said. "That would explain why he abducted the Talents instead of paying them like the other potioners do." The scheme was slowly coming into focus.

"No matter what his reasoning was," Caleb said, speaking up for the first time, "we can't let this continue. Tell me more about the warehouse, sir."

Danil obliged, describing the building and its defenses in great detail. Like all good Academy-trained Impersonators, Danil had paid close attention to his surroundings, and he was able to provide a fairly complete picture of the secretive operation. He knew how many guards there were, which ones were Talents themselves—not many apart from Benson—and how some of the other Talents had been lured in.

"It was never the same way twice," Danil said. "I was nabbed from the Academy in the middle of the night. Someone else responded to a notice offering to pay Talents for their blood. Another went home with a beautiful woman. One was stolen from a boat in the middle of the harbor and delivered to the warehouse wrapped in a carpet."

"Ober is intelligent," Caleb said. "It's like him to cover his tracks, avoid patterns."

"So that's who's responsible?" Danil asked. "They never once said his name. I listened, asked everyone. Not a whisper of it."

"He wouldn't want it connected to him," Caleb said. "Or to his family." He rolled his shoulders as if shrugging off the association and leaned forward.

"Did you hear any hints of what their end goal could be?"

"We had plenty of time to think it over," Danil said. "The prevailing theory was that they were trying to create superior soldiers."

Caleb nodded. "Multiple Talents in a single individual would be formidable."

"A fifth Talent," Mica said quietly.

"So this mad potioner tortures a bunch of Talents until they're both extra fast and extra strong in order to make his own army?" Peet said. "I don't buy it."

The others looked up, surprised.

"Why is that?" Caleb asked.

"If someone did to me what he did to this poor bastard," Peet grimaced apologetically at Danil, "there isn't a chance in all the Windfast Empire I'd ever fight for him."

"Can't argue with that," Danil said.

"Maybe the Talents are just the first step," Mica said. "What if he's using them to figure out some sort of potion he can give to his own loyal men?" She looked at Caleb. "Maybe without their knowledge."

Caleb went very still. Peet and Danil talked over Mica's suggestion, their voices seeming to fade away as she watched the young lord process what had been done to him—and what could well have been done to others. This must be the closest he had ever come to uncovering the source of his strange, erratic Talents.

"Let us put an end to this," Caleb said at last. "I have a dozen fighting men in my employment. We must keep this as clean as possible. Peet, if you know any Muscles and Shields who'd like work tonight, I'd be grateful if you could rouse them. I will pay them well."

"I reckon they'd do it for free," Peet said fiercely. "That vile cretin can't come after Talents and expect us not to do something about it."

"It's all right," Caleb said. "The Pebble Islands are good for it."

He outlined a quick, efficient plan to take control of the warehouse. He clearly had a good mind for strategy, and he wasn't allowing whatever distress he may be feeling over his uncle's betrayal to get in the way. Mica was impressed. She'd never seen this side of him before.

"We may experience opposition from the City Watch," he said as they wrapped up their discussion. "I need the Shields to hold them until we determine who's actually in on the scheme and who believes we're attacking an innocent business. And remember: do not mention Princess Jessamyn's name."

"Done," Peet said. "See you at dawn!" And the young Blur rushed out, leaving the door swinging behind him.

Caleb turned to Mica. "You should stay—"

"Not a chance," she interrupted. "I'm coming with you."

"You can't be seen," Caleb said. "Ober knows who you are. We don't want him connecting this with the princess."

Mica contorted her features, turning herself into a mirror image of Caleb himself, if a bit smaller. "Problem solved."

Caleb's mouth opened in surprise as she flashed his own grin at him.

"Now that's one of the stranger things I've seen."

"You get used to it," Danil said sleepily as he settled back on his pillows. For a moment, Caleb's square features appeared on his face too.

Caleb looked between the two Impersonators and threw up his hands. "Have it your way. Let's go."

CHAPTER TWENTY-FOUR

The combined forces met at dawn outside the warehouse district. The rain had stopped, and the gray skies were giving way to a deep rose tinged with gold.

Peet had made short work of his recruitment task. Two dozen local Talents leapt from their beds and tramped through the mud at his call, eager to fight back against those who had threatened their friends and family members. They carried an assortment of humble weapons, from clubs to butchers' knives, though in many cases their bodies would be weapon enough. Mica spotted Edwina among the volunteers. The squat little Mimic had added a collection of gruesome scars to her face, and she brandished a heavy stick as she awaited the order to move. Mica wondered if the scars were actually part of her real face. Rufus had been an Army Elite, and she was beginning to suspect that Edwina had been one of Master Kiev's imperial spies, just like Mica.

Most of Caleb's men were Talents too, Blurs and Shields who responded to the young lord's direction with a swiftness and ease that spoke of excellent training. Caleb divided them up so they each led a small force of volunteers and ordered them to approach the warehouse from different directions.

"Hold as many guards as you can for questioning," he told them. "We want to keep this clean."

"Yes, my lord." The Shield who had command of Caleb's retainers snapped off a salute. A few years older than his liege, he had long brown hair and a lanky build, and he wore a coat with the Pebble Islands' sparrow sigil stitched on the chest. "I'll take the north approach."

"Thank you, Stievson. Did you bring my weapons?"

"As you commanded." Stievson held out a fine sword in a polished leather sheath, which Caleb slung around his hips. It suited him, Mica thought, and she remembered how she'd once matched her steps to his and judged him to have a soldier's stride.

"We'll wrap them up right quick, my lord," Peet called. "Can't let the bastards get away."

"All right then." Caleb caught Mica's eye and gave her a brief nod. "Let's go."

Mica fell in beside Caleb as they marched into the warehouse district, clutching curved knives in each of her hands. None of the men commented on their lord's Impersonator shadow. The warehouse district was suspiciously empty, as if the workers sensed trouble brewing. Their boots squelching through the mud sounded loud in the absence of the morning rush.

They were still a block from their destination when a messenger from one of the groups rushed back to find Caleb and Mica. Their party had surprised a pair of workers carrying a crate down to the docks. It contained a captured Talent, a Blur who had bolted the moment the crate was opened. The workers had been taken into custody.

"They didn't waste any time once they knew they'd been found," Mica said. "Danil and I made a lot of noise getting out of there."

"They probably thought they could clear the warehouse and ship out before you brought help," Caleb said. He turned back to the messenger. "Tell your team to go straight to the docks and find the ship where the crates are being loaded. I'll send another group to help commandeer it."

"Aye, my lord."

"This is good for us," Caleb said as his men rushed to do his bidding. "They're spread out. Frantic. We'll make quick work of them."

"Lead the way, my lord," Mica said.

Caleb grinned, the first time he'd smiled since he learned what his uncle had done. "It is so strange to hear you speak in my voice."

"I can wear a different face, if you like. I have plenty."

"No, keep that one," he said, suddenly serious. "My men will protect you with their lives if I fall."

"That's not going to happen," Mica said. "You're mostly impervious anyway."

"The moment I start relying on that is the moment I take a sword to the gut, remember?" Caleb touched his side, and Mica recalled the feel of the rough scar cutting through warm skin. The flesh of her own skin puckered as she added the mark beneath her shirt as a reminder. She didn't intend to let anyone stab him today.

The warehouse was already in chaos when they arrived. Guards, both in City Watch uniforms and in plain clothes, were hurriedly hauling out the crates and dismantling the potioner's grotesque workshop. If Mica and the others had waited a few hours longer to attack, all the Talents—and all the evidence—would be gone.

When the first team of local Talents rushed the doors, the guards tried to run, but the others were waiting to intercept them. Caleb had planned the attack well, and once they fell to the task, overwhelming the guards and freeing the remaining Talents was relatively simple. Mica suspected Caleb and his men could have taken control of the warehouse without the help of the Jewel

Harbor Talents. Even her soldier brothers would have been impressed with their discipline and skill.

Caleb himself clearly trained often with his men. Mica had seen him fight with a makeshift weapon before, but he wielded his own sword with calm grace, occasionally interrupted by bursts of unnatural strength and speed. She understood now why he avoided dancing as much as possible. No one could watch him move without seeing that something was different about him. He adapted quickly as his strength and speed shifted, and at least once a sword glanced right off his skin without cutting into it. Still, Mica knew it was only a matter of time before the bursts of Talent stole the last of his strength. She stayed near him through the assault, ready to pull him out of danger if his body gave way. He seemed equally aware of her, moving to block attacks when her knives wouldn't suffice. It felt right somehow, as if they'd been born to fight side by side.

As they cut their way down the center aisle, Mica caught sight of Edwina advancing on her husband's kidnappers, laying into them with her stick like a baker flattening dough. They stood little chance against her fury. Before long, the clash of swords and smack of fists gave way to cries of joy as the last of the guards were captured or sent running. Only one person struggled on in the face of defeat: Haddell the potioner.

The old man had fought viciously, throwing acid at any who challenged him until a pair of Caleb's sword-wielding Shields managed to wound him and chase him from his morbid workshop. The potions he tossed at them over his shoulder burned their clothes away in patches, but they eventually cornered him at the back of the warehouse, the last of his poisons spent.

Caleb ordered the Shields to stand down and advanced on the potioner, backing him up against the redbrick wall. Mica stayed by his side, breathing heavily from the fight. If her strength was spent, Caleb was sure to fall at any moment. But he could be about to learn why and how he'd been cursed.

"It's all over," Caleb said as he strode toward the potioner. The man's blue eyes were wild, and he was bleeding from a stab to the gut. He wouldn't last much longer without help. "There's no point in fighting. I need to know what you've been trying to do here."

"Trying?" The old man laughed maniacally. "I have been succeeding!"

"Tell me more," Caleb said. "I'll allow you to save yourself with a healing tonic, if you cooperate."

The potioner gave a sticky cough and grinned, his scars stretching. "You don't even remember me, do you, boy?"

Caleb didn't react, his grip on his sword holding steady.

"I've worked with your uncle a long time," the potioner said, "since he first started developing his theories. You used to visit us in my workshop when you were small."

"You must be Haddell," Caleb said calmly. "I remember. How many other potioners are engaged in this project? Or are you his only one?"

"His best, his best." Haddell cackled madly, giving the impression that he was a harmless old loon. But Mica didn't fall for it. She had heard his gruff, gravelly shout earlier. She knew the madness was an act, an impersonation.

"Ober knows his stuff, he does," Haddell went on. "He's gotten better since his first experiments. But *you'd* know all about that."

Caleb's shoulders tensed. "What do you mean?"

"You were one of the first." The man giggled, and blood bubbled at the edge of his lips.

Mica got ready. He'd try something as soon as he thought Caleb was distracted. She edged closer, trying not to attract attention. Sure enough, the old potioner's hand began inching toward his pocket.

Haddell grinned at Caleb. "I didn't think he should try it on one so young, not when the formula was so new, so untested. But he wanted to. Yes, he was sure of himself, even then."

"Whatever he did, it didn't work very well," Caleb said, some of his calm slipping. "You were right."

"I was." The potioner bowed his head, and his fingers closed on something in his pocket.

There was a glint of glass. A tiny bottle. Mica tensed. She'd only have one chance.

"He felt guilty about your condition. Oh yes, for years. He did try to make it up to you. I suspect he loves you, if it makes you feel better."

"It doesn't," Caleb said. "Where are the others he has used to test this formula? Timbral Island?"

"I'm sure you'd like to know." The potioner beckoned him with a wrinkled hand, as if about to share a secret. "Maybe you'll find the others, if you look where you least wish them to be."

Caleb frowned, leaning in a little. "Where I—?"

Haddell threw the tiny bottle at Caleb so fast Mica almost missed it. She leapt forward just in time to swat the bottle aside. It shattered against the brick wall, which immediately began to disintegrate, issuing clouds of acrid smoke. By the time the smoke cleared, the old potioner had slumped to the ground and breathed his last.

"Mica!" Caleb looked between her and where the brick was being eaten away by the potion. "You could have been—"

"So could you," she said.

"I should have seen it coming. Thank you."

They retreated a few paces from the dead potioner and the acrid smoke, Mica feeling slightly giddy from the near miss. She hadn't been sure if the bottle would break open on her hands when she knocked it aside. She looked up at Caleb. His hair was tousled, and his square face was smudged—and he'd never looked more handsome.

"I have your back, you know," she said.

He stared at her for a minute, looking a little dazed too. Then he barked a laugh.

"My back. I get it."

Abruptly, Mica remembered she was still wearing Caleb's features. She went red and immediately switched to her freckled city woman form.

"Don't ever tell another Mimic I said that," she muttered. "It's the worst joke in the book."

Caleb chuckled, and she saw a hint of that youth from the hilltop in Gullton, good humored and gallant despite what he'd been through tonight.

"Anything for the woman who saved my life."

They smiled at each other, surrounded by carnage in that grim warehouse, and the moment felt weighty somehow. Significant.

Feeling suddenly shy, Mica looked away from the young lord to appraise the results of their actions this morning.

The fighting was done, and the remaining Talents were being freed. Mica saw Edwina order a young Muscle girl to break open a crate, and her husband tumbled out, looking slightly rumpled but whole. Others hadn't fared as well. Danil wasn't the only one to lose a limb. Mica wouldn't soon forget the sight of these battered and broken people who'd been kept in darkness for so long. Worse, she had a feeling this was only part of a larger scheme.

The Jewel Harbor Talents tended to the wounded while Caleb's men tied up the captured guards and marched them to the center of the warehouse. Too many wore City Watch uniforms. It would take time to unravel how deep Lord Ober's influence ran among Jewel Harbor's defenders. And where had he taken the rest of the Talents? His own island or somewhere less obvious? The fighting may be done, but Mica's work was only beginning.

She made her bottom lip grow and shrink as she considered what to do next in these still moments after the battle.

"It drives me crazy when you do that."

"What?" Mica turned. Caleb had come closer. He was looking at her bottom lip, which she'd been contorting almost without thinking about it. She let it settle into shape—her shape, not the one matching the rest of the face she wore.

He reached up to touch her lips, brushing them with the pad of his thumb. She stopped breathing.

"Mica," he said softly.

"Yes?"

He didn't say anything more, only looked at her, yet she had the feeling that he was looking at her and really *seeing* her, past the impersonation and her mission and his noble status. A lump formed in her throat. She could hardly express how much she wanted to be *seen*.

She slowly changed her eyes back to her own plain hazel.

Caleb leaned in, as if the strange color had been a barrier holding him back. He took her chin gently in his square hand and kissed her on the mouth. Mica hardly dared to move, afraid one more shift of her features would make him stop.

The kiss was feather light, almost chaste, as if it were a solemn thing to bring their lips together. Mica's eyes fluttered closed at the exquisite touch.

He pulled back far too soon, scanning her face. Clouds were forming in his eyes, as if his uncle's betrayal was finally catching up to him. Mica wanted to fling her arms around his neck, to kiss him again and promise they'd figure it out together. But before she could move toward him, he released her and walked back to rejoin his men.

It took a few hours to clean up the warehouse and question the guards. They insisted they had no idea where the ships took the Talents they removed from the city, and not a single one mentioned their lord's name.

Caleb promised the gathered Talents that he would bring the perpetrators to justice. They hurried to shake his hand and offer their thanks before dispersing to their homes. He had earned the respect and admiration of many tonight. Rumors about the noble rescuer of captive Talents would spread. There'd be no mention of the Impersonator who'd fought at Caleb's side or the role she had played in uncovering the plot. Mica recalled Master Kiev's speech from her Assignment Ceremony. This was how it should be.

When Caleb's knees buckled at last, Stievson and the others carried him back to the Silver Palace without comment. Mica hadn't had a chance to talk with him about what the potioner had said.

You were one of the first.

Ober and Haddell must have succeeded in generating multiple Talents in others. How many were there, and did they have more control over their abilities than Caleb did? What if Ober already had men who were fast, strong, and impervious, and who wouldn't be knocked flat after using those skills?

She would talk it over with Caleb as soon as he recovered. After what they had accomplished tonight, she had little doubt they would work together again. She was already looking forward to it—and to the next time he'd press his lips against hers. She was surprised at how little she cared that he was a fancy lord now.

It wasn't until she returned to her rooms and fell into bed that Mica remembered she had forgotten to retrieve Jessamyn's potions from the rooftop of the second warehouse.

CHAPTER TWENTY-FIVE

R umors ran wild about the raid on the mysterious warehouse of horrors over the next few days. No one had connected the incident with Lord Ober, but everyone knew the dashing Lord Caleb had saved dozens of captive Talents from an evil potioner.

"I hear he stabbed the madman himself," Lady Elana said when a group of ladies gathered to discuss it in the conservatory. "He fought side by side with his own guards."

"Incredible," said Lady Amanta.

Mica moved a little closer, pruning shears clutched in her hands. She was impersonating a gardener this afternoon, an easy task after her recent adventures.

"And remember how he led the charge on the harbor cruise?"

"It must have been terrifying," said Lady Amanta.

"Yes, but he was so brave." Elana sighed.

"Caleb has *always* been the heroic type," said Lady Ingrid, who was usually loath to agree with Elana on anything. "I'm not at all surprised."

"When did he become so attractive, though?" Elana said.

"Those waistcoats he wears . . ." She twirled a finger through her red hair, a dreamy smile on her lips.

"I bet Jessamyn is looking at him differently now." Lady Amanta gave a bawdy chuckle, and the others tittered in agreement. Mica clipped the leaves off a nearby rosebush a little too aggressively.

It had occurred to her that the kiss could have been an impulsive act in the aftermath of battle, nothing more. Caleb was still a member of the nobility, Mica was not, and the princess herself could end up choosing him as a consort. But Mica couldn't reason away her feelings. Besides, Caleb was a true gentleman, not just a noble. He wouldn't kiss her like that unless he meant it.

"Who was responsible for that horrid place anyway?" Lady Elana asked.

"I heard the potioner acted on his own," Lady Ingrid said. "He was a lunatic, after all."

"Raving," Lady Amanta agreed.

Mica figured it was just as well that no one knew how lucid Haddell had been when he committed his atrocities. So far none of the rumors mentioned a noble mastermind behind the operation or tied the princess to the raid. Jessamyn seemed content to allow the mad potioner narrative to spread. If Lord Ober was angry that his nephew had taken it upon himself to clear out the warehouse, he hid it well. Caleb was safely sequestered in his rooms, protected by Stievson and his loyal retainers while he slept off the effects of using his Talents.

Mica still didn't understand why they couldn't arrest Lord Ober. She said as much to the princess as they prepared for a royal feast in the princess's dressing room a few days after the raid.

"Lord Ober could be assembling an army of loyalists with exceptional abilities," Jessamyn said. "Which of these goes better?" She held up two different strings of pearls against her metallic gold gown.

"That one." Mica pointed without really examining the choices. The necklaces looked the same to her anyway.

"Thought so." Jessamyn looped the pearls around her neck.

"About Lord Ober...?"

"We can't tell how far he got on his little scheme. We mustn't imprison him until we know whether a large force of super soldiers will descend on us to rescue him."

"Are you so sure he's building an army?"

"What else would a man as ambitious as Lord Ober do with a potion like that?" Jessamyn opened her case of crowns and tiaras and surveyed them with a critical eye. "It has happened before. Don't they teach history at the Academy? I really must speak to my father about that place."

"Why is it so important for his island to stay in the empire?" Mica asked. "Why not let them go off and be the independent Kingdom of Timbral?"

Jessamyn gave a longsuffering sigh. "Haven't we talked about why the Windfast was formed in the first place, Micathea?"

"To fight the armies of Obsidian."

"Exactly. Any islands that break away would be vulnerable to the dark kingdom, and every piece of the empire we lose makes us a little weaker."

Mica thought of her brothers and her parents, who fought side by side with men and women from all over the empire. They were Talented and disciplined, but the dread armies from across the sea were vast.

"So it comes back to Obsidian again?"

"Always." Jessamyn settled on a crown at last, silver with a large pearl dangling from the center. "That's better. Now, remember: I shall oppose Lord Ober tonight when he thinks I've agreed to support him. I need you to keep a careful watch on Lords Dolan and Nobu, and on Lady Wendel. I believe they are on the fence about the wisdom of escalating hostilities. I want to know how they react when I disagree with Lord Ober's war games proposal."

"Yes, Princess." Mica moved to the mirror to tie a scarf around her hair. She would impersonate a serving girl tonight so she could listen in on the gossip. The nobles rarely looked at the men and women pouring their drinks. "But are you sure he'll still suggest the war games after what happened?"

"He can't allow the warehouse scandal to affect him. He has spent days drumming up support for his war games proposal. If he pulls out now, his allies will wonder why."

Mica frowned. "But *you* promised to support him, Princess. Are you sure it's a good idea to go back on your word? I'm afraid if Lord Ober gets angry—"

"I expect he will be very angry indeed, especially when he realizes I've persuaded my father to take my side in advance."

"Aren't you playing with fire here?"

"That has never stopped me from opposing a bad idea before." Jessamyn gave Mica a wicked smile in the mirror, resplendent in her gown and pearls. "*I* am not afraid of Lord Ober."

And she turned and sauntered out of the dressing room.

The feast took place in the banquet hall in the heart of the Silver Palace. Hundreds of candles were arranged around the walls, filling the room with dancing light. The scent of roses and burning wax hung in the air. All the usual nobles were there, dressed in costly gowns and silk coats, clutching crystal goblets in jeweled hands. Mica was surprised to find that the grandeur had become commonplace over the past few months. Her brothers would never believe she walked among such finery without blinking.

Princess Jessamyn was in rare form that night. She circled

among the guests before the feast, enchanting the lords with secret smiles and whispering conspiratorially with the ladies. Her metallic gown shimmered in the candlelight, perfectly complementing her dark-red hair, which fell in loose curls down her back. She exuded pure charm, making everyone at the banquet want to be near her and drink in a little of her magic. She even shared a toast with Lord Ober and Lady Euphia before inviting everyone to take their seats.

As the nobles feasted on roasted meats and fine cheeses dripping with honey, Mica moved slowly down the long banquet table, pouring drinks and listening to snippets of discussion. The conversations were rife with the witty banter with an undercurrent of falsehood that Mica had come to think of as the language of the Silver Palace. No one could ever say exactly what they meant or appear too earnest. For some, there was nothing more pathetic than sincerity. It was why Elana and Ingrid were giggling together despite their mutual hatred, why the emperor and his daughter hid the closeness of their own relationship, and why Caleb stood out so sharply amongst the Rivens and Dolans of the imperial court.

When Mica paused to refill Elana and Ingrid's glasses, the ladies were *still* gushing about Lord Caleb's heroics, even though the man himself wasn't there. Mica was disappointed he wasn't yet well enough to attend the feast. She'd wanted to see if he recognized her in her current guise. Perhaps if Caleb identified her in yet another face, it would prove he too had deeper feelings.

Focus on the task at hand, she reminded herself. *You have to thwart Lord Ober. Then you can think about his nephew.*

The more Mica grew to care for Caleb, the more she wanted to find out exactly what his uncle had done to him. It was Ober's fault Caleb was left bedridden after using the volatile abilities he never should have had in the first place. She hoped there was a chance his curse could be lifted.

The nobles feasted on, their laughter echoing around the vast hall as the candles burned low. They gossiped and teased and engaged in frivolous chatter while Mica waited impatiently for the showdown. It wasn't until the dessert wines were brought out that Lord Ober leaned toward Emperor Styl and suggested mobilizing imperial forces for war games on Talon.

The babble died down at once, as if everyone had been waiting for this point in the evening.

"It will remind the King of Obsidian that we are powerful," Lord Ober said after outlining his proposal, "but it stops short of open hostilities."

"And what do your peers think of the idea?" Emperor Styl asked, his face as inscrutable as ever.

Several nobles were quick to voice their agreement, probably those Lord Ober had approached in advance. Mica took careful note of everyone who spoke up for Ober. The most vocal supporter of the proposition was Lady Ingrid of Talon.

War games would be great for her island's economy, Mica thought, surprised at how easily the realization came to her. She was finally starting to understand how these nobles operated. *But what is Lord Ober getting out of the war games?* There was still a missing piece here, and she wasn't sure what it meant.

"We must show we will not be intimidated," Lord Ober declared as approval for his proposal spread. He drew himself up, handsome and distinguished in the candlelight, far more charismatic than the marble-faced emperor. "We shall remind our own people, as well as our enemies, of the strength of the Windfast Empire."

The nobles nodded, looking to the energetic lord and murmuring about how war games could be just what the empire needed. Lord Ober certainly knew how to command a room.

Then Emperor Styl raised a hand, and the banquet hall instantly went silent.

Every face turned toward the head of the table, and Mica revised her earlier opinion. Emperor Styl may not be charming, but he used intimidating gravity as effectively as Jessamyn and Ober used charm. When he spoke, even the most arrogant nobles listened.

"Your proposal has some potential," the emperor said, tapping his fingertips together, "but I query the wisdom of escalating tensions right now."

"I understand these concerns, Your Majesty. Perhaps we could seek your esteemed daughter's counsel?" Lord Ober bowed gallantly to the princess, not hiding the complete confidence on his face. "Princess Jessamyn, I know the whole court values your opinion. What do you think of my proposition?"

"Thank you for asking, my lord." Jessamyn took a dainty sip of her dessert wine. "I believe mobilizing our forces, even if it is only for war games, will exacerbate an already delicate situation. I do *not* think we should do it."

The chivalrous smile slipped from Ober's face.

"Some were quick to call for violence after the harbor cruise incident," Jessamyn continued. "You were among them, Lord Ober, but that turned out to be an act of pure pettiness by a disgruntled servant."

Cold wrath crept into Ober's eyes at the realization that Jessamyn had played him. The sight made Mica want to reach for her hidden knives. It only got worse as the princess went on.

"You were so convinced Obsidian was responsible that you nearly pushed us into an unjustified conflict then too."

"That's true," someone murmured. "Lord Ober wanted us to take action."

"So rash."

"Yes, we don't need a fight."

"Our empire *is* strong," Jessamyn said, speaking to the rest of the nobles now. "We needn't resort to posturing by sending our soldiers running around Talon for no reason. Let us put aside this idea of playing at war."

"Hear! Hear!" Lord Fritz shouted.

Lord Dolan raised a goblet. "The princess is as wise as she is beautiful!"

Jessamyn gave him a radiant smile, and several other nobles rushed to agree. Lord Ober remained silent, watching her accept the compliments of those sitting around her, his face reddening beneath his sculpted beard.

He was still watching the princess when Emperor Styl said, "My daughter is indeed wise. I'm sorry, Lord Ober, but I will not approve this war games proposal today. Let us focus on strengthening the empire without needless posturing."

"Of course, Your Majesty." Lord Ober inclined his head slightly, never taking his eyes off Princess Jessamyn. "I live to serve the empire."

After the feast, the nobles strolled up to the ballroom to spend the rest of the evening dancing and drinking. Lord Ober lurked in a corner of the promenade, speaking to anyone who approached him, but not seeking out conversation as he usually did. Mica circulated around the balcony, refilling wine goblets and keeping a close watch on the Timbral lord. She wished mindreading were a Talent. She wanted to know if he was starting to suspect Jessamyn was responsible for *both* of his recent setbacks.

Lord Ober remained in a foul mood all evening. He even refused to dance with his wife, whispering a sharp retort in her ear when she asked him to join her. Lady Euphia's face went pale beneath her too-thick powder, and she turned and left the banquet hall.

Mica couldn't help wondering whether Lord Ober's anger was disproportionate to the situation. Why had he been so determined to initiate the war games? Could it have been a cover for his own plans involving the multi-Talented army Jessamyn was so convinced he was building? Whatever it was, Jessamyn had made a dangerous enemy. They had already seen what Ober was capable of.

Mica was supposed to stay behind to help clean up after the last of the nobles vacated the ballroom, but when Lord Ober left a few minutes after the princess retired for the night, Mica shifted to a face she had never used before and followed him.

She half expected Lord Ober to attack Jessamyn in the corridor, but he strolled in the direction of his own quarters in the west wing instead. Mica flitted along behind him, a shadow in a shadowy hall. Ober didn't look back, and he paused only once to speak to a passing Shield. Mica edged close enough to hear him asking about the Shield's elderly parents, sounding as amiable as ever. The pleasant tone in Ober's voice struck Mica as suspicious given how angry he had seemed earlier. He couldn't have been replaced by an Impersonator, could he? She hadn't taken her eyes off him all night

Impersonator or not, Lord Ober didn't take any detours on his way back to his chambers. He went straight inside and did not reemerge. Mica watched from around a corner for as long as she could, but the door showed no signs of opening.

What are you up to in there?

Lord Ober would not accept defeat this easily, but Jessamyn and Caleb had both insisted he was a cautious man. He would plan his retaliation with the same meticulous care he had used in hiding his connection to the warehouse. Though a sense of uneasiness lingered in the pit of Mica's stomach, at last she concluded that he would not take action tonight.

As she abandoned her vigil, Mica considered stopping by Caleb's rooms to see how he was feeling. But that may cross a line in a way that couldn't be explained by the afterglow of battle. Besides, she had a feeling she needed to be at the princess's side tonight.

"It's about time you got back!" Jessamyn said when Mica reported to her chambers. "Tell me everything."

While Mica filled the princess in on what she had observed during the feast, Jessamyn waltzed around her sitting room as if the tale of her triumph gave her life. She was especially pleased when Mica described how Lord Ober's face had gone brick red when he realized Jessamyn had turned on him.

"That's what he gets for trying to neutralize me."

Mica was nervous rather than gleeful. She couldn't help feeling they had missed something, some weakness.

"Do you think he suspects you had the warehouse raided? He knew you were with Caleb that night."

"It is too much of a coincidence for him *not* to connect the events," Jessamyn said, "but he cannot prove it any more than I can prove he was behind the warehouse in the first place. Oh, I do wonder what his next move will be." She strolled to her side table, where the tea service she had shattered a few nights ago had already been replaced with a new one—silver instead of breakable porcelain. She poured herself some tea, chuckling over this game she and Lord Ober were playing.

"We still need to be careful," Mica said. "Maybe I should impersonate Lady Euphia, see if I can get him to tell me something."

"I doubt he tells that silly biddy anything," Jessamyn said breezily, "but you may try."

Mica frowned, thinking over Jessamyn's words. She remembered Lord Ober rebuking Lady Euphia for asking him to dance. How had such a calculating man ended up with her? Was it possible she too was hiding something beneath a frivolous face?

"Go get some rest, Micathea." The princess sipped her tea, clearly untroubled. "We shall have schemes aplenty in the morning."

"Yes, Princess." Mica started toward the servants' quarters, though she had no intention of resting. She planned to leave through the back staircase to visit Danil at Peet's. He would be setting out to join Sapphire soon.

But as Mica pulled back the tapestry, something caught her eye on the side table. A small glass vial lay on its side next to the silver teapot. It had Magic Q's curling logo on the side. She snatched it up.

"Where did this come from?"

"What *are* you talking about?" Jessamyn took another sip of her tea. Her cup was almost empty.

"This vial." Mica held it up, hands shaking.

"It's to help me sleep. You know I have various potions for—"

"But where did it *come* from? You ran out. I didn't bring back the last—"

"Calm down, Micathea. Quinn personally delivered replacements for the potions you so carelessly lost. There's a reason I am her most loyal customer."

Mica felt as if the floor were falling away as she stared at the empty vial, the teacup Jessamyn had already drained. "How . . ." She stopped to clear her throat. "How did she know I lost the others?"

Jessamyn froze. They looked at each other, and pure stillness filled the room for one heartbeat. Two.

Then the silver teacup hit the floor.

And Jessamyn's face began to melt.

CHAPTER TWENTY-SIX

M ica ran through the palace as fast as she could, her features shifting wildly, panic nearly blinding her. Jessamyn's screams seemed to chase after her as she sprinted toward the west wing.

Mica had left the princess with Banner, the Shield holding her in his arms as poison spread through her body. Jessamyn had still been alive, but Mica didn't know how much longer she'd hold out. She could still see the horrifying way Jessamyn's skin had blistered and slid, as if she were being held too close to a fire.

Don't think about it. Keep moving.

Mica forced Jessamyn's features onto her own face as she turned the final corner and adopted the princess's angriest strut.

"I must see Lord Caleb at once," she declared to the guard posted outside the door. It was Stievson, the Shield with long brown hair she'd met a few days ago at the warehouse.

"I beg your pardon, my lady," he said, "but I am under strict orders—"

"I am not some *lady*," Mica snapped. "Honestly, I must speak to Lord Caleb about your training. Let me pass at once."

Stievson ducked his head apologetically, long hair swaying. "Yes, Princess Jessamyn."

Mica put her hands on her hips, continuing to glare at him. "*Well?*"

Stievson winced, jumping forward to open the door for her. "Forgive me, Princess Jessamyn. Allow me, Princess Jessamyn."

Mica sauntered past him without another look. She didn't pay attention to the austere décor in Caleb's antechamber, which was unoccupied, or even check to see if he was awake in the inner room. She went straight to a side table where numerous vials and bottles were arranged beside a water pitcher. Caleb was the only person in the palace she knew for certain had powerful health tonics on hand at all times. Her hands shook badly as she dumped all the vials into a sack and carried them out again. Stievson looked surprised to see her leave so soon, but she didn't pause to explain.

She wished for Blur speed as she raced headlong through the opulent corridors toward the princess's rooms. She might have a potion in her bag that would grant it temporarily, but she didn't have time to find out. She hoped Lord Ober hadn't tainted Caleb's potion supply. He must be angry with his nephew for dismantling the warehouse, but Mica didn't think he'd poison him outright. No, Ober had laid the blame squarely at Jessamyn's feet.

Please don't let her be dead.

Mica hadn't realized how much she had come to care for the princess. Jessamyn could be frustrating, but Mica admired her too. She was daring in the face of the powerful, deftly walking the tightrope of imperial politics for the good of the empire. And she had saved Mica's life, delivering a deadly blow without hesitation to rescue her hired Talent. That was the kind of princess Mica could stand behind.

Please, please don't let her be dead.

She kicked the door open and rushed over to Banner, who

still sat on the carpet where she'd left him, holding Jessamyn in his arms.

"Is she—?"

"We don't have much time," Banner said.

The princess had gone quiet, no longer screaming or whimpering. Her breath was a low rattle. Mica couldn't bear to look at her face.

She dumped the potion bottles onto the plush carpet and set aside anything with a label mentioning healing or energy. It looked as though Caleb had been trying all kinds of treatments to manage his condition. She wished she could trust a potioner to tell her which to use, but Quinn was the only one she knew, and she had delivered the poison in the first place.

Mica pulled open Jessamyn's cracked lips to pour the first draught down her throat. The princess coughed up half of it before Mica could get her to swallow a few drops. She unstopped another bottle and hesitated.

"Use them all," Banner said.

"This one is for Shield—"

"Just do it."

Mica poured the healthful doses into Jessamyn's mouth one by one.

After she administered the potions, Mica steeled herself to really look at Jessamyn's face. The skin on the left side had bubbled and slid, rendering her features completely unrecognizable. On the right, Jessamyn's delicate complexion was marred with burn-like patches of rough red skin. It looked as if a similar pattern continued down her body. Her neck, her hands, her ankles. Wherever skin was visible, it was either patchy and burned or waxy and misshapen.

Neither Mica nor Banner spoke as they waited for some sign that the potions were taking effect. The Shield cradled the princess's head tenderly, smoothing back her sweat-damp hair.

Mica wondered if, while Brin had been pining after Banner, he had been pining after someone else.

The seconds ticked past. Mica couldn't tell if the healing potions were helping, but the damage didn't seem to be getting any worse.

Come on, Princess. You can fight this.

Swallowing a lump in her throat, Mica took Jessamyn's less-damaged hand, which was covered with raised red marks, as if it had been splashed with acid. The princess's eyes remained closed, but the poison no longer seemed to be spreading.

You have to pull through.

Jessamyn was too vivacious to die. She couldn't be defeated by the likes of Lord Ober.

A picture formed in Mica's mind of Lady Euphia marching out of the ballroom after Lord Ober whispered in her ear. It had happened right in front of her. She had missed the danger, dismissing Euphia as quickly as everyone else did.

Aren't you supposed to see through people's masks?

Mica wondered if Quinn had betrayed them too, or if Euphia had sent an Impersonator to the princess's door with the potion. No matter who carried out the orders, *Mica* had been the one who told Lord Ober the identity of Jessamyn's trusted potion supplier. This was her fault.

The princess's breathing seemed to ease a little, but every breath Mica took felt rougher and more ragged. She pressed her forehead to the princess's hand, fighting back tears.

"I'm sorry," she whispered, not caring that Banner could hear. "I'm so sorry."

Were the marks on Jessamyn's hands smaller? A few of the welts on her face looked a little less angry than they had moments ago, less red and inflamed.

Mica swore to herself that she'd never let the princess down again if she'd only wake up. She held her breath, clutching Jessamyn's mottled hand, begging for another chance.

The princess's eyelids twitched.

"Princess?"

Another twitch.

"Princess, can you hear me?"

Her lids stopped fluttering.

"Jessamyn?" Mica raised her voice, afraid she'd imagined the tiny spark of life. "Jessa!"

Then the princess opened her eyes. "Honestly, Micathea. Where are your manners?" she rasped. "I expect to be addressed by my formal title at all times."

Mica sat back, relief flooding through her. Banner burst into tears.

Jessamyn turned her head from side to side, wincing as the movement pulled at her damaged skin. She looked between her Mimic and her Shield.

"Well? Who is going to tell me why I am not dead?"

Jessamyn forbade Mica and Banner from leaving her chambers until they knew how bad her condition was. She didn't want so much as a whisper to get out that she had been poisoned—or that she had survived.

"He is more powerful than I thought if he dared an assassination attempt," she said as they settled her in her grand canopy bed. "We must wait for him to show his hand."

Mica wasn't sure what that meant, but she was too relieved Jessamyn had survived to argue. She thought for sure Lord Ober would be arrested now. If he wasn't, Mica had half a mind deal with him herself.

"Ober has a plan," Jessamyn insisted. "We will see what it is soon enough."

Mica wondered if she was in too much pain to think straight. The health potions had stopped the progress of the poison and reduced the worst of the burn marks, but they didn't seem to be healing any more than that. Jessamyn was unrecognizable as the beauty who had spoken up at the feast in a golden gown and pearls.

Mica paced around the antechamber, exercising her impersonations and impatiently waiting for—whatever the princess expected to happen. She wanted to know what was going on in the rest of the Silver Palace. She wanted to check on Caleb, Danil, and Quinn. She wanted to kill the man who had tried to murder her princess. Most of all, Mica wanted to avoid thinking about how *she* had enabled it. *She* had given away the princess's secret potioner and then left her potions at the warehouse for Ober to find.

Banner seemed almost as anxious as Mica. He fretted over the bedridden princess, ordered sugary treats from the kitchens (not allowing Alea, the maid who delivered the food, so much as a glimpse inside the bedroom), and even offered to spoon-feed her. Jessamyn thanked him graciously for every bite, her bearing positively regal as she lay back on her pillows.

Mica was too nervous to eat. She fought against her guilt, pacing and pacing as the sun rose above Amber Island in the distance.

She watched the slow progress of daylight through the vast window, itching to take action. But Jessamyn told her to wait a little longer. Lord Ober would grow impatient. He would make his move. Mica didn't know how they'd know what it was when they were cloistered here, but the princess could display the patience of a gargoyle when she wanted to.

What is she waiting for?

Lord Ober couldn't show his hand any clearer than he already had. He was a traitor to the Windfast Empire. He had mutilated scores of Talents and poisoned the princess. If nothing else, that ought to be enough to have his head removed from his shoulders and every inch of his island buried in salt.

But still, Jessamyn waited.

When the sun was a full, golden ball above the harbor, about to tip past its zenith, a knock sounded on the door.

"Ah," Jessamyn said. "I suspect we are about to learn something very interesting."

Mica hurried to the door and found Peet bouncing on his toes in the corridor.

"I have an urgent message for the princess!"

"Stay out there!" Jessamyn shouted. There was a low murmur of voices and a rustle of fabric, then she said, "I will receive you now, good sir."

Mica escorted Peet through the sitting room to the bedchamber, where Banner had pulled the curtains around the canopy bed to hide the princess from view.

Peet looked slightly confused as he spoke through the curtains to the unseen princess.

"A threat has been made against your life by agents of the Obsidian King, Your Highness." Peet bowed, even though Jessamyn couldn't see him. "Half a dozen spies heard the whispers overnight and reported them to their noble employers. Rumors are spreading that the Obsidians plan to assassinate you."

"Interesting," Jessamyn said. "That's even bolder than I anticipated."

"There's more, my princess," Peet said. "The nobles are already spreading this assassination rumor, but I heard from a reliable source that the story was planted for their informants to pick up. As far as the spies around the Obsidian King know, there are no plans to murder Your Imperial Ladyship."

"Ha!" Jessamyn said. "I bet Ober is pacing around his chambers right now, waiting for someone to discover my body. By the time they do, the nobles will already be convinced Obsidian is responsible. They won't even pause to investigate."

Peet gaped at the curtains. "Your . . . your body?"

"Quickly, Micathea," Jessamyn called. "You must make an appearance. Wear my favorite black dress, the one with the silver details. You're going to put a stop to this nonsense once and for all."

"Won't everyone suspect an Impersonator if the rumor of your death is already out there?"

"You will just have to convince them all, including my father, that you're really me. Quickly now. Get to the throne room. I am certain Lord Ober is planning a big show. You *must* be there to interrupt him. And Micathea?"

"Yes, Princess?"

"Your performance must be utterly flawless."

CHAPTER TWENTY-SEVEN

Mica strode toward the throne room, her dark skirt swishing around her ankles. The night-black gown had a wide silver belt and epaulets, creating the impression of armor. Jessamyn's dark-red hair floated around her shoulders, and a silver crown rested atop her head. She looked like a princess on her way to war. Mica wasn't surprised this was Jessamyn's favorite dress.

Banner had refused to leave Jessamyn's side, so a different palace Shield escorted Mica, a new fellow with a shaved head and large eyes who had no idea she wasn't really the princess. Peet had raced off to fetch his source, one of Master Kiev's spies, who could corroborate the story of the planted assassination rumor. But the evidence wouldn't matter if any of the nobles in the throne room realized Mica wasn't really Jessamyn. They would figure out the princess had been poisoned, and the damage would be done. There'd be no convincing them that Lord Ober rather than the Obsidian King was responsible then. The end result would be Mica's brothers marching to a war they probably wouldn't win.

She could not fail.

The Shield pulled open the door, and Mica burst into the throne room.

Emperor Styl looked up at her from the dais and smiled. The expression transformed his normally grave face, and for a brief moment he looked almost doting. So far, so good. Jessamyn had clued Mica in on the secret code she shared with her father. Only *she* wore silver crowns. She'd sent Mica to do her bidding wearing gold and jewels and pearls atop her head, but whenever the emperor saw a silver shine, he knew a Mimic wasn't replacing his daughter.

"This is the only time I've ever broken his trust," Jessamyn had said as she set the silver diadem on Mica's head. "Do not let me down."

Now, as Mica strode down the golden carpet, every eye turned to follow her progress, and gasps rippled through the assembly. The rumors that the princess had been murdered must have preceded her.

Also, she looked utterly devastating.

Mica had taken the princess's regal beauty and enhanced it as much as she could while staying within the realm of believability. Bright eyes. Shiny hair. Glowing skin. Perfect lips turned up in a knowing smile. All who saw her couldn't help but feel bewitched. Every little touch Mica had added made them more likely to want to please her, more likely to take her side. Beauty was a tool, as she had long been taught, and today she would make it into a weapon.

Lord Ober stood near the dais, not ten feet from the throne. Blatant shock crossed his face at the sight of her, but it disappeared quickly, replaced by suspicion.

"Daughter." Emperor Styl's clear voice called attention back to the front of the room. "Lord Ober was just telling me that threats have been made against your life by the King of Obsidian. Some think your murder is looming."

"I'm afraid reports of my imminent demise are much exaggerated," Mica said.

"Princess Jessamyn." Lord Ober offered her a smooth bow. "I am pleased to see you, of course, but I believe we should take these threats seriously. The last thing any of us wants is to see you come to harm."

"I appreciate your concern for my health, my lord."

"We all wish to see you thrive. In fact," Lord Ober turned back to address the emperor, "I believe we can do more to see that the princess is protected. Perhaps she should retire to the imperial villa over in Winnow Bay until we can determine who's trying to harm her. We must protect the heir to the throne at all costs."

"How kind of you, Lord Ober," Mica said dryly. She couldn't help being impressed at how quickly he tried to turn the situation to his advantage. Mere seconds after his assassination attempt had been thwarted, he was already cooking up a new way to get rid of her. "However, I am afraid you are still mistaken, my lord."

"About what, my princess?"

"Haven't you heard?" Mica gave her best imitation of Princess Jessamyn's longsuffering sigh. "Why am I always the most informed person in this court? You *must* get better spies."

"I beg your pardon," Lord Ober said, his voice flat.

"*I* learned straight from a trusted Imperial Impersonator that the Obsidian threat against my life was fabricated. It is nothing but a rumor."

Murmurs spread through the throne room. The lords and ladies whispered furiously to each other, some summoning members of their entourages, as if to confirm their spies' reports.

Mica raised a hand, waiting for the crowds to quiet before continuing. She wanted them all to hear this. "Once again, you have exaggerated the danger posed by the Obsidian King, my lord. You're becoming quite paranoid about him." She glanced at Lord Ober's distinguished features and prominent nose, and hatred bubbled up within her. He had come far too close to killing her princess. She wasn't going to let him get away with it. Her voice rang loud and clear across the assembly. "One might almost think, Lord Ober, that you are trying to provoke my father into a war."

A hush fell over the crowd.

The emperor certainly wasn't smiling now.

"Are you certain the rumors are fabricated?"

"Yes." Mica met his gaze. The emperor's eyes were exactly the same shade of brown as his daughter's. "I am having my informants double-check the information thoroughly, but there seems to be no Obsidian threat. I suspect they will find the *source* of the rumors quite close to home."

She looked straight at Lord Ober, and she knew no one in the throne room missed the implication. They were hanging on her every word, ready to believe whatever she said. Hatred churned like potion in a cauldron within her. She wanted Ober's head— and with this face, she could make them give it to her.

Then a voice rose broke the expectant silence.

"How do we know you're really the princess and not an Impersonator?"

Mica had anticipated the challenge, but it was not Lord Ober who voiced it.

She turned. Lord Caleb stood at the front of the crowd, his face pale, as if he hadn't fully recovered from his latest illness. Dread ripped through her as he stared at the mask she had assumed. Somehow, he always knew when it was really Mica. He couldn't have picked a worse time to point it out.

"I wish for proof that this is really Princess Jessamyn." Caleb met her eyes, and Mica fought against the urge to shake her head, to warn him not to push it. He was supposed to be on their side. Why was he helping his uncle now, especially after what he'd done to the Talents in that warehouse?

Apparently, her brief hesitation confirmed his suspicion.

Worry and a hint of betrayal showed in his eyes. He opened his mouth. But before he could give her away, a loud voice interrupted him.

"You think I don't know my own daughter?" Emperor Styl boomed. "She is no Impersonator. Jessamyn, please continue what you were saying before you were so rudely interrupted."

Mica started in surprise, not missing the shock on Caleb's face at the emperor's words. Mercifully, he kept quiet as Mica spoke once more.

"Thank you, Father. As I was saying, Lord Ober's actions may be a provocation, or paranoia, or they could be a clumsy attempt at political posturing." She gave a very Jessamyn-like sigh of pity, making her eyes a little bigger and more luminous, reeling her audience back in. "Perhaps it's best if Lord Ober retreats to his own Winnow Bay villa for a season of rest while we investigate. It will be good for him. Life in the Silver Palace can be stressful at times."

A few of the nobles chuckled, and Lord Ober's face darkened.

"You may be right," Emperor Styl said. "I do hope you'll take my daughter's advice seriously, Lord Ober. I'm sure she only has your best interests at heart."

Lord Ober looked as though he were swallowing glass as he said, "I'm sure she does. Thank you, Princess."

He bowed and marched stiffly out of the throne room, whispers chasing after him. Mica watched him go, hoping she was doing the right thing. She had pulled back from calling for Ober's head only because she couldn't be certain what Caleb would do. If he'd question her legitimacy, he must still have mixed feelings about his uncle. He may try to stop an execution. Lopping off heads wasn't Jessamyn's style anyway.

As the nobles whispered about Lord Ober with a certain wry amusement, Mica began to see why Jessamyn wanted to do it this way. By calling him out on a clumsy conspiracy, she'd made the once-powerful Ober lose the nobles' respect. His influence had been hamstrung, and it would be easier to arrest him without creating chaos among his allies. In the long run, embarrassing him was far more effective than calling him a traitor or making him a martyr.

Even so, Mica knew Lord Ober was still dangerous. And he wouldn't forget this.

Caleb, too, strode out of the throne room without looking at her again.

"Let us put to rest this notion that the Obsidian King is out to do us harm," Emperor Styl said. "As my daughter says, this is mere paranoia. We have a strong army and intelligence network. The Windfast will not cower before baseless rumors."

And he leaned back upon his throne, his face marble-carved once more.

Mica returned to the princess's chambers as soon as she could, eager to see how Jessamyn was faring. Banner admitted her to the inner room as a woman she didn't recognize emerged, carrying a basket full of potions. She had pure-white hair, rheumy blue eyes, and hands as wrinkled as walnuts.

"She's a healer," Banner said by way of explanation. "The princess trusts her not to tell."

Mica nodded at the old woman and hurried to the princess's bedside, hoping the healer had managed to do some good.

Jessamyn's face didn't look as though it had improved much at all. Her skin still sagged like melted wax on one side. Sticky brown ointment covered the burn-like patches, and her eyes were red, as if she'd been crying. But she smiled triumphantly when Mica described what had happened in the throne room.

"Well! You didn't mess that one up."

Mica bowed, figuring that was as close as she'd get to praise.

"How are you feeling, Princess?"

"I wish I could say I've felt worse." Jessamyn touched the sagging skin on the left side of her face and winced. "I've certainly never *looked* worse. The healer doesn't think this damage can be fixed, at least not with any potion she knows of. I . . . I am afraid this may be the new me." She blinked rapidly, holding back tears.

Mica shuffled her feet beside the bed, unsure how to act. She had never seen the princess cry before. Jessamyn always seemed so vibrant and strong, hiding her vulnerabilities so well that Mica had no idea what they actually were. But the princess had relied heavily on her looks. What must it be like not to have them anymore?

"I'm so sorry this happened to you." Mica needed to confess that she had been the one who told Lord Ober about Magic Q, but she couldn't bring herself to do it now, when Jessamyn looked so sad. Instead, she said, "I never really thanked you for saving my life back on the harbor cruise."

"Yes, that was rude of you." Jessamyn smiled a bit. "I was rather brave, wasn't I?"

"Yes, Princess."

"I still dream about that man sometimes." Jessamyn lowered her voice, seeming frailer and smaller in her sick bed. "I wake up sweating, feeling the blow ringing in my bones."

"I understand," Mica whispered, thinking of Benson's death in the warehouse.

"No matter," Jessamyn said. "It was worth it, in defense of a friend."

"Thank you, Princess."

They looked steadily at each other for one heartbeat. Two.

Then Jessamyn cleared her throat. "On to business then. Now that you have *finally* mastered your impersonation of me, I will need you to do it full-time."

Mica's jaw went slack. "I beg your pardon?"

"That's right. The situation is much too delicate right now to

262

announce my poisoning. We must make sure Ober is under control, and as soon as he is, I need to shore up every alliance I have ever made. There's also the matter of corruption in the City Watch. Really, there is far too much on my plate to deal with the fallout of what has happened right now."

"You want to keep the poisoning a secret?"

"Keep up, Micathea. Hmm, maybe you *aren't* up to the task. I need you to attend all my appearances in my face until I find a way to heal this mess or it is convenient to reveal the truth."

"You're asking me to be you *all* the time?"

"Isn't that what you're here for?"

Mica didn't answer. This task felt different from what she had been doing so far. She had played scores of different roles in the Silver Palace, impersonating whomever Jessamyn demanded. But she had still been herself. She had still been Mica. Jessamyn was asking her to give up her entire identity to become not an impersonator, but a full-time imposter.

"I do not ask this lightly," Jessamyn said. "The empire is in crisis, and it will remain so until we dig Lord Ober's influence out by the roots. I cannot do that looking like a victim. The nobles much worship me, not pity me."

Mica squeezed her own features back onto her face, needing to make this decision in her own skin. She glanced at the mirror on the princess's wall, at her snub nose, hazel eyes, nut-brown hair. Then she looked down at the disfigured lady.

This was it, the moment to choose how much she really wanted to serve the empire. When she had entered the Academy, Mica had talked about serving her homeland, but she had imagined the adventure and even the glory—not the kind that would get her recognized on the streets of Jewel Harbor, but the kind where history would remember her for accomplishing something significant. When Master Kiev had said this assignment was her way to serve, even though it didn't involve adventures in far-off lands, she had resisted the idea. She had complained. She had pushed back against Jessamyn's orders. But when she finally cooperated with the princess, they had saved the captive Talents and broken the dominance of the most powerful lord in the empire.

But now? Now she was being asked to give up her very self, the only thing she always had, no matter what people could see. If Jessamyn's face never recovered, she could wind up pretending to be the princess for the rest of her life. Was she willing to take it that far?

"I need to think about it," Mica said.

Jessamyn opened her mouth to respond, when someone pounded a fist on the outer door.

"Jessa! It's Caleb," called a muffled voice. "Are you all right? Don't make me break down this door!"

Jessamyn raised an eyebrow at Mica. "You'd better think fast."

"I'll take care of this." Mica quickly resumed her Jessamyn impersonation, closed the door between the bedroom and the antechamber, and instructed Banner to admit Caleb to the sitting room.

He marched in looking murderous.

"Where is the princess?"

"Have you taken leave of your senses?" Mica said in her very best Jessamyn voice. She was getting quite good at it.

"That wasn't her in the throne room," Caleb said. "Are the rumors true? Has someone hurt her?"

"Of course that was me in the throne room," Mica said. "Really, I'd expect my dearest friend to know better."

Caleb hesitated, as if doubting himself for the first time. He looked closely at her, and Mica paid extra attention to the exact turn of her lips. She had been working on this impersonation since he pointed out the flaw, and she was pretty sure she had it perfect this time.

He brushed a hand through his hair, making it messier than ever, and narrowed his eyes. Mica gave one of Jessamyn's signature sighs, as if she were terribly put-upon and no one else was as sensible as her.

"Are you satisfied yet?"

"I suppose," he said slowly. "After all that talk about Obsidian, I thought . . . I'm glad to see you're all right."

Mica suddenly understood why Caleb had doubted her enough to call attention to a possible imposter in the throne room. He believed the rumors about the threat. He thought Jessamyn had been murdered and replaced. It stung that he suspected her of being a traitor after all they had been through, but she had to admire him for being loyal enough to challenge her in front of the court. That was the kind of dedication Jessamyn inspired in her friends.

Mica knew what she had to do.

"Is there anything else?" she asked Caleb. "I *must* prepare for my dancing lesson. I have a new dress that will make Lady Elana curl up in a corner and weep."

Caleb grinned, and the remaining tension went out of his shoulders. "I'm sure you do. Sorry to trouble you." He started to go, then paused. "Will your Impersonator be hiding in the balcony again?"

"Why do you ask?" Mica said as nonchalantly as she could manage.

"I'm chasing new leads to understand my . . . condition after what Haddell told me. I thought she might like to help." A faint smile crossed his lips. "Besides, she's good company."

Mica's heart thudded painfully at his words. *Why did he have to say this now?* She never should have let her feelings for him grow. He was a weakness, one she wouldn't be able to afford in the days to come. If she was going to commit to this imposter assignment, she had to *become* the princess. Which meant she could no longer be Mica—at least for now.

She took a deep breath. "Micathea doesn't work for me anymore."

Caleb's smile faded. "What do you mean?"

"She decided palace life wasn't for her." Mica waved her hand vaguely at the window. "I'm sure she's off on some daring spy mission by now."

"Did she leave any way to reach her?"

Mica's chest squeezed like a fist, and it took all her willpower not to morph back into herself and throw her arms around Caleb's neck. But she said, "I can't be expected to bother with that kind of information."

"So she just . . . left?" He looked so disappointed. Why did he have to make this harder?

"I don't know why you care," Mica said, her voice brittle. "It's not as if she's a member of the nobility anyway."

"I guess not." For a moment, suspicion flickered in Caleb's eyes. Then it was gone.

"It was nice to have known her." He bowed. "I'll see you at the dancing lesson, Jessa. May you thrive."

Mica waited until the door closed behind him before she whispered back in her own voice. "May you thrive, Caleb."

Then she drew herself up and went to inform the princess of her decision.

EPILOGUE

Mica wore her own face when she went to see Quinn. She had spent all day as Jessamyn at an autumn garden party at the palace, preening in an orange dress and sipping spiced cider with the ladies. But she put on a brown Mimic's skirt to walk to Potioners Alley. She had unfinished business with Magic Q.

The gossip at the garden party had centered on Lord Ober's departure from Jewel Harbor. He and Lady Euphia had set sail within hours of the showdown in the throne room the previous week, before he could be quietly arrested. Rumor had it he was sailing to his holdfast on Timbral Island. He may have left in disgrace, but the scandalized court would eventually forget his disastrous attempt to stir up trouble with Obsidian. He would return. They could only hope he hadn't yet perfected his sinister concoction, or he might bring a multi-Talented army with him.

Potioners Alley had a sleepy quality this evening. Darkness was falling, softening the shadows on the cobblestones. The usual odors seemed muted, as if the entire place were holding its breath as Mica walked into Quinn's shop.

The door was unlocked, but the shop was empty. Mica had never seen any other customers there, come to think of it. The place was too eerie to make people want to linger, with its potions glistening a hundred shades of red.

"Magic Q?" Mica called in her own voice. "Is anyone here?"

There was no answer. Mica hesitated at the door to the workshop, wondering whether she should don an impersonation. But Quinn had never seen her real face anyway. She pushed open the rough wooden door.

The high windows illuminated the workshop with hazy, golden light. The table was still as cluttered as it had been the last time Mica was here, but the vials and instruments had a thin layer of dust now, hinting at disuse. Only a few carefully labeled potion bottles lined the shelves. The stacks of parchment, notes, and diagrams that had once covered the desk were gone. Those papers, more than anything else, had given the workshop an industrious, lived-in appearance. Now, it was just an empty apothecary.

Mica sighed, stirring the dust in the workshop. There were no signs of struggle, no broken bottles or overturned tables. The person who had packed up the papers had done it deliberately. Perhaps Quinn would use them to create even more elaborate concoctions. Or perhaps she was dead, and someone knew her notes would be useful.

Though Mica had half expected to find Quinn's body, she feared it was worse for the empire that she had gone willingly. Was she working for Lord Ober now, picking up where Haddell left off? How had he persuaded her to betray the princess? Promises of money? Threats? Opportunities for career advancement? The potioner who had made a name for herself in Jewel Harbor might find a whole new kind of notoriety in Lord Ober's employ.

Mica wouldn't let them get far. She'd do whatever it took to stop Lord Ober and his infernal potioners before they hurt more Talents or inflicted Caleb's curse on other innocents. It would be easier this time. She had all the resources of the Windfast Empire at her fingertips, now that she was a princess.

ACKNOWLEDGMENTS

This book would not be possible without the support of my family and my writing community. I am grateful to Willow, Amanda, Mandy, Jen, Betsy, Debra, MaryAnna, Vishal, Sarah, Brooke, Michele, and Rachel for your feedback, encouragement, and good company. You make Hong Kong a great place to be a writer.

Thank you to my online writing community, especially my friends from the Author's Corner. I've learned so much from you guys, and I can't wait to meet more of you in real life.

I'd like to thank the teams at Red Adept Editing and Deranged Doctor Design and my agent Sarah Hershman for agreeing to embark on this new series with me. I couldn't have asked for a better group of professionals to help me turn this story into a book.

My parents and siblings continue to be my biggest cheerleaders. Thanks especially to my youngest sister, Kylie, for keeping me company while I wrote my outlines, and to my oldest sister, Chelsea, for giving me such detailed notes. Also, thank you for making me change Mica's name. You were right.

No acknowledgments section would be complete without

thanking my husband. He's funny and wise and inquisitive, and I'm lucky I get to hang out with him.

And finally, thank *you* for reading, especially if you've been with me for a few books now. You make it possible for me to keep doing what I love, and I'm so grateful for your support. I'm excited to start this new adventure with you!

Jordan Rivet

Hong Kong, 2017

ABOUT THE AUTHOR

Jordan Rivet is an American author of young adult fantasy and post-apocalyptic adventures. Originally from Arizona, she lives in Hong Kong with her husband. A full-time writer, Jordan can usually be found making faces at her computer in the local Starbucks. She hasn't been kicked out yet.

www.JordanRivet.com
Jordan@JordanRivet.com

ALSO BY JORDAN RIVET

STEEL AND FIRE

Duel of Fire

King of Mist

Dance of Steel

City of Wind

Night of Flame

THE SEABOUND CHRONICLES

Seabound

Seaswept

Seafled

Burnt Sea: A Seabound Prequel

Made in the USA
Middletown, DE
31 July 2018